Missing

By Bob Adamov

Next **Emerson Moore** Adventure

Golden Torpedo

ISBN: 0-9786184-5-9
978-0-9786184-5-2

Library of Congress Number:
2014960019

Cover art and Dustjacket by Denis K. Lange
www.langedesign.biz

Cover Illustration by Ted McLaren
www.mfa.fineartstudioonline.com

Submit all requests for reprinting to:
BookMasters, Inc.
PO Box 388
Ashland, Ohio 78735

Published in the United States by:
Packard Island Publishing, Wooster, Ohio

www.bookmasters.com
www.packardislandpublishing.com
www.BobAdamov.com

Visit Bob Adamov on Facebook

First Edition – April 2015

Printed in the United States

Acknowledgements

For technical assistance, I'd like to express my appreciation to former Navy SEAL Chris Heben, Attorney Joe Weinstein, former Wayne County Deputy Sheriff Charlie Hardman, John Clark at the Grosse Ile Yacht Club, and my buddy, Mike "Mad Dog" Adams.

I'd like to thank my team of editors: Cathy Adamov, Peggy Parker, Hank Inman of Goldfinch Communications, Andrea Goss Knaub, Jackie Buckwalter, and Mike Steidl. And a special thank you to editor John Wisse for his special seasoning! Also, thank you to cover designer Denis Lange of Lange Design and Toledo artist Ted McLaren for the wonderful cover painting.

Dedication

This book is dedicated to my beautiful, loving and caring sweetheart of a wife, Cathy, to the victims of human trafficking, and law enforcement officers killed in the line of duty and their families.

Donations

The Lucas County Human Trafficking Coalition and Second Chance will receive a portion of the proceeds from the sale of this book. Visit www.lchtc.org.

If you would like to help support the following organizations, please send your donation to:

Lucas County Human Trafficking Coalition and Second Chance
c/o The Toledo Area Ministries
3043 Monroe Street
Toledo, OH 43606

For more information, check these sites:

www.ohioseagrant.osu.edu
www.MillerFerry.com
www.cusslersociety.com
www.VisitPutinBay.com

They that wait upon the Lord shall renew their strength; they shall mount up with wings as eagles; they shall run, and not be weary; and they shall walk, and not faint. – Isaiah 40:31

Lake Erie Islands

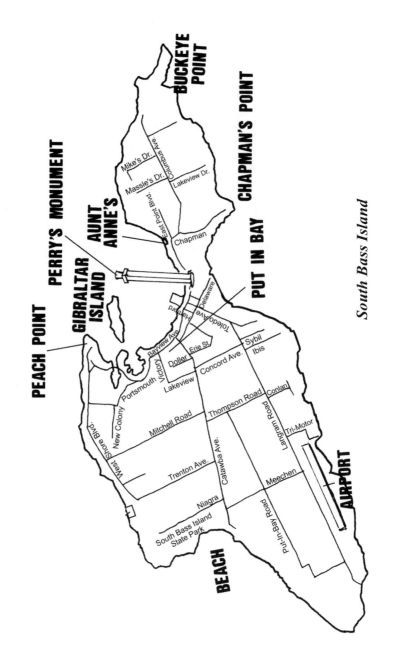

South Bass Island

The Beer Barrel Saloon
Put-in-Bay, Ohio

It was late May, the beginning of summer season at the popular Put-in-Bay resort village located 55 miles east of Toledo on South Bass Island in Lake Erie's western basin. A noisy crowd filled the cavernous Beer Barrel Saloon – Home of the World's Longest Bar – as the featured band, The Menus, played to an overflow audience.

The bar stools were filled with partying men and women of various legal ages. One especially attractive brunette in her late twenties had her hands full of rambunctious male adoration. Five guys in their thirties had been plying her with drinks and she was well inebriated.

"Come on. You've got to see our boat," one of the men sincerely pleaded as he tugged her off her bar stool.

"Yeah, you'll love it. We can party on it, Connie," another one chimed in as he intently looked at the woman with the large, chocolate brown eyes.

"I really shouldn't. I need to go home, fellas," Connie stammered as she wobbled on her feet, first one way, then another, until she was falling against one of the guys.

"I don't think she knows what she's doing," another said as he hungrily eyed Connie's body with a lascivious appetite and deep thirst.

The predatory male wolfpack guided her from the bar area toward the exit door so they might soon feast upon their prey away from public view.

A six-foot-two, tanned dark-haired man slid off his bar stool. He was in his early forties and lived with his aged aunt on the island at East Point. His name was Emerson Moore, an investigative reporter for *The Washington Post*. He had been watching the male wolfpack manipulate the woman with alcohol and guessed what they had planned for her. She was a local island woman whom he had run into on several occasions. Her name was Connie Mueller. She was a knockout!

"Hold on guys," Moore announced as he approached the five men near the Barrel's doorway. He didn't want to get involved, but couldn't help himself. He had the "rescue the damsel in distress" syndrome.

"What?" one of them asked as he spun around to face Moore.

"Where do you think you're going with my cousin?" Moore asked, even though she wasn't his cousin.

"She wants to party with us, dude," the man answered. "Go away!"

Moore looked at Connie, who was being held up by two of the men. "Connie, do you want to go with these guys?"

"No," she slurred. "I need to go home now."

"Sorry to spoil your fun, but the lady wants to go home," Moore said as he took a step closer to them.

The men had imbibed too much alcohol to think wisely. One of them replied, "Butt out, buddy. She's going with us."

"I don't think so," Moore said as he removed one of the men's arms from around her waist.

"Hey jerk!" the guy deliriously yelled as he threw a drunken punch at Moore, missing him as Moore easily sidestepped the blow.

Moore pushed the man aside, who then dropped to the floor. As Moore started to remove the arm of the second man from around Connie's waist, two of the remaining wolfpack jumped on Moore's back and they all tumbled together to the floor. As the men grappled on the floor, feet and fists flew wildly. The fight didn't last longer than thirty seconds as the bar's bouncers raced over and quickly broke it up, separating the fighters.

"What happened here, Emerson?" one of the bouncers supportively asked. He knew Moore as a good friend of the Beer Barrel's owner.

Moore briefly explained and the bouncers escorted the five drunken men through the Delaware Avenue exit and off the premises. Moore turned to the sobbing and drunk woman. "Connie, would you like me to take you home?"

"Yes. Please. You know where I live?"

"Out by the airport," Moore replied.

"Yep," she said as she leaned on Moore with a modest sense of relief.

"Come on outside. I've got my golf cart parked on the side."

The two walked out of the Catawba Avenue exit and boarded Moore's golf cart. Connie leaned against Moore, held somewhat tightly onto his arm and then directed him to her mobile home, which was set a short distance back off the road. A solitary outside light was heavily covered by mayflies and dimly illuminated her front porch.

After parking, Moore helped Connie out of the cart. As she drunkenly stood in place, she draped her arms around his neck.

"Emerson, you are such a nice guy."

"No problem. Just wanted to help you before those guys took advantage of you."

She nuzzled her face close to Moore's. "Would you like to take advantage of me?" she asked her good-looking rescuer with a little suggestive snicker.

"Now, Connie. You've really had too much to drink," Moore said as he pulled back. He wasn't one to prey upon drunken women. Trying to change the topic, Moore spotted a fully-chromed Harley-Davidson low-rider motorcycle parked near the trailer and next to Connie's Kawasaki Drifter 800 with fat fenders. "Hey, nice bike," he said as he tried to pry her off of him.

"It's Boozer's. I want a kiss," she demanded and then suddenly locked her lips onto Moore's astonished lips.

Moore immediately pulled away. "Who's Boozer?"

The sudden slamming of the mobile home's screen door startled Moore, who immediately turned toward the front porch. There stood a burly, bearded man with his long hair pulled back in a ponytail. He was wearing a tank top and jeans. He was also wearing a very distinct scowl on his face.

"I'm Boozer. What do you think you're doing there with my woman, meathead?"

Before Moore could answer, Boozer ran back into the mobile home, the screen door slamming shut behind him.

"Honey, he helped me," Connie yelled before realizing Boozer had run back into the trailer. Her demeanor changed quickly as she gained some temporary, but measurable and immediate sobriety and nervously advised Moore, "He's gone to get his shotgun. He's kind of jealous!"

Moore turned to run to the golf cart. "I didn't know you had a live-in boyfriend, Connie!"

"You don't have time for that." She pointed to a small metal shed. "Hide there! I'll cool him down!"

Moore ran into the rusty shed and closed the door behind him. From his tenuous hiding place, he heard the screen door slam shut again as Boozer rushed out of the mobile home. He could hear the couple argue as she pleaded to explain and Boozer cursed about her and Moore embracing. As the voices soon neared the shed, Moore began to worry.

"Honey, I'm telling you that he helped me get away from those guys."

"I don't believe you, Connie!" Boozer saw the golf cart was still parked in the driveway. "Where did he go? Kissing my woman! I'll fix his sorry ass," Boozer spouted angrily as he swung the shotgun at hip level, looking for a target.

His head swung back to look at the shed. "Is he in there?"

"No, he ran over there," she pointed in the opposite direction.

"Then you don't mind if I shoot the shed to pieces, do you?"

"No, don't do that! Please, Boozer!" she screamed.

Boozer unloaded the first barrel of his shotgun and it ripped through the rusty door. He then charged at the shed and tore open the door to find it empty. He saw that the rusty rear wall had a large hole in it that Moore created to escape and disappear into the night.

Boozer stalked around the shed and the yard in search of Moore. Then he turned to Connie, who was acting a little less drunk and was anxiously following him. "You get in the house. I'm staying out here tonight and waiting for him to come back for his golf cart."

Sobbing, Connie entered the trailer and Boozer settled down in a chair with the reloaded shotgun on his lap. It would be a fruitless use of his time since Moore had headed with due diligence back to his aunt's home. He had no plans of returning to retrieve his golf cart that evening. He had had his fill of excitement for one night.

The Reel Bar
Put-in-Bay

"Here's your burger, Emerson," Ray Fogg said as the tall, dark-haired singer and comedian served the burger and fries to Moore, who was seated near the bar. Fogg and his partner, Andy Christensen, had purchased the former Tony's Garage on Catawba Avenue a couple of years earlier. They had remodeled it with reclaimed barn wood, stone, antique lighting and vintage décor like fishing memorabilia and old signs.

Fogg, a longtime island entertainer, also relocated his raucous show to the restaurant and bar, which was packed with patrons that day and was part of the reason why he was helping the staff deliver food to the tables.

"How's your burger, Emerson?" Mike "Mad Dog" Adams asked as he swung his butt onto the chair next to Moore. Adams was the legendary island entertainer who had been singing and cracking jokes around the corner at The Round House Bar for over thirty-five years.

"These are the best!" Moore said between bites of the Reel Burger served on a branded bun.

"Is it raw?" Adams asked as he began setting up Moore.

"Not at all," Moore responded, unsuspecting. "It's perfect!"

"Not raw like your adventure with Boozer and Connie last night?" Adams asked with a chuckle before placing his Black Bean burger order with a server.

Moore turned to look at the muscular singer who was wearing a white ball cap, blue shorts and a pink T-shirt. The shirt was lettered with "Save the TATAS." He had an earring in one ear and his hair was pulled back in a ponytail. His eyes twinkled and a warm smile emitted from his bearded face.

"How in the world did you hear about it?" Emerson queried.

"Coconut Pomps told me."

Adams was referring to his good friend, assistant and infamous island taxi driver Tim Pompei whose nickname was Coconut Pomps. It was Pomps, who had luckily spotted Moore when he was walking home the previous night and had given Moore a ride. During the ride, Moore had related the story about Connie Mueller and Boozer.

"I should have known," Emerson admitted somewhat reservedly. "The police are retrieving my golf cart for me today."

Adams nodded his head with feigned amusement and a grin on his face. "Heard you got a real blast out of it." Adams chuckled at his comment.

"More than I expected! You would have enjoyed watching me put a back door in that shed. Good thing it was old and rusted," Moore said. Then he added, "That was a little too close for comfort. And all I was doing was rescuing a damsel in distress."

"You like doing that stuff, don't you?"

"It's the Boy Scout in me."

Adams took a sip of his coffee and cocked his head as he looked at Moore. "You really do need to loosen up a bit, Emerson," he advised.

"I could never be as loose as the Mad Dog!" Moore grinned as he reached for his coffee cup and took a drink.

"No freaking way, buddy! Can't have another Mad Dog on the island. People would wonder what the world was coming to!" Adams smiled.

"I'll just be a rabid dog," Moore responded.

"Now you're talking," Adams said as he looked with great anticipation at the burger that had been placed in front of him. "Working on any exciting stories?"

"Yes. I've got to follow up with my editor in D.C. He wants me to do a story on Jimmy Diamonds. Ever hear of him?"

Adams stopped eating. "Yeah, and he's bad news, Emerson. You be careful if you get around him. He plays for keeps. Get it?"

Moore swung around on his barstool with a sense of purpose now and looked at Adams. "How do you know about him, Mike?"

"It's not like I know the guy personally. But, I've heard stories about him when I played in clubs in the Detroit area. I've actually seen him once or twice."

"Did he come to one of your shows?"

"As a matter of fact, yes, he did," Adams recounted. "He stood out. Very classy dresser. Had two bodyguards with him. Big boys, I mean really big and mean looking dudes. Not the kind you want to mess with, my friend."

Moore grinned a bit sheepishly. "Did you pick on him during your act, Mike?"

"Come on, Emerson, seriously? I'm not crazy enough to pick on a guy like that. In all of my years in the business, you get a feel for the ones you can pick on and the ones you can't. Diamonds is definitely in the 'can't' department."

"I bet."

"You be careful, Emerson, if you go messing around with him. I've heard stories about people ending up in the Detroit River when they got crosswise with him."

Moore confidently arose from his seat and paid his bill. "Thanks, Mike. I always try to be careful when I'm doing my stories."

"Not careful enough. You have a history of pushing the edge a little too much, buddy. You're lucky to be alive. Just be extra careful with this guy, Emerson. Heed my warning," Adams cautioned with a serious tone between bites of his burger.

"Okay. Okay," Moore said. "I get it."

"Hey, I meant to ask you. Did you ever go back to the art classes?" Moore asked.

"No, I'm sticking to painting houses."

Moore beamed at the comment. "You know what that means in mobster slang, don't you?"

"No, I don't, Emerson."

"Painting houses means you're a killer. You splatter blood all over the floors and walls," Moore snickered as he relayed the results of his recent research on organized crime.

"I'll just stick to splattering paint all over everything," Adams said. Suddenly a sly smile appeared on Adams' face as he thought about another painting opportunity. "Now, I might just change my mind if I could start a body painting business like they have in Key West. That's the kind of paint splattering I'd really enjoy."

"No surprise there," Moore cracked.

"Hey, Bob's here!" Adams called as island entertainer Bob Gatewood walked onto the stage and set down his guitar. Gatewood waved at Adams and Moore and started to walk in their direction. He was doing a special mid-afternoon show for his good friend, Fogg. Gatewood's song *"Friends of the Bay"* had been recently chosen by the village council as the official song of Put-in-Bay.

"Hi, gents," Gatewood said affably as he walked over to the table.

Before they could respond, Fogg walked over and spoke to Adams and Moore. "You two are in for something special this afternoon."

"Something more special than your singing, Ray?" Adams chided his friend good-naturedly.

"Aw, come on Mad Dog, the only thing more special than my singing is my smile," Fogg countered with a grin.

"Now, that would be the Island Rock God talking," Adams jested back.

Fogg explained, "We're on stage together this afternoon. We did it last year on Labor Day and we decided to do it today, too."

"Great!" Moore said as he looked forward to hearing the two buddies sing.

"And I'm going to sit back and lead the applause," Adams chimed in.

Fogg and Gatewood headed to the stage to finish setting up. Within fifteen minutes, they were entertaining the crowd.

About halfway through their first set, Moore looked at his watch, then leaned toward Adams and said, "I better be leaving, Mike. Got to see if the police have my golf cart."

"Go on, git," Adams said as he continued to focus on the music.

Moore walked out of the restaurant and strode along Catawba Avenue. Crossing an alley, he went down a set of steps to the police department.

"Looking for your golf cart?" Chief of Police Chet Wilkens asked as he encountered Moore in the small lobby. It was the size of a large closet.

"Good guess," Moore chuckled.

"It's out back. The guys picked it up after you phoned in this morning."

"I appreciate your guys getting it for me, Chief. I didn't think it was a good idea for me to go back there, at least not until Boozer cools down and listens to Connie's story."

"You're probably right. You want to press charges?"

"No. Let it go. No harm done, except to one poor old, rusty shed."

"Good. Boozer's not a bad guy. He's come a long way from his wild days," Chief Wilkens advised.

"I'd hate to think what his wild days were like," Moore replied. "I'd better go."

He departed the lobby, found his golf cart and drove it back to his aunt's house located a few doors from Perry's Monument, the 352-foot-tall Doric column that was the centerpiece of the island. He pulled the cart into the garage behind the house and walked along the side of the house to the front, which overlooked the bay. When he reached the dock, Moore sat down with his feet dangling over the edge and called his boss, *Washington Post* Editor John Sedler.

"Sedler here," the voice answered, almost gruffly.

"Hi, John. It's Emerson."

Sedler's business-like tone changed upon hearing Moore's voice. "Let me guess. You're sitting on the porch and enjoying the island breeze there in Put-in-Bay."

"Close. I'm sitting on the dock and enjoying the island breeze," Moore pleasantly said as he watched the Jet Express with a load of visitors round Gibraltar Island as it entered the harbor, crowded with an array of watercraft.

"Yes, and I'm sitting here in D.C. with the smog-filled breeze of too much traffic and political punditry!" Sedler enviously countered.

"You could always move your office out here with me," Moore teased. He knew it wasn't practical.

"Oh, sure I could!" Switching from chit-chat to the business at hand, Sedler asked, "Did you get a chance to do any more research on Jimmy Diamonds?"

"Yes. I've been building a file on him. I'm trying to set up a meeting with the Detroit Police Department and the U.S. Attorney's Office there to see what I can glean and substantiate."

"Looks like Diamonds has built himself quite an empire with Detroit as his base of operations."

"That's what I saw, and he's running into some territory wars as he expands outside of Michigan," Moore added.

"On top of everything, the guy's an egomaniac," Sedler advised.

"And that may work to my advantage in getting an interview with him. The guy thinks he's Teflon. Nothing sticks to him."

"Do what you can. And Emerson?"

Moore interrupted Sedler. "I know. You want me to be careful."

"Like you ever take my advice," Sedler said. He knew his ace investigative reporter had narrowly escaped death in several of his previous reporting adventures.

"I'll be careful," Moore said as they ended their call.

Moore stood and walked into the house. He heard his Aunt Anne humming in the kitchen as she worked. His seventy-something aunt was full of energy and so pleased that Moore had moved in with her several years ago following the separate deaths of her husband and of Moore's wife and son. Moore enjoyed using her home and the island as his base of operations. He ran up the steps to continue his research on his laptop.

Jimmy Diamonds' Warehouse Office
South Side Detroit, Michigan

Pulling his ringing cell phone out of his pocket, Fat Freddy tapped the screen and answered it. He was fidgeting from one foot to the other, having so much nervous energy at times that he could short out a motion detector. Fat Freddy dutifully turned to Jimmy Diamonds and said, "They just pulled in. You want me to bring him up here?"

"No, Einstein! I want you to take him out and wine and dine him!" Diamonds boiled. Some days he felt like he was the only one with any brains.

"Of course I want him up here, unless you want to stand in for him!"

"No way, Jimmy. I'll get him," Fat Freddy said quickly as he waddled out of the office. Fat Freddy knew what was in store for the visitor and believed the visitor was getting what he deserved.

Fat Freddy Fabrizio was a five-foot, five-inch-tall, generously overweight Italian-American with short-cropped, salt-and-pepper hair and dark brown eyes which had seen their share of horrific murders. He had moved steadily up in Diamonds' crime organization to become one of Diamonds' most trusted men and a member of the racketeer's inner circle.

"And make it fast!" Diamonds ordered his top henchman, who was already closing the office door behind him. Reaching into a drawer, Diamonds pulled out a small plastic bag filled with cocaine and dumped a small amount of the white powder on his desk. Retrieving a credit card from his wallet, he cut the coke into two lines and replaced the card into his wallet.

He took a $100 bill, folded it in half, then rolled it into a little pencil-thin tube and placed one end on the line of coke. As be bent over with the other end of the bill inserted in one nostril, he slowly moved the rolled C-note along the line as he snorted the coke. Diamonds repeated the procedure with the second line. Snorting as he stood, then pinching together and gently wiping his nostrils with a thumb and index finger, he put the C-note back into his pocket and cleaned off the desk. He now was going to calmly enjoy confronting his visitor. He had hungry eyes, like a buzzard waiting for its prey to slowly die.

Diamonds' real name was James Diamonte. He picked up the Diamonds moniker from his early career in crime when he specialized in heisting precious diamonds. Sometimes, his name was shortened to Jimmy D. He didn't care either way.

Diamonds was a large man of about six feet with broad shoulders and silver hair combed back. He was known for his penchant for $200.00 haircuts, $1,000 women and other expensive tastes. He had an intimidating thick, wide forehead and steely blue eyes that seemed to angrily look through you with laser-like precision. He had a thin smile on his rotund face and a jacket slipped over his shoulders as he waited for the unsuspecting visitor and the chance to hold him accountable.

His office was on the top floor of a two-story warehouse on the city's South Side off Fort Street. It had several large windows overlooking the Detroit River so that Diamonds could watch the passing river traffic. He could also look across the river at Canada and downriver at the Ambassador Bridge, linking the United States to Canada.

Below his window, he could keep a watchful eye on the dock where his 47-foot Meridian 441 Sedan rocked quietly in the river. She was named *Diamonds Forever.* One of the joys of Diamonds' dangerous life was piloting the sleek craft between its dock and his home on the river on Grosse Ile, an island located where the Detroit River emptied into Lake Erie. Besides, he had reasoned to himself, traveling the river would make a hit on him much more difficult.

Diamonds' office was a large, walnut-paneled room. It was ornately decorated in contrast to the starkness of the warehouse and the run-down warehouse district. Diamonds believed in living large. His office had a hot tub near the large windows and a custom built fish tank stocked with his pet red-bellied piranhas, known for their aggressive, carnivorous behavior.

Diamonds loved the ferocious perch-shaped piranhas from the Amazon Basin. He related to their voracious appetite for meat. They were always in the hunt for victims just as he was. The piranhas' razor-sharp teeth were wedge-shaped like a shark's, and combined with powerful jaw muscles, enabled them to rapidly snap through flesh and bone as they ripped apart their victims. Piranhas embodied evil ferocity, a trait Diamonds especially admired.

The door to his office opened and Fat Freddy returned. He was accompanied by two men, Carmine Marino and Tony Parella. Marino had his arms bound together behind his back.

Tony Parella was a wiry, smart-mouthed wannabe with thinning black hair and snaky, cobra-like eyes. Deadly eyes. He was also a member of Diamonds' inner circle, but Fat Freddy didn't like his pushy ways. He also didn't like it that Parella would call him "Fats" or "Doublewide." He had warned Diamonds to watch his back around Parella, but Diamonds ignored the advice. Diamonds thought, in some ways, that the upstart reminded him of himself in his younger days.

A solitary chair had been placed near the piranha tank and Marino was pushed onto it. Parella and Fat Freddy stood together behind the chair, as would soldiers at their post.

"Here's Carmine, Jimmy," Fat Freddy said as he looked down at the man who was sweating profusely.

"Carmine, how's it going?" Diamonds asked as he slowly strode around his desk and stood in front of the man.

Before Marino could respond, Parella leaned slightly downward toward Marino's ear and cracked, "It's going down the toilet, isn't it, Carmine?"

Diamonds shot Parella a look that clearly told Parella to shut up.

"Not so good," said Marino, as he continued to look straight ahead at Diamonds. Marino squirmed in his seat, uncomfortably so, as if he was about to have an uncontrolled bowel movement.

"That's an understatement!" Diamonds said conclusively as he looked down on Marino.

"I can explain, Jimmy!" Marino said excitedly.

"Oh, I think you're going to do more than explain," Diamonds countered with an evil snicker.

"Listen, Jimmy! I made a mistake. I'm coming clean with you now," Marino implored.

"Cut the crap! The only reason you're coming clean with me is that you got caught with one hand in the cookie jar. You stole from me, Carmine!"

"I was just borrowing some of the money from the coke sale."

"You don't touch one nickel of my coke money! Nobody does!" Diamonds screamed.

"I was going to pay you back!" Marino whined.

"Then why didn't you ask me to borrow the money? Huh, Carmine?" Diamonds turned and gazed out the window as a freighter plied up the river. He took in a deep breath and tried to settle his wrath. It didn't work. He then spun around to face Marino again. "I think you just got damn greedy, Carmine!" he screamed.

"No. That wasn't it at all. I was going to pay you back and with interest!" Marino swore.

"Sure you were. You know, Carmine, what them Arabs do in the Mideast when someone steals?" Diamonds didn't wait for an answer. "They take him down to the public square and cut off the offending part. So in your case, it would be your hand for stealing."

Marino pulled back in his chair. "Jimmy, please don't. I'll do anything you want!"

Diamonds walked to his fish tank, which held four piranhas. While looking at them in the tank, he asked, "Carmine, do you like fish?"

Eyeing the predators in the tank, Marino nervously responded, "Yes, I do, Jimmy."

"You know what these fish are?"

"Yes, piranhas. I've seen them before when I've been here in your office."

"Piranhas are kind of different to work with. You need to keep them in groups of four or more and they like to attack the weaker member of their group. It's survival of the fittest, right, Carmine?"

"Yeah, right, Jimmy."

"Sometimes, you'll find a piranha with one eye missing, like this one." Diamonds held up a small fish bowl containing a one-eyed piranha. "This one was attacked by the others because it was the weakest. He survived only because I rescued him with a net." Diamonds looked at Marino. "Carmine, do you have a safety net?"

"Jimmy, I'll pay you back. I promise."

Diamonds held up his hand, palm outward toward Marino. "Stop. I don't believe you have a safety net. Watch what happens when I dump this poor guy into the tank with these others who haven't been fed in days."

As Diamonds emptied the fishbowl into the large tank, the four piranhas attacked and immediately devoured the one-eyed piranha.

"See what happens, Carmine?" Diamonds asked as he set the empty fishbowl on a nearby table. "So what should I do with you? Stick your offending hand in the tank? Stick both of your hands in the tank?" Diamonds' eyes had a dangerous and glazed look.

In contrast, Marino's eyes were wide with terror. He steadily shrank back in his chair. "Jimmy, please!" he begged.

Walking slowly to his desk, Diamonds sat on the edge and stared at Marino. "Tell you what I'm going to do. I won't stick your hands in the tank today. I'm going to give you a little break."

Marino relaxed.

"Yeah, I'm going to let you be the first to test my new hot tub. What do you think about that?"

"Sure, anything. I'll do anything for you, Jimmy." The words flooded out of Marino's mouth as he felt a sense of relief and his body relaxed. He didn't know how short that relief would be.

"Good. Now stand up, Carmine," Diamonds instructed.

Marino stood and then was surprised when Fat Freddy bent down and began wrapping duct tape around his ankles to tightly bind them together.

"What are you doing?"

"Be patient. Fat Freddy knows what to do."

"Are you going to drown me?" Marino asked as he looked toward the hot tub.

Laughing sinisterly, Diamonds responded, "No, you don't have to worry about drowning." Diamonds' eyes stared like daggers at Marino. "Maybe I'll turn on that radio and toss it in the water. Maybe electrocute you!"

"Jimmy, no! No, Jimmy, please!" Marino yelled.

"No, I won't do that, either," Diamonds said as he walked over to the hot tub and unplugged the radio. He took the radio and placed it on his desk. "See, Carmine, nothing to worry about." Diamonds then nodded to Fat Freddy.

Next, Fat Freddy surprised Marino by placing a strip of duct tape across his mouth. Marino's eyes suddenly had a shocked look. The look turned to undeniable terror when Diamonds made his next comment.

"But you might have to worry about the three dozen or so piranha swimming in the hot tub. They haven't been fed for days."

With desperate, muffled screams, Marino tried to twist away while Fat Freddy and Parella held him securely and then started moving him next to the hot tub.

Before they dumped Marino into the hot tub, Diamonds walked over to Marino. In his hand, he held a knife. Slowly he drew the knife across Marino's cheek, cutting it deeply enough to draw blood. "A little blood in the water drives them into a feeding frenzy."

Diamonds smiled at the horrified Marino. "It shouldn't take too long. Hope the water's warm enough for you, Carmine," Diamonds chuckled as he nodded his head and the two men immediately pushed a struggling Marino into the tub.

The three watched as Marino tried to avoid his deadly moment with fate. He tried to wiggle free as his muffled screams echoed off the plate glass windows. The water churned violently with the attacking piranhas and Marino's death throes.

Within a few short minutes, the water stopped swirling and returned to a peaceful, but deadly calm. The once crystal clear water now had a deep red, wine-stained appearance.

Diamonds next spoke calmly to Parella. "Tony, go ahead and net my pets, then put them back in the big tank. You can clean out any remains from the tub and drain it. Then, put clean water in it."

"Will do."

"Be sure to dump whatever remains are left downriver and not in front of my docks."

"Let's go," Diamonds said as he turned to Fat Freddy.

"Where to?"

"Lunch. We're going for some of them good sliders over at the Green Dot Stables before the crowd gets there."

"Enjoy lunch, Fats! Pretty soon I'll have to call you triple wide," Parella snickered.

Fat Freddy stopped and turned to stare at Parella. He took two steps toward him when Diamonds' hand gripped Fat Freddy's arm. "Let it go, Fat Freddy. He's just having fun." Diamonds quietly enjoyed seeing the tension between his top two men.

Fat Freddy turned away from Parella. He was miffed. "I'll get the keys to the car."

Diamonds shook his head negatively. "We can walk the two-and-a-half blocks over to West Lafayette." Diamonds saw Fat Freddy wince. "What's wrong? You don't want to walk?"

"Jimmy, it's real hot out there."

Diamonds threw Fat Freddy a look that meant business.

"But then again, I could use the exercise," Fat Freddy said as he hurried over to Diamonds.

"Isn't that an understatement," Diamonds said as he walked through the door, quickly followed by a waddling Fat Freddy.

Diamonds and Fat Freddy walked out of the office and left the building.

Twisted Sisters Gallery
Marblehead Peninsula

After taking a mid-morning Miller Boat Line Ferry from Lime Kiln Dock on South Bass Island to the Catawba Peninsula, Moore had driven his dark green Mustang convertible with a tan top to Marblehead on an errand for his Aunt Anne. She had purchased a painting at the Twisted Sisters Gallery while on a recent outing to the mainland with the South Bass Island OWLS (Old Women's Literary Society). Moore was picking it up for her on that crisp summer morning.

As he drove past the Kelleys Island Ferry terminal in Marblehead and pulled into the gallery parking lot, Moore thought how much he needed to enjoy the change in scenery. For the last two days, he had been heads-down on the Internet, researching Jimmy Diamonds through various media stories and following up with phone calls to a number of sources in the Detroit area. His head was spinning from the research as he also was anxiously awaiting a return call from the Detroit Police Department's Organized Crime Section.

"Good morning!" a cheery voice called out as Moore walked into the gallery filled with local paintings, photography, beach glass jewelry, unique wood art and other eccentricities, including marshmallow roasting sticks and walking sticks made from golf clubs. "I haven't seen you in ages, Emerson."

Moore identified the source of the warm greeting as vivacious gallery co-owner Sherry Warner. Her enthusiasm and life energy bubbled over, much like his Aunt Anne's.

"Hi, Sherry," Moore said with a smile as the entrance door closed behind him.

"You here to pick up your aunt's painting?"

"Yes," he answered as he looked at the diverse collection of artwork around the gallery. He enjoyed taking in the creativity, especially that of local and regional artists.

"I have it right here," Sherry said as she picked up a piece to show him. It was a tropical painting of a skiff tied to the shore in emerald green waters.

"I like it," Moore said appreciably.

"New artist for us. Ted McLaren in Toledo. We just started carrying his tropical paintings. The one your aunt bought is called *Islander Water Taxi*."

"Very tranquil."

"That's what I need around here, Emerson. Some tranquility," Warner teased.

"I'll say you do," a voice spoke from behind Moore.

Moore curiously turned around to face the entranceway and saw Donna Schoonmaker, the other co-owner, walking in. She was carrying two cups of coffee.

"If I had known you were coming, Emerson, I'd have brought another coffee from Avery's for you," the dark-haired and dark-complected Schoonmaker said, referring to the adjoining café which was a popular hangout for locals.

Moore smiled. He enjoyed visiting the two ladies, who were in their early fifties, and hearing them banter between themselves. They were so entertaining.

"That's okay. I'm stopping at the Peninsula Restaurant for a late breakfast," Moore explained. He wanted to see his friend, Char, who waitressed there.

Moore's cell phone buzzed.

"Excuse me, ladies," Moore politely said with a serious tone as he stepped outside the gallery to take the call. "Emerson Moore," he answered.

"Mr. Moore, this is Marc Bona returning your call." Bona was the second-in-command of the Detroit Police Department's Organized Crime Section. The five-foot-eleven-inch tall officer had a runner's build. He ran two miles each morning so he could indulge comfortably with his love of pasta and bread.

"Mad Dog Adams suggested I call you. I swear that guy knows everyone."

"I enjoy his show when I'm in Put-in-Bay and he's helped out with some of the police benefit shows in Detroit," Bona smiled as he recalled the entertainer. His hazel eyes looked through his wire-rim glasses at a picture of the Detroit Red Wings on the far wall of his office.

"I work for…"

Bona interrupted Moore. "I know all about you, Emerson. Checked you out before I returned your call. Nice job with helping break up that human trafficking ring in Toledo and Naples. There was some spillover here in Detroit that we did mop-up duty on. Now, what can I do for you?" he asked as he ran his left hand through his close-cropped black hair.

"Jimmy Diamonds."

"Yes, sir?"

"I'm working on a story about him and wondered what you could tell me."

"You know his nickname?"

"The Teflon King?"

"You've done some homework, I see."

"I have. Where do you stand on the Diaz murder?"

Moore was referring to the recent murder of Mexican drug lord Eduardo Diaz in Detroit and attempts to link the murder to his crosstown rival, Jimmy Diamonds. Moore had discovered numerous articles in the media during his Internet research.

"Now, hold on there, son. I'd think you'd be one of the first to know that we can't comment on an ongoing investigation."

"Thought I'd give it a try," Moore grinned to himself.

"Anything that we want to say about that would be released during a press conference and we've had a couple of them."

"I saw that. Doesn't look like you've been able to nail him yet," Moore said as he pushed gently for more information.

Bona chuckled. He liked the reporter's persistence. "Like I said, I don't have anything more to tell you at this time."

"I'll keep digging."

"Be careful, Mr. Moore. We're pretty sure he and his boys play very rough."

"That's a theme I've been hearing. I'll be careful."

"Sorry I couldn't help you more."

"I understand," Moore said as he ended the call. This was going to be much tougher than he thought.

"Finished your call?" Schoonmaker asked after Moore reentered the gallery.

"Yep. I'm all set," he said as he took the painting she was handing him. "Thank you, ladies," he said as he turned and walked out of the gallery. Moore placed the painting in the Mustang's back seat and then he settled into the driver's seat. He started the car and headed to the Peninsula Restaurant to see Char and have his late breakfast.

As he drove the short distance to the restaurant, his mind replayed the recent phone conversation with Bona. He began forming in his mind a plan to meet Jimmy Diamonds.

Jimmy Diamonds' House
Grosse Ile, Michigan

After clearing Diamonds' henchman at the front gates to the Diamonds' island estate on East River Road, Moore drove slowly up the drive through well-manicured and landscaped grounds to the large mansion. He saw several peacocks roaming the grounds and knew that they were also a back-up to Diamonds' security system. They would cry out when intruders were on the grounds.

He parked in front of the main entrance and walked toward the front door, taking in the panoramic view of the Detroit River. He saw a large, expensive boat docked across the street and in front of the house. He assumed it belonged to Diamonds. Somebody's in the money, Moore thought to himself.

This wasn't Moore's first visit to this idyllic island. He often thought he wouldn't mind having a home there even if it was in Michigan. But then again, he enjoyed living in Put-in-Bay, especially since he was a big Ohio State football fan.

Moore confidently walked up the few steps to the front door, guarded by two armed men. One of the men opened the door and Moore entered the mansion.

"Wait here," one of the men instructed Moore.

Moore did as he was told. He quickly spied the surveillance camera mounted on the wall next to expensive paintings. It was trained on him. Ignoring it, Moore peered into one of the rooms and saw that it was an enormous dining area with a "five-mile-long" table.

"Emerson Moore?"

A voice behind Moore caused him to curiously turn and respond. "Yes."

"I'm Freddy Fabrizio, Mr. Diamonte's assistant. Would you follow me, please?" Without waiting for a reply, Fat Freddy turned and began walking down the hallway past a sweeping staircase that led to the second floor suites.

Moore quickly followed him to the rear of the mansion where Fat Freddy made a turn into a short entryway and stopped.

Fat Freddy reached into a drawer and produced a scanning

wand. "Would you please set your portfolio down? I'll need to scan you before we walk into the office," he said.

Moore set his portfolio on a vacant shelf and stood while Fat Freddy ran the wand over him. "Checking to see if I'm wired?" Moore asked as he winced at the smell of garlic on Fat Freddy's breath.

"That and to see if you're armed," he responded.

"You could have just asked me," Moore said, a bit irritated.

"We don't take chances with anyone coming in for a meeting," Fat Freddy said as the wand began to beep near the beltline under Moore's sport coat. With a look of concern, Fat Freddy stepped back. "You packing?"

"No."

"What do you have here?" he asked as he reached over to pat Moore's side.

"My cell phone," Moore answered exasperated.

"Hand it over."

"Why? I have it in silent mode."

"Doesn't matter. It's a recording device," Fat Freddy said as he held out his hand.

Moore withdrew the cell phone and its holder, and then handed it to Fat Freddy. "It's no big deal."

"And it shouldn't be," Fat Freddy said as he continued to wand Moore. "Okay, looks like you're clean. Thank you." He set Moore's cell phone on the shelf. "You can have it back when you're done with the meeting."

Moore picked up his portfolio as Fat Freddy knocked three times on the office door before opening it. Following Fat Freddy, Moore entered the equally ostentatious office. It was filled with rich mahogany furniture and lavishly decorated. One of the French doors, overlooking a large swimming pool and outdoor patio area, was open. The aroma of someone smoking a cigar was blown into the room by a fresh breeze.

"Jimmy? Our visitor is here."

Through the open doorway, Moore saw a hand extinguish a cigar in a standing ashtray. The hand disappeared and, a couple of seconds later, Jimmy Diamonds entered the room with a purposeful swagger. He was the king of his castle.

"Mr. Moore, what a pleasure it is to make your acquaintance, sir," Diamonds said with graciousness and respect as he walked over to firmly shake Moore's hand.

"Likewise," Moore responded, assessing the fifty-something crime boss in front of him.

Diamonds was wearing a $1,500 Hickey Freeman suit. The gray suit, a bit dated in style for some, was perhaps made more fashionable and complimented by a $140 Forzieri white dress shirt and a $150 Lorenzo Cana blue tie. His powerfully built frame was starting to show the results of his overeating and lack of exercise as Moore noted a bulge protruding from his mid-section.

"Have a seat, Mr. Moore," Diamonds hospitably offered as he sat in one of the two custom-designed Italian leather chairs in front of his opulent desk.

Sitting in the other chair and facing Diamonds, Moore opened his portfolio and withdrew a pen so he could take notes. "I appreciate you giving me the time to meet with you."

"Anything for the media. You folks seem so fixated by my success," Diamonds' ego responded.

"You are very successful, Mr. Diamonte," Moore agreed.

"Glad to spend some time with someone from Put-in-Bay. It's been a long time since we visited there." Turning to Fat Freddy, he asked, "Isn't that right, Fat Freddy?"

"Yes."

"And did we raise hell there, or what?"

A large smile crossed Fat Freddy's face as he recalled their last visit to Put-in-Bay. "Especially with those two divorcees from Monroe!"

Smiling in return as he nodded in remembrance, Diamonds looked at Moore and asked, "You ever hear that Mad Dog guy play at the Round House?"

"Yes. Several times," Moore replied. "He's a friend of mine."

"He is? You tell him I said 'hello.' He won't remember me, but I kept buying him rounds of shots when he played here in Detroit."

"I think a lot of people do," Moore suggested.

"Yeah, probably. I love it when he has women come on stage and blow the conch shell. That's so frickin' funny!" Diamonds said.

"I like that part, too," Fat Freddy added.

"Mad Dog sure knows how to play to the crowd," Moore agreed.

"What can I do for you today, Mr. Moore?" Diamonds asked. "It's not often a newspaper like *The Washington Post* sends someone to Grosse Ile to interview me. I usually get the local rags writing about my philanthropic activities."

"And I understand they are legendary," Moore continued to play to the ego.

A wide smile crossed Diamonds' equally wide face. "They are. I give a lot of money out, locally. A lot."

Pulling a sheet of paper from his portfolio, Moore glanced at it. "I have compiled a listing of many of the organizations that receive contributions from you."

"Pretty impressive, huh?" Diamonds continued to smile broadly.

"Yes. I did notice one trend," Moore said with conviction as he wrinkled his brow.

"Oh yeah? What's that?"

"The largest contributions from you are to various law enforcement organizations," Moore said.

"Yeah, and what of it, Mr. Moore?" Diamonds' smile was now replaced by a more serious look.

"It's almost like you want to stay on their good side," Moore cautiously observed.

"Yeah, I want them to know they are appreciated by an important local benefactor. Me. Is there a problem with me contributing to them?"

"None whatsoever. I'm just talking about appearances, sir. But, let me switch to disappearances," Moore said as he prepared to drill in.

"Hey, I want to go on the record. I had nothing to do with the disappearance of Malaysian Airlines flight MH370," Diamonds joked.

Fat Freddy laughed at his boss's joke.

Moore cringed at the poor taste of the "joke." Pulling another sheet from his portfolio, he read off several names. "These individuals were linked to organized crime in Detroit and have disappeared in the last eight months."

"Why are you asking me about organized crime? I'm a successful businessman. That's got nothing to do with me," Diamonds replied with measured calm.

"It certainly doesn't," a feminine voice spoke softly from the open patio door.

The men turned to look and saw a tall, blonde woman in stiletto heels and a revealing, white bikini. Her ocean-blue eyes looked piercingly from Diamonds to Moore, as she sauntered into the office. She didn't bother to put on the black mesh cover-up that dangled over one arm. She was one of those women who was very aware of the tantalizing effect her charms had on men, and she relished bathing mindfully naked in their attention.

"Don't stop talking, boys, just because I'm here," she continued.

"You can be so distracting, Veronica," Diamonds said as he ogled his voluptuous girlfriend.

"Who's your friend, Jimmy?" Veronica asked as she looked at

the handsome reporter present before her.

Before Diamonds could respond, Moore abruptly stood and shook the hand she extended to him. "I'm Emerson Moore, of *The Washington Post*."

"Well, it is quite my pleasure to meet you, Mr. Emerson Moore," she said seductively as she bent forward, openly showing her ample cleavage.

"Come on. Get out of here, Veronica. We've got business to discuss," Diamonds said as he waved her away. He didn't like her coming into his office and distracting his guest, even though he was proud of her assets.

"Easy, Jimmy dearest. I was just being polite." She turned from Diamonds and back to Moore. "I do hope I get to see you again." She looked back at Diamonds. "And when I'm wanted."

"Cut the crap. You know you're wanted. Move along, sweet pea," Diamonds said with a tone conveying that he was finished with her interruption.

"Later, gentlemen," Veronica said as she sashayed out of the room, crossing one shapely leg directly over the other, much like a runway fashion model.

Diamonds watched the seductive sway of Veronica's curvaceous hips as she left and closed the door behind herself. Moore, on the other hand, had returned to his notes in front of him. He wouldn't let himself get caught staring at Diamonds' eye candy. He knew better and was intently focused on the task at hand of interviewing his host.

"Hot, isn't she, Mr. Moore?" Diamonds boasted.

Thinking quickly before replying, Moore said, "She is very attractive. I'm sure she is an asset for you."

"Yeah, she's got a really hot…," Fat Freddy began before Diamonds cut him off.

"You don't need to say any more, Fat Freddy." Diamonds looked from Fat Freddy to Moore. "What's your next question, Moore?"

"There have been rumors that you're the kingpin of organized crime in Detroit and that you've been working to consolidate your power base," Moore said as he lowered the sheet of paper he had been studying and trained his eyes on Diamonds.

"Nothing but rumors. You go back and check your records again, Mr. Moore. Nothing has ever stuck to me. I run an import and export business," Diamonds said confidently as he settled back into his plush chair and smiled calmly.

"Is that why you've been dubbed the 'Teflon King?' Nothing sticks to you." Moore countered.

Before responding, Diamonds evaluated the probing reporter in front of him. He was playing mental chess and thereby decided he'd outsmart his inquisitive visitor. Diamonds leaned forward in his chair. "Listen, Mr. Emerson Moore. I'm a law-abiding citizen in Detroit. I haven't broken any laws and I don't plan on breaking any. So, the feds or IRS, and even John Sedler at *The Washington Post*, can check me as much as they want and they won't find anything because there's nothing to be found. I know you guys all like a juicy story, but you're barking up the wrong tree here."

"I see," Moore said. "Are you aware that there's a Colombian gang infiltrating Detroit's illegal drug trade?"

Waving his right hand, Diamonds replied, "I may have read something of it in the *Detroit Free Press*. I read lots of things, Mr. Moore."

"I read about it, too. What I read was that there was a power play going on between your organization and theirs, and then suddenly it ended."

"I don't know what you're talking about," Diamonds said.

"You ever hear of a guy named Eduardo Diaz?" Moore pushed.

Thinking for a moment before answering, Diamonds answered slowly. "No, I don't believe I have."

"Maybe you'd know him better by his street name. Ever hear of El Loco?"

Internally, Diamonds' stomach was beginning to twist. Outwardly, no one could tell he was feeling any discomfort. "Nope. Never heard of him."

Nodding his head, Moore continued, "It seems that Mr. Diaz and his crew were making inroads into the Detroit drug trade, one that is allegedly controlled by you alone."

After a momentary pause, he continued. "One night, Diaz left a downtown restaurant. His two bodyguards were gunned down on the spot and it appeared that Diaz was captured by unknown assailants. His body was found two days later in an abandoned building on the south side. His head had four bullet holes in it. You know anything about it?"

"No," Diamonds replied as he waved his hand dismissively. "But it's a good story, isn't it? Lots of true stories like that here because Detroit's a tough town. Tough people. Unfortunately, things like that happen, Mr. Moore."

"Mr. Diamonte, there are strong rumors circling that you personally offed him. Did you?"

Diamonds' patience reached its limit and he jumped to his feet as anger exploded like an erupting volcano. He unleashed a series of expletives at Moore for trying to link him to Diaz's murder.

Fat Freddy stepped to Diamonds' side and tried to help him regain his composure before Diamonds advanced to the next stage and became physically violent. He had witnessed it before and knew the signs. "Jimmy, come on. Sit down."

Diamonds' face burned red. "I allow you into my home and treat you with respect and this is what you do? Everything I do for this town and this is how you treat me? You – " Diamonds sat back down with assistance from Fat Freddy.

Realizing the inevitable degree of Diamonds' anger, Moore clicked his pen, then set his pen and portfolio on the desk and arose from his chair. "This might be a good time for a break. Can you please direct me to your bathroom?"

"Good idea," Fat Freddy said as he picked up the phone and punched in a number. "Tony, could you come in?"

Within seconds, the office door opened and Parella entered. "You needed me?"

"Yeah. Could you escort this gentleman to the bathroom?"

"Sure." Parella looked at Moore. "You want to follow me?"

Moore walked out of the office and followed Parella a short distance down the hall to the bathroom door.

"Right in there unless you want to squeeze your lemon in that planter," Parella said as he pointed to a large planter in the hallway.

"No, I'll use the bathroom," Moore said as he walked in and a smirking Parella took up position outside the bathroom door.

Moore stepped inside, closing the door behind him. He smiled at how well his plan had worked. He had hoped to stir up Diamonds so that he'd explode and say something he shouldn't say. The agitation worked to a point, but he wasn't able to get or confirm any breakthrough information with absolute certainty. Moore believed though, that he was on the right track.

Meanwhile, Diamonds was raging in his office at Fat Freddy. "Who does he think he is? He comes in here and accuses me like that."

"Easy, Jimmy. Calm down. You don't want to slip and say something you don't mean to say, do you?"

Diamonds was still furious. "I don't slip. No one can link Diaz to me that night. We were too careful when I killed him. We killed the witnesses. You should have been there."

"I'd rather have been there than in the hospital with that heart issue."

"You still got them pills they gave you?" Diamonds asked.

"Yeah. Sometimes, I eat the nitro like candy. I don't know why they don't flavor them."

Hearing the door open, they turned to face Moore as he entered the office. As Moore neared Diamonds and examined the emotions on his face, Moore could see that his plan to step away allowed Diamonds to cool down.

"Ready to start again?"

"No, I am not," Diamonds responded in a firm tone. "I answered your questions. We're done. I have business to attend to. Something has come up that needs my attention."

"I see," Moore said with mild disappointment as he picked up his pen and portfolio. He clicked his pen and placed it in his shirt pocket. Shaking hands with Diamonds, Moore said, "I appreciate the time we spent together, Mr. Diamonte, although I didn't mean for it to be so combative. I'm just doing my job."

"Combative? That was nothing," Diamonds said. He wanted to say more, but decided to simmer down. "Fat Freddy will escort you to the door."

Moore followed him out of the office and down the hallway to the front door. "Thanks, Freddy," Moore said as he shook hands and walked through the open door and to his car.

After driving down the driveway and a couple of miles from the estate, Moore found a quiet spot to turn off and park. He then reached for his pen and connected it to his tablet and listened to the audio recording of the interview.

Moore's eyes widened when he heard the conversation that took place while he was in the bathroom. He had Diamonds on tape confirming he had killed Diaz. Moore reached for his cell phone and called Bona.

"Bona here."

"This is Emerson Moore. Are you in your office?"

"Yes, why?"

"I think I just nailed Jimmy Diamonds on the Diaz murder for you," Moore said eagerly.

"How's that?"

"I'll show you when I get there."

"Come on in. I'll be waiting," Bona said.

Police Headquarters
Detroit, Michigan

Bona's head was bent over his desk as he read through a file. The knock at his door caused him to raise his head. Through the glass on the door, Bona saw Moore standing somewhat anxiously and he waved him to enter.

"So, you've got the goods on Jimmy Diamonds, do you, Mr. Moore?" Bona asked with much skepticism. He watched Moore drop with enthused exhaustion into an empty chair on the other side of the desk as if he had just completed running a marathon.

"I do, but let me tell you first about my meeting with him to set the stage," Moore suggested. He then explained to Bona what had transpired at Grosse Ile.

"After I got Diamonds mad at me, I thought we needed to cool down. I told him I had to use the bathroom. That's when I got him," Moore related.

"In the bathroom?" Bona asked incredulously. Leaning forward in his chair, Bona said, "You do know this sounds weird, don't you?"

Moore extended his arms and held up both hands, palms outward toward Bona, much like a traffic cop. "Stop! You're heading in the wrong direction."

"Okay, go on."

"I have a tool," Moore said.

"You bragging?" Bona asked in a teasing manner.

"No. Wait!"

Moore removed his pen recorder from his pocket and connected it to his iPad. It was time now for a little show and tell. "Just listen to this," he said as he played the recorder.

Bona listened closely. A wide smile filled his face when he heard Diamonds confirm he had killed Diaz. After the recording ended, Bona looked up at Moore. "I'd like to have this if you don't mind. It's exactly what we needed to nail him. You've done well, Emerson."

Moore confidently smiled with deep satisfaction in noting he had helped come up with the evidence needed to convict Diamonds. He disconnected the recorder and gave it to Bona. "Thanks, Marc. I do have a favor to ask."

"Sure, I'll return your recorder once the trial is over," Bona said.

"No, that's not it."

"Okay then, what's your favor? Ask away."

"I'd like to be there when you arrest Diamonds for the murder of Diaz. I'd like to cover it and then write about it for *The Post*, exclusively."

"That can be arranged." Bona looked at his watch. "Give me an hour or so to get everything set up."

"Okay."

Bona rose from behind his desk and walked around to Moore. "Let me show you to an empty office down the hall, Emerson. You can camp out there while we get organized."

"Great," Moore confirmed as he stood and followed Bona down the hall and to an empty office. Once Bona left, Moore sat behind the desk, took out his cell phone and called his editor, John Sedler.

"Sedler here," the gruff voice answered.

"It's Emerson, John."

Sedler's tone softened. "Hello, Emerson. Did you get a chance to interview Jimmy Diamonds yet?"

"Get a chance? Wait until you hear this! I think I just broke the Diaz murder case wide open. I've got a recording of Jimmy Diamonds confessing to the murder."

"What?" Sedler asked, stunned.

"Yep. I nailed his butt!" Moore excitedly blurted into his phone. He then went on to repeat the story he had given Bona and confirmed to Sedler that he was going to exclusively cover the arrest of Detroit's notorious crime boss that afternoon.

"Good. No, I mean great job, Emerson!" Sedler proudly exclaimed as he sat back in his chair. He was beaming. He couldn't get over the uncanny ability of his ace investigative reporter to land new breaking stories with solid reporting. He was mighty proud of his protégé.

They chatted for a few minutes more before ending the call. An hour later, as Bona had indicated, Moore found himself in an unmarked police vehicle with Bona and several officers en route to Grosse Ile where a special Detroit Police and Wayne County Violent Crime Task Force and SWAT team soon arrested a shocked Jimmy Diamonds and took him into custody.

Afterwards, Moore wrote the story about his day's activities. The wire services and large media broadcasters like Fox and CNN also carried the breaking news with credit given to *The Washington Post* and Moore's reporting.

Third Circuit Court, Criminal Division
Detroit, Michigan

Following his arrest and initial court appearances, Jimmy Diamonds faced a jury trial on a charge of first-degree murder. To get a conviction, the prosecuting attorney would need to prove the murder involved premeditation and came at the hands of the Detroit crime boss.

Michigan's Third Circuit Court was located in the Frank Murphy Hall of Justice in downtown Detroit. The courtroom was packed with spectators and reporters as the trial began with opening statements from both attorneys. When they finished, Judge Joseph Wilson instructed Wayne County assistant prosecutor, Jill Fitz, to call her first witness.

"Thank you, Your Honor. The state calls Mr. Emerson Moore," the tall blonde said.

Wearing a dark blue suit, white shirt and blue-and-white striped tie, Moore respectfully rose and walked to the witness stand where he was sworn in.

As he sat, Fitz approached him. "Would you tell the jury your name, please?

"Emerson Moore."

"Where do you reside?"

"Put-in-Bay, Ohio."

"And what is your occupation?"

"I'm an investigative reporter for *The Washington Post*."

"Mr. Moore, would you tell the court where you were on June 2nd of this year?"

"Yes, I met with Mr. Diamonte."

"If Mr. Diamonte is present in this courtroom now, would you please point to him?"

Moore pointed to Diamonds, sitting at the defense table and appearing to have no interest in the current proceeding.

"Let the record reflect that Mr. Moore pointed to the defendant, Mr. Diamonte," Fitz said as she looked at the court reporter.

"And where did the meeting with Mr. Diamonte take place?"

"At his home on Grosse Ile."

"Was there a particular place in the home where the meeting occurred?"

"Yes, in the study on the first floor of the house."

"Who asked for this meeting?"

"I did."

"Why did you want to meet with Mr. Diamonte?" Fitz asked matter-of-factly as she turned her back to Moore and looked toward the jury.

"I wanted to interview him for a story for *The Post*."

"And what was the focus of your interview?"

"I wanted to ask him about his numerous contributions to law enforcement charities. I suspected they were a cover for payoffs."

"I see," Fitz said as she spun around to face Moore. "Was there anyone else present at the meeting?"

"Yes, Freddy Fabrizio."

"If Mr. Fabrizio is present in this courtroom now, would you also point to him?"

Moore pointed to Fat Freddy, sitting in the first row of seats behind the defense team.

"Let the record reflect that Mr. Moore pointed to Mr. Fabrizio, a spectator in the courtroom," Fitz said to the court reporter.

"Was Mr. Fabrizio present during the entire time of your interview?"

"Yes."

"Would you give the jury a brief overview of your interview?"

"Sure," Moore said as he relaxed in his seat. "We started with a brief discussion about Put-in-Bay and their visits to the island."

Fitz interrupted. "What island is that?"

"Put-in-Bay is located on South Bass Island in western Lake Erie near Port Clinton and Sandusky."

"Please continue."

"Then, I shifted into what I thought were his overly generous contributions to law enforcement agencies and the disappearance of a number of Detroit gang members in the last eight months. I specifically narrowed the discussion to Eduardo Diaz and his death."

"And what happened when you did that?"

"Mr. Diamonte became very agitated."

"Agitated? What do you mean by that, precisely?"

"He went off on me and began swearing like a Marine drill instructor," Moore explained.

"And what did you do?"

"When situations start to get out of control, I've always found it's a good time to briefly remove oneself from the situation so that tempers can cool. I told them that I needed to use the bathroom."

"So, you went to the bathroom?"

"Yes. They called one of their cohorts to escort me to it, so that I wasn't wandering around the residence by myself."

"Did Mr. Diamonte and Mr. Fabrizio remain in Mr. Diamonte's study?"

"Yes, they did."

"Was there anyone else present with them?"

"No, not to my knowledge."

"What happened when you returned from the bathroom?"

"Things had calmed down. Mr. Diamonte told me that he had to immediately conclude our meeting because something had come up that needed his attention."

"What happened next, sir?"

"Mr. Fabrizio escorted me to the front door and I drove away in my car."

"And then?"

"After a few miles, I stopped," said Moore.

"Why?"

"I wanted to replay my meeting with them and see if they revealed anything while I was out of the study."

"And how could you do that?"

"My pen is a recording device. I use it to tape my interviews."

"Mr. Moore, did you purchase this device for the purpose of taping Mr. Diamonte?"

"No, not at all. I've had it for nearly a year. I like it because it doesn't make my interviewees nervous since they don't know it's a recording device as well as a writing instrument."

"Mr. Moore, is it your practice to tape your interviews?"

"Yes, it is."

"Do you tell your subjects they are being recorded?"

"I typically do not."

"Did you tell Mr. Diamonte or Mr. Fabrizio that their conversation with you was being recorded?"

"No, I did not."

Walking to a table in front of the judge, Fitz picked up a silver pen and then proceeded back toward Moore on the witness stand so that he could see it. "I hand you what has been labeled as Exhibit A for identification purposes. Is this your pen, Mr. Moore?"

The reporter took the pen in hand and carefully examined it, then handed it back to his inquisitor. "Yes. It has a scratch on the side," Moore replied.

Fitz placed the pen on the table and began to connect it to a speaker as she looked without obvious emotion at the judge "If it pleases the court, I'd like to now play the recording for the jury."

The judge looked at the defense attorney, who reluctantly nodded his agreement. "You may proceed, Ms. Fitz," the judge said.

Fitz played the recording and the room fell eerily silent as everyone listened to the conversation between Diamonds and Fat Freddy.

"Who does he think he is? He comes in here and accuses me like that," Diamonds stormed.

"Easy Jimmy. Calm down. You don't want to slip and say something you don't mean to say, do you?" Fat Freddy asked.

"I don't slip. No one can link Diaz to me that night. We were too careful when I killed him. We killed the witnesses. You should have been there."

"I'd rather have been there than in the hospital with that heart issue."

When the recording ended, Fitz turned off the pen and faced Moore. "Could you, Mr. Moore, identify the two voices we just heard?"

"Yes. The first voice belonged to Mr. Diamonte. The second was Freddy Fabrizio."

"And whose voice stated that he had killed Eduardo Diaz?"

"That was Mr. Diamonte."

"Could you speak up and again repeat that comment for the jury?"

"Yes, that was Mr. Diamonte saying that he killed Eduardo Diaz."

"And did Mr. Diamonte make this statement in your presence during your interview?"

"No, he did not. I left my pen on record when I left the study to go to the bathroom. That's when the statement was made."

"Thank you, Mr. Moore." Fitz turned to the judge. "That's all I have for this witness," she said as she returned to her chair at the prosecution table.

Diamonds' defense attorney, Bill Salvatori, slowly rose from his chair. He held a pad of notes in his left hand that he was reading as he asked his first question. "Mr. Moore, were you wanded when you entered Mr. Diamonte's home?"

"Yes, I was."

"Doesn't that tell you that Mr. Diamonte was concerned for his privacy?"

"Mr. Fabrizio told me that it was a safety scan as they looked for weapons."

"Didn't he also tell you that they were looking for recording devices?"

"Yes, but I was thinking it was more along the lines of being wired, like for a drug deal."

"Why didn't Mr. Fabrizio find your pen?"

"It was in my portfolio."

"And where was your portfolio when you were being scanned?"

"I had set it on a shelf."

"Did you purposely conceal the fact that you had a recording device?"

"No. I honestly didn't think about it."

"When did you realize, Mr. Moore, that you, in fact, had the recording device?"

"When I pulled it out of my portfolio to take notes."

"And when you realized you had it, why didn't you tell either my client or Mr. Fabrizio that you had the device?"

"I didn't think it was a big deal. I use it a lot."

"Mr. Moore, were you trying to entrap Mr. Diamonte?"

"No, I was trying to gather information for my story."

"And your story was about generous philanthropic donations?"

"No." Moore squirmed a bit.

"What was your story about?"

"The impact Mr. Diamonte was having on the marked increase in homicides and organized crime activities in Detroit."

"So, you were out to get Mr. Diamonte?"

"No, I was out to get the truth."

"Did you get the truth?"

"I didn't get to the rest of my interview questions because Mr. Diamonte promptly cut the interview short."

Salvatori stepped back and looked at the jury. "I believe you will see, as this case progresses, that there is no basis in fact contained in the recording you have heard. Mr. Moore doesn't realize how the tables were intentionally turned on him."

Fitz adamantly spoke from her seat. "I object, Your Honor."

"Sustained," the judge retorted.

Looking at the judge, Salvatori said, "We're finished with this witness for now, but reserve the right to call him back to the stand, Your Honor."

The judge nodded and turned to Moore, "You may step down, sir." He then turned to the prosecutor. "Ms. Fitz, you may call your next witness."

One of the prosecutor's assistants, who was standing at the back of the room, suddenly ducked out of the courtroom. He reappeared within seconds. A dapperly dressed Hispanic man was at his side.

"Your Honor, the state calls Mr. Ricardo Ramos to the stand."

"What's this all about?" Diamonds fumed as he jerked Salvatori around in his chair. Despite his calm demeanor earlier in the courtroom proceedings, Diamonds now was becoming more visibly agitated.

"I don't know," Salvatori replied as Ramos walked down the center aisle. "Do you know him?"

"Yeah. He was one of Diaz's top guys. What's he doing here?"

"Your Honor, we don't know anything about this witness," Salvatori pleaded as he rose from the defense table.

"Ms. Fitz, would you like to explain?" the judge asked.

"Yes, Your Honor. Mr. Ramos contacted our office yesterday and has invaluable and specific information relevant to this case."

"I see. You may proceed," the judge said as he glanced at the defense team.

Fitz motioned Ramos forward and he was sworn in, then seated on the witness stand.

"Could you state your name?" Fitz asked.

"Ricardo Ramos."

"And your residence?"

"I live here."

"Mr. Ramos, could you tell us where here is?"

"Oh, yeah. Detroit."

"And what is your occupation, Mr. Ramos?"

"I'm unemployed."

"Mr. Ramos, could you tell the court where you were on April 15th of this year?"

"Yes, I met with Jimmy."

"Jimmy?" Fitz asked.

"Jimmy Diamonds. He's sitting right there." Ramos pointed at Diamonds.

"Let the record show that Mr. Ramos pointed to the defendant, Mr. Diamonte," Fitz said as she looked at the court reporter.

Turning back to Ramos, Fitz asked, "And where did the meeting with Mr. Diamonte take place?"

"In an alley in Detroit. It was late at night."

"Could you be more specific?"

"Yeah. It was behind El Manquello's Restaurant on Bagley."

"Was there anyone else present at the meeting?"

"No. Not really. He had a driver, but he got out of the car and stood in front of it so Jimmy and I could talk privately in the car."

"Mr. Ramos, could you look around this courtroom and tell us if you see the driver?"

Ramos scanned the crowded courtroom. "No, I don't see him."

"And what was the purpose of your meeting with Mr. Diamonte?" Fitz asked as she turned her back to Ramos and looked toward the jury.

"Jimmy wanted to see me. He asked me to kill Eduardo Diaz."

"I did not," Diamonds bellowed as he jumped from his chair in anger and pointed his finger, then emphatically shook it in accusatory fashion toward Ramos, who then began to cower in the witness box. "I never had a meeting with that low-life!"

"Keep your client under control please, Mr. Salvatori," the judge demanded as Salvatori gently pulled Diamonds back into his chair and began whispering to him.

Spinning around to face Ramos, Fitz asked, "What exactly did Mr. Diamonte say to you?"

"He asked me to kill Eduardo Diaz."

"And what was your understanding as to why would he ask you to kill him?"

"He knew that I was a friend of Diaz and hung out with him."

"Did you work for Mr. Diaz?"

Ramos hesitated. "No," he finally replied.

"Did Mr. Diamonte offer to pay you to kill Mr. Diaz?"

"Yes."

"And how much was he going to pay you?"

"Fifty thousand dollars. Half up front and the rest after I did it."

"Liar! I've never met this man. He's making up all of this," Diamonds shouted with intense objection from his chair. His face was red with anger and the bailiff in the courtroom began moving toward the defense table to restrain the nearly out-of-control defendant.

"Mr. Salvatori, please control your client. If he continues to be disruptive, I'll have the bailiff remove him from the courtroom immediately. Do you understand, sir? It is your final warning," the judge said firmly, looking directly at the accused.

"Yes, Your Honor. I do understand," Salvatori said as he tried to calm down his client. Salvatori spoke quietly, "Jimmy, you need to get in control of yourself, no exceptions. Please, Jimmy."

"He's lying through his teeth! I never met him! It's a set up!" Diamonds stormed quietly.

The judge looked toward Fitz and said, "You may continue questioning the witness."

"Thank you, Your Honor." Fitz turned back to Ramos and asked, "And what did you say to Mr. Diamonte's offer to kill Mr. Diaz?"

"I told him no way. Eduardo was a friend of mine."

"I see. Why do you think Mr. Diamonte wanted Mr. Diaz killed?"

"Drugs. Jimmy was losing drug business to Eduardo."

Salvatori stood from his seat and interrupted. "I must object, Your Honor, and move to strike this testimony. That's supposition. There has been no connection of illegal drug selling to my client."

"Objection sustained," the judge said as he turned to look at the jury. "I'm instructing you to disregard the comment regarding Mr. Diamonte losing drug business to Mr. Diaz." Looking back at Fitz, he said, "You may continue."

"Let me rephrase my question. Did Mr. Diamonte tell you why he wanted Mr. Diaz murdered?"

"Yes."

"Why?"

"He said that Diaz was selling drugs in his territory."

"I see. I'm finished with this witness, Your Honor," Fitz said as she walked back to the prosecutor's table and sat in her chair.

"Mr. Salvatori?" the judge asked.

Salvatori and Diamonds had their heads together as they quietly conversed.

"Mr. Salvatori, do you have any questions for this witness or should I dismiss him?" the judge asked.

Rising from his seat, Salvatori approached the witness. "I apologize for the delay, Your Honor. Mr. Ramos, at what time on April 15th did this alleged meeting take place?"

"Let me think a minute." Ramos paused before continuing. "It was around ten o'clock at night."

"Are you sure?"

"Yes. Absolutely."

"Mr. Ramos, would it surprise you if I told you that Mr. Diamonte was at a fundraiser for the police that night at ten o'clock at his Grosse Ile residence?"

"Yes, it would, because he was with me."

Salvatori turned to the jury. "I'll be calling several witnesses who can refute Mr. Ramos' testimony that Mr. Diamonte was with Mr. Ramos that evening at ten o'clock. We will show that Mr. Diamonte left the fundraiser and went to the airport where a chartered plane was waiting for him and he flew out that night." Salvatori suddenly whirled around and faced Ramos. "Mr. Ramos, do you know what perjury is?"

"Yes."

"What is it?"

"Lying."

"Did you just commit perjury?"

"No! What I said happened. You're just going to have his friends come in and they're going to make up stories about where he was. I'm telling you that he met with me!" Ramos stormed with frustration.

"Calm down, Mr. Ramos." Turning to the judge, Salvatori said, "That's all I have at this time for this witness, Your Honor."

The trial continued for the rest of the afternoon with a variety of witnesses and the Wayne County medical examiner testifying on behalf of the prosecution until they rested their case around four o'clock. The judge then adjourned the trial for the day.

The trial reopened at nine o'clock the next morning with defense attorney Salvatori calling several witnesses who provided alibis for Diamonds' whereabouts on the evening on April 15th to contradict Ramos' assertion. At noon, the judge adjourned for lunch.

Before returning to the courtroom after lunch, Salvatori and Diamonds went into the men's restroom where they checked and found it vacant. Fat Freddy guarded the entrance so that they wouldn't be interrupted.

Reaching into his pocket, Diamonds produced a small plastic bag filled with cocaine. When Salvatori saw him pour it on the countertop by the sink, he said, "Jimmy, you can't do that here."

Using his credit card to create two lines, Diamonds said with a stone face, "Lesson number one. You don't tell me what to do. I'm going to be on the stand next and I need a little boost." He took a $100 bill and rolled it into a tube, then bent over the first line and snorted the coke. He repeated the process with the next line.

Smiling as he looked into the mirror, he wiped the white powder from his nostrils. "Now, I'm ready for those S.O.B.s."

"You shouldn't do this in front of me, Jimmy," Salvatori said.

"I got extra. You want to take a snort?"

Perturbed with his client, Salvatori turned. "Let's go."

The two men, followed by Fat Freddy, returned to their chairs in the courtroom where shortly thereafter Diamonds was called to the witness stand.

Salvatori approached him. "Could you please state your name for the court?

"James Diamonte."

"And where do you reside, Mr. Diamonte?"

"Grosse Ile. I've got a place that looks over the Detroit River."

"And what is your occupation, Mr. Diamonte?"

"I own an import and export business."

"And where is that business located, sir?"

"In Detroit."

"Where in Detroit?"

"South side. Off of West Fort Street. It overlooks the river."

"Thank you, Mr. Diamonte. Do you know Mr. Ramos?"

"No!" Diamonds responded emphatically. "I never met the S.O.B."

Judge Wilson leaned forward from the bench and spoke to Diamonds. "Mr. Diamonte, watch your language, please, in this courtroom."

Diamonds nodded his understanding in return.

"Then, you didn't meet Mr. Ramos on April 15th of this year?"

"No! I never met him any time."

"Why sir, do you think Mr. Ramos testified otherwise?"

"He wants to see me locked up for some reason."

"Any idea what that reason would be?"

"Not a clue!"

"Mr. Diamonte, could you please tell the jury where you were on April 15th of this year?"

"Yes, I was at a party at my home."

"Thank you. And, you've heard several witnesses earlier testify that they were with you at your party, correct?"

"Yes."

"How long did that party last, Mr. Diamonte?"

"It started at eight o'clock and lasted until two o'clock in the morning."

"Did you leave the party at anytime?"

"No way! Why would I leave a party at my house? You saw

some of the female witnesses. You think I would want to leave a party with women who look that beautiful?"

A few chuckles could be heard in the courtroom.

"Mr. Diamonte, did you know the deceased, Mr. Eduardo Diaz?"

"Not personally. I read some stories about him in the *Detroit Free Press*. That's all I knew about him."

"Thank you. Did he pose a business threat to you?"

"Based on what I read in the newspaper, we're not in the same line of business. So, he couldn't be a threat to me."

"Mr. Diamonte, did you have a meeting with Mr. Emerson Moore on June 2nd?"

"Yes."

"And where, sir, did the meeting with Mr. Moore take place?"

"At my home on Grosse Ile."

"Was anyone else, Mr. Diamonte, present during this meeting?"

"Yes, my associate. Freddy Fabrizio."

"And what, sir, was the purpose of your meeting with Mr. Moore?" Salvatori asked as he turned his back to Moore and then next toward the jury.

"He wanted to interview me about my philanthropic activities."

"And did he do that, Mr. Diamonte? Did he ask you specifically about your many charitable and philanthropic activities?"

"That's the way it started," Diamonds said innocently as he stared stonily at Moore, who was seated in the courtroom.

"How did it end? That is, Mr. Diamonte, how did the interview with you and Mr. Moore end?"

"He started to accuse me of bribing the police."

"Do you have an understanding of why he would have done that, sir?"

"He was just looking for a cheap headline. A juicy story. You know how these newspaper guys need headlines to sell newspapers. It doesn't even need to be true."

"Mr. Diamonte, have you ever bribed a law enforcement officer?"

"Never!" Diamonds said firmly.

"Did Mr. Moore leave the room at any time during his meeting with you in your residence?"

A smile crossed Diamonds face. "Yeah. He had to use the bathroom. I think he had the runs," Diamonds snickered quietly as he attempted to embarrass Moore.

"Thank you. What happened next when Mr. Moore left your study?"

"I looked down at his pen and recognized it as a common recording device. I see them all the time when I go to the Brookstone store. I whispered to Freddy that we're going to have a little fun with Moore and to play along with me."

"And what did you do, or say?"

"Moore was looking for a headline, so I gave him one."

"Could you please explain, sir?"

"It's like everyone heard when the tape was played here in the courtroom. I made some make-believe comments in front of the pen that made it sound like I killed Diaz."

"Did you in fact kill Mr. Diaz, Mr. Diamonte, or cause harm or injury upon him in any other manner?"

"No, sir, I was just joking. I was tired of his insulting questions and wanted to get him worked up. I should never have done it, obviously I realize that now," Diamonds said ashamedly and with his head bowed. He was doing his best to look repentant before the court and jury, but it wasn't working.

"It looks, sir, like your joke backfired and unfortunately resulted in you being brought into this courtroom and accused of a serious crime, doesn't it, Mr. Diamonte?" Salvatori asked.

"Yes," Diamonds said as he turned directly toward the judge.

"It was God-awful poor judgment on my part," he further stated as he then turned completely around in his witness chair and faced the jury. "I am very sorry because I should never have joked about something as serious as another human's death. Life is precious."

"Thank you, Mr. Diamonte," Salvatori said as he finished questioning his client and returned to his seat.

Judge Wilson nodded at the prosecuting attorney to begin her questioning and Fitz approached the witness stand.

Fitz began by asking, "Mr. Diamonte, are you known by any other names?"

"Yes."

Salvatori shot up from his chair. "I object."

Looking at the judge, Fitz asked, "May we please approach the bench, Your Honor?"

Salvatori joined Fitz for a sidebar with the judge.

Speaking quietly, Fitz said, "Your Honor, the prosecution is trying to show Mr. Diamonte's connection to organized crime and the death of Mr. Diaz."

"I'll allow it, but proceed carefully," the judge ruled. "Objection overruled."

Salvatori returned to his seat while Fitz proceeded.

"Mr. Diamonte," Fitz began.

"Yes?"

"Could you answer my question?"

Diamonds looked at his attorney, who reluctantly nodded his head to Diamonds. "I've got a couple of nicknames. Jimmy Diamonds and Jimmy D."

"And where did those nicknames come from?"

"A couple of my friends. They thought they were being funny." Diamonds withheld revealing that he had a third nickname that wasn't widely known. It was Jimmy Death.

"And why did they give you those nicknames?"

"I don't know."

"Isn't it true that those are the kind of nicknames given to members of organized crime?"

Salvatori quickly arose from his chair again and protested. "Your Honor, I object to this line of questioning."

"I'd like both of you to approach the bench," the judge ordered.

Both attorneys walked to the bench and the three of them whispered in hushed tones. When they finished, they returned to their places and Fitz changed her line of questioning.

"Mr. Diamonte."

"Yes?"

"In your deposition, you indicated that you believed Mr. Diaz committed suicide; is that correct?"

Diamonds looked at his attorney before answering. Seeing his attorney nod, he replied. "Yes."

"Come, come, Mr. Diamonte. Do you really believe it was suicide?"

"Yes."

"Could you explain to me how it could be suicide when he was shot four times in the head?"

A thin smile appeared on Diamonds' mouth. "His aim was off," he answered in feigned seriousness.

The courtroom crowd tittered.

The judge pounded his gavel. "I'll have order in my court." He leaned toward the witness stand. "Mr. Diamonte, this is not a joking matter."

"I know that, Your Honor."

The judge glared at Diamonds and then nodded to Fitz to continue.

"Mr. Diamonte, I need your help on this one. If this was a suicide as you allege, why couldn't we find the weapon?"

"That's easy. Diaz hid it before he died."

The courtroom filled with laughter again as the judge pounded his gavel and again restored order in the courtroom.

"I'm finished with this witness, Your Honor," Fitz said as she returned to the prosecution's table.

"You're excused," the judge said to Diamonds, who stepped down from the witness stand. As he walked past the prosecution's table, he threw them a sidelong grin of triumph. He was still feeling the effects of the snort of coke he had earlier enjoyed.

The defense team called Fat Freddy to the stand to confirm Diamonds' comments that they were joking when he and Diamonds had the taped conversation. After the prosecutor cross-examined with nothing pertinent surfacing, the defense attorney rested his case and the two opposing attorneys each made their closing arguments to the jury.

Having received the judge's instructions, the jury left the courtroom to start their deliberations. Two days later, the jury returned its verdict and found Diamonds guilty of the premeditated murder of Eduardo Diaz. The judge scheduled sentencing for the following afternoon when he sentenced Diamonds to forty years in prison.

Diamonds was immediately taken into custody and sent to a holding cell pending his transfer in two days to the Chippewa Correctional Facility in Kincheloe, Michigan.

Wayne County Jail
Detroit, Michigan

The armored prisoner transport van pulled away from the jail complex onto Clinton Street. A stoic guard sat next to the driver. Both were armed. Behind them a solid wall separated them from their human cargo. Locked in the rear of the vehicle were Jimmy Diamonds, another guard and Emerson Moore. Since Moore had broken the story that led to Diamonds' subsequent conviction, he was given special permission to ride in the transport vehicle the day after sentencing and exclusively interview Diamonds on the drive to the Chippewa Correctional Facility.

Rumors recently had circulated that Diamonds' henchmen would attempt to free him during his trip to prison. To lessen the chances of an escape, the police had sent out two decoy vehicles with police escorts over the last two hours. It would have worked, except Diamonds had a paid informant in the police department.

The van, containing Diamonds, Moore and the three guards, left the garage with no escort and took a circuitous route to start its journey. It turned and drove east along Beaubien Street. The vehicle turned right onto Atwater Street, which ran in a southerly direction, downriver and parallel to the Detroit River and next to the Detroit Riverwalk.

As the van crossed Renaissance Drive West and started over the Detroit-Windsor Tunnel, the guard in the passenger seat asked,

"What's this about?"

"Construction, it looks like," the driver said as he braked the van to a stop.

A man wearing a neon yellow safety vest and yellow hardhat stood in the street directing traffic. He was holding a flagger's stop sign as a front-end loader backed onto the street. The flagger approached the van driver's window.

"You want to open up?" he asked over the beeping of the backing front-end loader.

"Can't do it!" the driver defiantly said through the bulletproof glass as he shook his head from side to side.

The flagger pointed to an open doorway of a nearby building. "You might want to reconsider that, friend."

"What the hell!" the driver exclaimed as his wife and the other guard's wife were pushed through the doorway by two masked gunmen.

"Ten seconds to open the window and toss out your guns or they die," the flagger shouted. He had dropped the flag he had been holding and was now holding a handgun.

"Please don't hurt her!" the driver moaned.

"Not for me. I was going to divorce mine. This can make it easier on me. I'll get her insurance money," the passenger whispered.

"Screw you! I'm saving my wife," the driver uttered with clenched teeth and determination.

"Five seconds," the flagger announced. "Four…three…two…"

The driver opened the windows on both sides as he depressed a silent alarm with his left foot. Using the vehicle's GPS, police reinforcements would quickly be on the scene.

"That's more like it. Toss out your weapons. Now!"

Reluctantly, both men threw their weapons out of the vehicle.

"Now, get out of the vehicle and come around to the rear," the flagger said as he looked at his watch. The two gunmen with the two wives joined them at the rear of the vehicle.

"Tell him to open up," the flagger instructed as he laid the barrel of his weapon against the van driver's temple. "You've got ten seconds or your wives die."

The driver pounded on the van's rear doors. "Jeff, open up man!"

"What's going on, Lou?" Jeff called through the locked rear door. There were no windows in the rear of the van.

"We're being hijacked. They've got our wives out here. They're going to kill them if you don't open up now."

"Can't do it," the guard responded from inside the van.

"Jeff, don't fool around man! These guys mean business!" the driver yelled urgently.

A gunshot filled the air as one of the gunmen instantly killed the driver's wife.

"No!" the driver cried as he ran over to her limp body on the ground.

"You're up," the flagger said to the other guard.

"You might as well as kill her because I'm not going to tell him to open the door," he said as he saw his freedom from marriage at hand.

Without hesitation, the flagger discharged his weapon and instantly killed the second guard. "That's not what I was going to do, sucker."

Suddenly, the bucket of the front-end loader crashed down on the roof of the armored van, putting a large dent in it. At the same time, a liquid sloshed out of the bucket and the smell of gasoline filled the air. Next, the front-end loader tipped its bucket and allowed gasoline to pour into the large dent it had made in the roof and overflow down the sides of the van. The smell of gasoline flowed through the vents and permeated the interior of the vehicle.

"This is your last chance before we torch the vehicle. We'll burn you alive!" the flagger yelled through the closed door. "You have five seconds!"

Two seconds flew by and the door to the rear of the van burst open. The guard emerged choking for fresh air, quickly followed by Moore who also was gasping desperately.

"Get me the hell out of here!" Diamonds yelled from the bench to which he was shackled.

"Keys!" the flagger demanded from the guard, who promptly handed them over. The flagger jumped into the van and freed Diamonds after handing him a .45 caliber semi-automatic handgun. As they exited the van, they heard a shot fired and looked to where the wives had been held. The grieving van driver had pulled his hideaway gun from his ankle holster and shot the gunman, who killed his wife. The second gunman then abruptly aimed and shot the van driver as he pushed away the other wife, who ran screaming uncontrollably down the street.

Simultaneously, three Detroit police cruisers arrived and officers rapidly opened fire on the remaining gunman, the flagger, the front-end loader driver and Diamonds.

Moore looked around to find cover as bullets whizzed by. Before he could dive behind a car parked nearby, he felt a sharply stinging sensation along the side of his head, then fell unconscious to the ground. A stray bullet had caught Moore in the head. Blood began steadily flowing from his head wound.

"Jimmy, to the river," the flagger yelled as he pointed to a go-fast boat that was waiting with its engines idling and pointed downriver. He then threw an incendiary device into the back of the van and it exploded in a ball of fire, showering the area with debris.

"Is Moore dead?" Diamonds asked as he ducked and returned fire at the officers.

"Head wound, I think," the flagger yelled.

"Bring him with us. I owe him big time and is he ever going to pay for this!" Diamonds barked furiously.

The flagger ran to Moore and heaved the reporter's body over his shoulder while running with Jimmy Diamonds the short distance across the Riverwalk and to the waiting go-fast boat. Another Diamonds' henchman was at the boat with an automatic weapon, firing upon the officers. During the run to the boat, the front-end loader driver and the other gunman were hit and had dropped to the ground. They sustained mortal wounds and died within ten minutes of each other.

Jumping into the escape boat, Diamonds grabbed one of the

automatic weapons so that the boat driver could complete the next phase of their escape. The flagger also jumped aboard and dropped Moore's body in a heap on the stern deck. Blood was still flowing steadily, but not profusely, from his head wound.

The boat leapt out of the water and rapidly headed downriver away from the firefight where numerous reinforcements continued to arrive. No more than five minutes had elapsed when a police helicopter circled the area and flew downriver in search of the speeding getaway craft.

The helicopter flew over several of the marinas on the riverfront and around Grosse Ile. It then flew over Lake Erie and spotted the escaping boat heading south toward Toledo. It swiftly closed in on the boat and saw no one at the controls. It appeared that the throttle had been set wide open.

Using his loudspeaker, the pilot ordered the unseen boat driver to halt. Seeing no one on board and assuming it had been abandoned, the helicopter pilot matched the speed of the boat and dropped over it. His crewmate slid the door open and hooked up a police officer to the winch line before lowering him to the deck of the craft.

When the officer landed on the deck, he detached himself from the line and brought the boat safely and quickly to a stop. He thoroughly searched the craft and found no one aboard, but discovered a large pool of blood on the deck near the stern. Emerson Moore was missing.

Grosse Ile Yacht Club
Hickory Island, Michigan

After racing downriver, and before it was commandeered by the police, the getaway boat had stopped briefly at the Grosse Ile Yacht Club on Hickory Island. The club was located on a small peninsula at the southernmost point of the Detroit River where it empties into Lake Erie. It had a commanding and unobstructed view of the lake and the river's boat and commercial ship traffic.

The boat had swung around to the south side of the club and reversed its engines so it could glide up to the dock. A van with Wharton Heating lettered on the side was parked next to the dock. The flagger and the boat's helmsman carried Moore and followed Diamonds the short distance to the van. Diamonds opened the unlocked rear doors so that Moore could be placed in the rear.

"We did it!" a familiar voice called to Diamonds from the driver's seat. It was Fat Freddy.

"Yeah, we did. And look at the extra baggage I picked up," Diamonds chortled as Fat Freddy twisted in his seat.

"Is that who I think it is?" Fat Freddy asked.

"Yeah – our friend, Emerson Moore. We're going to have a little fun with payback," Diamonds said as he turned to walk to the side of the van.

Fat Freddy cringed, realizing the torture in store for Moore.

Before jumping into the rear of the van, the helmsman pulled a remote control device from his pocket and pointed it toward the idling go-fast boat, which had been pointed toward Lake Erie. He depressed the controls that operated a device he had set on the boat's throttle. As the throttle gradually opened, the boat gathered speed and headed out to open water.

The helmsman jumped into the rear of the van and turned his attention to Moore. The flagger bent over Moore as Diamonds slipped into the passenger seat. The Wharton Heating van then slowly drove away.

During the boat ride Diamonds had discarded his prison gear and dressed in khaki slacks and a polo shirt. He also donned a pair of Ray-Ban sunglasses and a University of Michigan ball cap.

Starting the van, Fat Freddy began to drive it to the Grosse Ile Municipal Airport, a short distance away.

"You make sure he doesn't die on me!" Diamonds yelled to the helmsman and flagger as the van headed to the airport.

"It looks like the bleeding has mostly stopped," the flagger said.

Later, police officers would talk to John and Ruth Clark at the yacht club. They had been sitting on the deck of their 48-foot Hatteras, *The Mad Hatter*, when they saw the arrival and abrupt departure of Diamonds' getaway boat. The couple also reported they saw the Wharton Heating van come and go from the immediate area. Police would next turn their attention to searching for the van.

When the van arrived at the airport, it drove across the tarmac to a chartered plane that was waiting in a deserted part of the field. Upon stopping next to the plane, Diamonds and Fat Freddy jumped out and raced to the rear of the van.

"We did it!" Fat Freddy cheerfully yelled aloud. "I told you, Jimmy, it would be a piece of cake!"

"It was messy," Diamonds yelled from the back of the now open rear doors of the van.

"Is he okay?" Fat Freddy genuinely asked with concern as he peered at the bloodied reporter.

"He's breathing," the flagger answered.

"Put him on the plane," Diamonds ordered the flagger and helmsman.

Fat Freddy's big eyes bulged in surprise when he saw the unconscious Moore being carried out of the van. "What are you doing with him?"

"Payback is a bitch!" Diamonds grinned with a malicious smile.

"What are you doing? I don't get it! If you want him dead, just let him bleed out!"

"We're going to nurse the S.O.B. back to good health and then I'm going to kill him like I've never killed anyone. You can count on that!" Diamonds said as he helped the flagger and helmsman place Moore in the back of the plane. "We've got to quickly get him medical treatment."

"I can arrange that. I'll have someone waiting for us when we land," Fat Freddy said as he followed Diamonds onto the plane and made a call on his cell phone. The plane taxied down to the runway and took off for a small private airfield near Grand Haven, Michigan.

The flagger and helmsman returned to the van and drove off the island. When they neared Fort Road, they pulled behind the rear of a building where they each jumped out of the vehicle. Together they peeled off the Wharton Heating decal and reentered the vehicle.

They headed toward I-75 South where they would safely complete their escape.

A van met the chartered plane when it landed in Grand Haven. It contained three occupants – a physician named Ranney, his nurse, and a driver. Ranney did his work quietly and with no questions asked for organized crime mobsters from Chicago, Indianapolis and Detroit. In return, he was paid handsomely for keeping his mouth shut.

Ranney supervised the transfer of Moore to the rear of his van, which was tricked out with all sorts of medical equipment and supplies.

Taking his vitals and examining the wound, Ranney said, "He should be okay. He's lost a lot of blood though." Turning to the van driver, he said, "We've got to get him back to my clinic, quickly."

The clinic was located nearby on Dr. Ranney's large, secluded farm. The farm provided recovering mobsters with a private safe haven. Armed guards continually patrolled the grounds.

"You take care of him, Doc," Diamonds said as he headed back to the plane to join Fat Freddy, who had already climbed aboard. "I want him healthy."

"Should be no problem," Ranney replied as he started to close the van's rear doors. "I'll give Fat Freddy a call and keep him updated on his recovery."

"You do that," Diamonds said as he climbed inside the plane.

Shortly thereafter, the plane again was airborne and flying low over Lake Michigan as it headed to Chicago. Diamonds planned on meeting with some of his mobster friends in the "Windy City" to plan his revenge and potential return to Detroit.

The van carrying Moore drove swiftly to the clinic where the doctor would treat him with professional care to make him healthy enough to die at the hands of Jimmy Diamonds, although Ranney wasn't aware of Diamonds' intentions.

Ranney's Clinic
Near Grand Haven, Michigan

It had been two weeks since Diamonds' escape from the prison transport van. The media had sensationalized the escape, the wild shootout and extensive manhunt for Diamonds and Moore that had immediately been launched. The ongoing search remained unsuccessful and was deeply embarrassing to their pursuers. Their search trail had gone cold after being traced to the Grosse Ile Airport. It was as if Diamonds and Moore had simply disappeared into thin air.

After a call from Dr. Ranney, Diamonds and Fat Freddy drove from Chicago to Ranney's clinic to hear the final report in person on Moore's recovery and prognosis.

They had been ushered into a private waiting area in the clinic where Ranney greeted them. As they looked through a large window overlooking a brick patio, they saw Moore seated motionless in a chair. He had a small bandage covering the wound on the side of his head. From a distance, it appeared that Moore was listlessly staring at Ranney's cows, grazing in the pasture.

"He's recovered well. The wound is healing nicely," Ranney effortlessly stated.

"That's good," Diamonds quipped with evil anticipation of

how he was going to torturously kill Moore.

"There's just one problem with our patient."

"What's that, Doc?"

"He's lost his memory."

"He lost his what? His memory!" Diamonds exclaimed with utter surprise and pure disbelief. Diamonds just stood there for a moment, speechless now, and listened to Dr. Ranney.

"We've conducted several diagnostic tests on him and it appears that he has suffered significant memory loss due to the traumatic brain injury he received. We call it TBI. It may have damaged a portion of the brain. It's hard to tell," Ranney said as he looked at Diamonds.

"Is it temporary or permanent?" Diamonds asked.

"That's hard to say. Traumatic Brain Injury is a very complex injury with a wide array of symptoms and disabilities. Sometimes, memory loss is a temporary way for the body to deal with the trauma it's gone through. If the brain was significantly injured, then it could be permanent. The sudden, physical trauma his brain incurred may have impaired his brain's ability to process and store information as well as recover information."

"Does he know who he is?"

"No," Ranney answered. "He has no clue whatsoever."

"So, he doesn't remember what happened, like the trial or my escape or his role in getting me busted?"

"Not at all. His memory is, quite frankly, sir … missing."

Frowning, Diamonds turned to Fat Freddy. "Missing! Moore's memory is missing! Who would have thought that could happen! That takes the fun out of killing him and I want Emerson Moore to know, deeply and personally, why I'm killing him!" Diamonds stormed.

"Yeah, he should be held accountable, Jimmy," Fat Freddy agreed.

A plan began to formulate in the back of Diamonds' mind. "So, how long will this condition last?" Diamond pushed as he turned back to the doctor.

"Hard to say. Sometimes, it takes surgery. Recovering from the traumatic experience can take weeks or months. Some don't ever recover."

"I see."

"Damage to specific areas of the brain such as the frontal and temporal lobes, amygdale and hippocampus can result in a number of symptoms. He may have symptoms like being vulnerable to agitation, volatile emotions, physical aggression, lack of impulse control, trouble functioning at home, nightmares or flashbacks. He could suffer fear, anxiety and depression and turn to alcohol and drugs to cope. You might see him become emotionally numb and disconnected to others. He just won't be himself. He won't know who he is."

"I'm counting on that," Diamonds said quietly.

"What?" Ranney asked.

"Nothing. I was just thinking out loud," Diamonds responded.

Ranney continued. "You may see a change in his personality. Sometimes people who were kind, loving and funny have post-injury personality changes. There can be bouts of depression, intense anger, and confusion. We call it the 'Jekyll and Hyde syndrome.' You may see two versions of him residing within himself. One could be rational and easy-going, but the other can be frightening and dangerous at times."

"You mean he could do something to himself … like commit suicide?" Diamonds asked.

"Not usually. It's more likely that he could explode at others and do something irrational, totally out of character. We've already seen that."

"Oh?" Diamonds asked.

"He became very frustrated one night and destroyed his room. Is that the type of behavior you've seen from him in the past?"

Diamonds didn't have a clue, although he guessed that Moore was more of a rational type based on what he observed. "No," he answered, "he's usually pretty steady."

"We had to rush in and physically restrain him. I gave him a sedative. When he woke, he was fine. You'll have to keep an eye on him."

"Sounds like the Incredible Hulk to me," Fat Freddy chimed in. Diamonds shot him a serious look and Fat Freddy zipped his mouth shut.

"I'd recommend you get him into therapy to help him recover his lost memory. He'll need to be evaluated from time to time to determine how he's progressing and whether surgery needs to be performed to help restore his memory."

"Thanks, Doc. I understand," Diamonds said. "What about doing basic things like driving or knowing places he has been?"

"I tested him. He should be able to function normally. He does recall some things. I've asked him where he's travelled and he seems to be able to tell me a few places. It's just that he has no recollection of the personal side of his life or about family members or what his job was or where he resided."

"I see," Diamonds said with an evil grin. "By the way, Doc, have you or any of your staff called him by his real name?"

"No, you never gave me his real name and you know that I don't ask questions."

"Good. Yes, that's what I like about you, Doc."

"You can visit with him if you'd like."

"I think we'll do that. Doc, my associate and I need to chat privately for a moment before we go see him."

"Take your time," Ranney said before leaving the room.

"What are you thinking, Jimmy?" Fat Freddy asked when they were alone.

"I've been talking to the boys in Chicago about helping me pay back some folks in Detroit. They're reluctant to do anything because the heat is on."

"Yeah, I understand that. Half of Michigan must be looking for you."

"There's another way to handle this pay back now."

"What's that, Jimmy?"

"Manny Elias."

"Who's Manny Elias?"

"He's the top hitman in the United States."

"Never heard of him. I thought Santoro was the top hitman. You going to hire Santoro to put hits on the guys in Detroit?"

"Nope. Manny Elias is our guy. He's the rock star of killers for hire."

"How come I never heard of him?" Fat Freddy asked.

"Because he's sitting right there." Diamonds pointed through the window at Moore.

"Moore? He's no hitman."

"He doesn't know that, does he? He doesn't remember anything."

"He doesn't know anything about killing people," Fat Freddy protested.

"No, he doesn't and that's because Manny Elias lost his memory on his last kill when he took the bullet to the skull. He's got to be retrained and then directed." Diamonds grinned as he watched Moore. "And I'll use him as my tool to get revenge. And by doing that, it's my perfect revenge for Moore, too. I'll make Mr. Good Guy into Mr. Bad Guy!" Diamonds said with a sinister smirk.

"I get it. Pretty cool idea, Jimmy. What about his killing skills? He probably doesn't have any. We don't even know if he knows how to use a gun. Or if he did, did he forget?"

"I know a guy in Florida who can help with that. We'll fly Manny there for training."

"I like it. He'll be out of our way while he's there learning how to kill people."

"You both will be out of my way."

"Huh?" Fat Freddy asked with a puzzled look on his round, chubby face.

"You're going with him. I need a babysitter in case his memory starts to come back. I want you checking him all the time. I don't need any more surprises from the former Emerson Moore. No, no. We aren't using that name again. It's Manny Elias from now on, understand?"

"Yep."

"Good, and don't slip! Let's go see Elias." As they walked, Diamonds cautioned, "One more thing, Fat Freddy."

"What's that?"

"I don't want him ever looking at any TV, newspapers or the Internet. Capisce? The last thing we need is for him to see himself in some headline or story. That would ruin everything."

"Got it, Jimmy. Capisce."

"And don't let him shave. Get him to grow a beard to help mask his identity when he starts doing the hits for me. And no haircuts either!"

"Understand, will do, Jimmy."

The two men walked out to the patio area and Diamonds greeted

Elias. "Manny, how are you doing?"

Elias didn't turn around.

"Manny, you okay?" Diamonds asked as he walked around Elias and stood in front of him.

Elias raised his head slowly and looked at Diamonds. "Are you talking to me?"

"Manny, don't you recognize me? It's me, Jimmy."

"Frankly, I don't recognize anyone," Elias said in a flat monotone. It was very apparent that he was emotionally flatlining because of his memory loss.

"You'll be fine," Diamonds said as he pulled a patio chair in front of Elias and dropped in it. He motioned to Fat Freddy to sit in the other vacant chair.

"When?" Elias asked.

"Come on. Snap out of it. You're acting like a freaking zombie. Where's that personality of yours gone?" Diamonds asked. He was relishing Elias' memory loss. "You remember Fat Freddy?" he asked as he pointed to his associate.

Elias turned his head and looked at Fat Freddy. "No."

"He's one of your best friends. Aren't you, Fat Freddy?"

"Yeah, that's right, Manny. I'm like your brother from another mother!"

Diamonds looked at Fat Freddy's hulking frame. "You want to rephrase that?"

"Yeah, sure, Jimmy." Fat Freddy turned back to Elias. "What I meant was that you and I hang out together. You've been like a twin to me."

For the first time, they saw a reaction from Elias as his eyes widened and he looked at the rotund Fat Freddy. "Not sure that the term twin describes us."

"There you go. That's the Elias we know and love," Diamonds said.

Elias looked from Diamonds to Fat Freddy and back. "So, who am I?"

"You're Manny Elias," Diamonds answered.

"Manny Elias," he repeated out loud. "That's the first time that anyone has told me my name. What happened to me?"

"You mean to tell me the doctor here never told you who you are?" Diamonds asked in mock surprise.

"No."

"Fat Freddy, we're going to have to give them hell for the way they've treated Manny. They should have told him sooner."

"Yeah. We can give them hell," Fat Freddy agreed as he played along with Diamonds.

"What happened to me?" Elias asked again.

"You were working for me and somebody shot you, but you killed him," Diamonds lied as he started to concoct the backstory about who Elias was.

Jerking back when he heard that he had killed someone, Elias asked, "Why did I kill somebody?"

"You do that all the time. Don't you remember?" Diamonds asked.

"No."

"Manny, you're the rock star of hired contract killers in the United States. You're the number one hitman. No one comes close to you when it compares to the hits you've pulled off."

Tilting his head in disbelief, Elias asked, "I just go out and kill people?"

"Just the ones who deserve it. You work for me."

Stunned, Elias asked, "How many people have I killed?"

Diamonds thought a moment as he prepared to continue with his lie. "Since you were a teen, I think you told me once that you were up to about 58 kills."

"No!" Elias said in remorseful shock.

Diamonds nodded his head. "I'm telling you the truth, Manny. I swear on my mother's grave."

"Did I kill women or children?"

"No, I have to give you credit. You'd never go after them. We had to get someone else to do those hits," Diamonds said as he decided to give Elias' apparent emotional turmoil a break. "And we'd only do it if we wanted to send a message to some guy by taking out a family member. Sometimes we'd take out their father or mother."

"Am I wanted?"

"No, you've been pretty adept at making clean kills. No one has been able to tie you to them," Diamonds said.

"I just don't remember. That's me? That's who I am?"

Reaching over to grab his shoulder, Diamonds said, "That's no problem Manny. It'll come back to you."

As Diamonds pulled his hand back from Elias' shoulder, Elias looked down at his own hands. They were just an average pair of hands, not roughened and not significantly noteworthy. "I don't know if I want those memories coming back to me. I don't know if I could kill someone. I'm not sure how to do it, or that I want to."

Diamonds felt anger boiling in him, and repressed his urge to knock off Moore right then and there. "Still a goody two-shoes," he whispered under his breath as he fought the urge to grab his gun. Instead, he took a deep breath and forced a smile.

"No problem. We're going to retrain you. I know a guy in Florida who can help you out. We'll want to keep it quiet so as some of my enemies don't try to sneak around and off you before you get your skills back. Listen, it's the only skill you have. You, um, never relished the kills, but you're good at it. It's what you do."

"What do you do?"

Leaning closer to Elias, Diamonds lowered his voice. "Now, don't you go and run off your mouth. The three of us are all involved in organized crime. Keep that close to the vest. The cover story is that we're honest, philanthropic businessmen."

Looking from Diamonds to Fat Freddy and back to Diamonds,

Elias said with mild disbelief, "We're the bad guys?"

"The baddest and meanest. Don't you worry, it'll all come back to you one day."

"When do I get my memory back?"

"It can come back any time," Diamonds responded. He wanted to give Elias some sense of hope, although the return of his memory would result in Elias' rather immediate death.

"Am I married? Do I have a family?"

"You're an orphan. You were married once, but she died of leukemia."

"Don't I have any family? None at all?"

"No, Manny. We're the only family you have and we care about ya."

"Yeah," Fat Freddy contributed. "We're like brothers."

Thinking for a moment, Elias asked, "Can I go home, wherever that is?"

"Not any more. The guys who wanted you dead blew up your home outside of Detroit. There's nothing left. You're going to start over just like us. Detroit is off limits for all of us for now. We all have to lay low and let things cool down."

"When do I get out of here? And where do I go if I don't have a home?" Elias asked.

"Tomorrow, I hope. I'll talk to the doc. And we'll get you set up in a new home after you retrain in Florida. We'll take care of you. Like family. But for now, I need to go pay the doc for taking care of you and make a couple of phone calls to get things set up for your Florida trip," Diamonds said as he stood, followed quickly by Fat Freddy.

"Thanks," Elias said as he rose from his chair and warily shook Diamonds' hand. "I appreciate you taking care of me."

"No problem. I'll take care of you all right!" There was an evil glint in Diamonds' eyes as he spoke.

"Thanks again!" Elias responded.

"No problem at all. Besides, you'll be paying me back with your services," Diamonds said with a malicious smile. "We owe some people. Owe them a lot."

Starting to walk away, Diamonds paused and looked back at Elias. "You remember anything else?" Diamonds studied him carefully, making sure he was really this clueless before going forward with the next steps in the plan. He realized that Elias would need to be monitored carefully for any hint that his memory as Emerson Moore was returning.

"Not really," replied Elias.

"What does that mean?" Diamonds snapped. "Yes or no?"

"No, sir," Elias said to clarify his answer. "I just wish I did."

That was the first time Elias had seen how hot-tempered Diamonds could be and realized he'd have to be careful and respectful with him.

"That's more like it. We'll see you tomorrow."

Diamonds and Fat Freddy visited the doc and arranged for

Elias' release for the next day. After paying the doctor, the two left and drove to a nearby shopping area where Fat Freddy purchased clothes, shoes and personal hygiene items for himself and Elias.

While Fat Freddy shopped, Diamonds remained in the car where he made several phone calls. He was able to arrange for Elias' training in Florida and scheduled a charter plane to fly Fat Freddy and Elias to a small airfield near the training location.

The next day, the two returned to the clinic and picked up Elias. Then they drove to the small airport nearby where Elias and Fat Freddy boarded the plane for the flight south. After the plane took off, Diamonds drove back to Chicago where he was staying with mobster friends while he planned his revenge and relocation to the Cleveland area. Detroit was too hot for him to return there for now.

Cedar Key Airport
Cedar Key, Florida

An hour west of Gainesville, Florida, was the sleepy island fishing village of Cedar Key with about 700 inhabitants. There were no fast food chain restaurants and the local grocery store was so small that it made Put-in-Bay's Island Market look like a Super Wal-Mart. Cedar Key's lack of businesses and entertainment establishments made South Bass Island look like Manhattan.

Nothing much happened on Cedar Key. It was a great place to get lost. The solitary main street was lined with a mixture of art shops and boarded-up businesses. The quaint village was also the home to a laundromat, post office and a couple of small restaurants on Third Street - the main business thoroughfare.

A sand spit virtually surrounded the small, protected harbor, called Marina Basin. On the Gulf of Mexico side of the spit, a few waterfront restaurants offered visitors a choice of seafood dining. A couple of gift shops were also on the spit.

The island's airport, George T. Lewis Landing Field, was nothing more than a 2,500-foot strip of asphalt. Warning signs were placed at the end of the airstrip directing pilots not to taxi their aircraft onto the adjacent village street.

A plane landed and taxied to the end of the airstrip where a green Jeep Laredo waited for its two passengers. The plane's passengers disembarked with their duffel bags and walked to the vehicle as the plane turned and took off.

"You Newton?" Fat Freddy asked the driver.

"Yeah. Call me, Newt," he replied. Newton looked like a hard case.

"I'm Fat Freddy and this is Manny Elias," Freddy said as Elias nodded at Newton.

Newton looked at Fat Freddy's chubby frame and commented, "Thanks. I would never have guessed you were Fat Freddy."

Fat Freddy ignored his comment as he and Elias threw their gear into the vehicle and took seats.

"There's nothing frickin' here," Fat Freddy said disgustedly as the Jeep drove east on Airport Road through the small village.

"That's why you're here. You're nothing, too," Newton said.

Newton was in his late thirties - tall, lean and mean. His blonde hair was close-cropped and his slate blue eyes had a touch of cruelty in them. Since his dishonorable discharge from the U.S. Army Rangers, he had been involved with contract work and had now been hired to help Elias "regain" his forgotten skills.

Fat Freddy leaned toward Newton. He placed the barrel of his handgun against Newton's neck. "You think so? Well, this here is something. Don't make me use it," Fat Freddy threatened.

A smile cracked Newton's stern face. "You still playing with cap guns?"

Fat Freddy shoved the end of his weapon under Newton's chin. "Here, let me help you hear it go bang!" Fat Freddy grumbled as his anger built.

"Trigger happy aren't you, my little fat friend? Careful, your boss needs me," Newton cautioned.

Fat Freddy's anger began to boil over as he suddenly thrust the barrel harder against Newton's chin, causing Newton's head to noticeably move backwards. "Keep pushing me and I'll show you how trigger happy I can be!" he stormed. "And Jimmy can find your replacement any time I ask him to."

Newton knew that he had pushed Fat Freddy a little too hard. He tried to lighten the mood. "Easy. Easy," he repeated. "I was just funnin' you."

Fat Freddy relaxed and settled back in his seat. He returned his weapon to his holster. "Just be careful how you push me. I don't take it lightly."

"I can tell," Newton said as he drove them across the first bridge, past Annie's Cafe and down the road lined with lush vegetation and tidal marsh full of black needle rush, marsh hay cord grass and glasswart.

"Well, doesn't this place look like a touch of paradise!" Fat Freddy growled sarcastically as he observed the area's lack of business development.

"That's why we're here and my business is here. It's remote. This area is off everyone's radar screen," Newton replied assuredly and calmly. "Out here, nobody cares who you are. They don't ask questions, and they don't want questions."

During the verbal altercation, Elias had moved to the center of the rear seat. He had been poised to aid Fat Freddy if things took a turn for the worse. When Fat Freddy relaxed, Elias sat back in his seat as they drove past several of the island's popular eateries like the Island Pizzeria, Kona Joe's Island Café, Ada Blue Café and Blue Desert Café.

Crossing Number Four Channel as they followed Route 24, they saw the tidal marsh transition to scrub and sand. The vegetation included live oak, gopher apple, palmetto and climbing buckhorn. A little farther out, the landscape changed to swamp hardwoods like red maple, red cedar, wild grape, swamp dogwood and slash pine.

Suddenly, Newton turned onto a sand driveway and stopped the vehicle. Leaving the motor running, he exited the vehicle and unlocked a swinging gate. He returned to the Jeep and drove through the open gate. Stopping the vehicle again, he then jumped out and closed the gate behind them. Next, he returned to the vehicle and drove nearly a half-mile along the lane before it came to an end.

Parking the Jeep in front of a low cracker-style house, he said, "This will be your home for the next month."

"Looks like the Ritz to me," Fat Freddy cracked as he stepped out of the vehicle and stared at the weathered house.

"One big difference between the Ritz and my digs," Newton said.

"What's that?"

"No maid service. It's all on you, my friend," Newton chuckled as he walked toward the house.

Elias, who had also stepped out of the Jeep, chuckled softly. He liked this Newton fellow.

Fat Freddy and Elias walked to the rear of the Jeep and grabbed their duffel bags. They followed Newton at a gradual pace across a cluttered front porch and into an equally cluttered house.

As he walked in, Fat Freddy nervously scanned the interior. "You got a TV here?"

"Nope. Don't have time for it."

"How about Internet?"

"Why? Do you need to use it?"

"No, I just wondered if you have it."

"I do, but it's in my office. If you do need to use it, you'll have to let me know. I always keep my office locked."

"No problem. I was just wondering, that's all," Fat Freddy said, relieved that Elias wouldn't have access to the TV or Internet.

"Take your pick of the two rooms down that hall," Newton pointed and walked into the kitchen where he grabbed a cold beer from the fridge.

As they walked down the hall, Elias commented softly to Fat Freddy, "Nice friend you have there."

"Not my friend!" Fat Freddy retorted quickly. "Jimmy knows him. You mind what you do here because I'm sure he's going to be reporting back to Jimmy," Fat Freddy added as he chose the bigger of the two rooms.

"I'm here to relearn. That's my focus," Elias said as he tossed his duffel bag onto the bed and walked to the kitchen.

"Beer?" Newton asked Elias.

"Sure," Elias said.

"Help yourself. Like I said, I don't provide maid service."

"I gathered as much," Elias said as he walked to the fridge and withdrew two beers. "Here you go," he said as he handed a beer to Fat Freddy, who entered the kitchen.

Fat Freddy took the beer. After taking a couple of gulps of the refreshing beverage, he asked, "You got any good Italian restaurants in this place, Newt?"

"Yeah. Back in town. A real pizzeria. They deliver, too. But I don't allow deliveries here," Newton responded.

"That don't sound like any real Italian restaurant to me. I'll cook you guys some real Italian meals," Fat Freddy said.

"Fine with me. I can run you into town to get what you need," Newton said as he tossed his empty beer bottle in a nearby trash-can. "You guys ready to get started?"

"Sure, what's on the agenda?" Fat Freddy asked.

"Physical training."

Fat Freddy groaned quietly at the thought. "That's for our friend Elias here. I got a bad back." Freddy allowed a groan to escape as he leaned over. "I wish I could join you two; I'd show up the both of ya."

Newton saw through the charade, but didn't comment. His assignment was Elias. "Go and change into workout gear and some good running shoes."

"Yeah. You boys run along. I'm going to grab another beer and sit out on the porch. You let me know if you need me to time you or anything," Fat Freddy said as he threw his bottle in the trashcan and grabbed another beer from the fridge.

Newton didn't comment as he headed to his room to change. Elias did likewise. Shortly afterwards the two met on the rear porch.

"Follow me," Newton ordered as he turned and started to jog down one of the many paths leading through the swamp.

After a few minutes, Newton came to a sudden stop. Elias almost crashed into him.

"What's wrong?" Elias asked as he used the back of his hand to wipe the sweat from his brow.

"There. On the trail." Newton pointed to a large rattlesnake.

Elias looked to where Newton pointed. He shuddered when he saw how big the snake was. "That's a big one!" he exclaimed.

"He's nothing. You should see his mother."

"I don't think so," Elias responded. "What do we do?"

"Take a breather. He'll mosey on in a minute."

"Anything else we need to watch for?" Elias asked as he looked into the nearby scrub and swamp.

"Keep an eye out for water moccasins and cottonmouths. You might see a gator, but we'll be in and out of the water pretty quick," Newton answered as he watched the snake slowly slither off the trail.

"We're going in the water?"

"Yeah. Up to our ankles."

"That's a relief," Elias said, glad it wasn't deeper. When he looked back at Newton, he saw that the trainer was already several paces down the path. Elias moved quickly to catch up.

Over the next two hours, Newton ran at a brisk pace through the woods and swampy areas, occasionally stopping to drop to the ground to do fifty push-ups.

Elias trailed behind Newton, barely keeping his fleeting figure in sight. Newton would finish his push-up set quickly and then harangue Elias for not keeping up with him and for struggling to do the fifty push-ups.

Elias didn't complain or comment. He didn't want to waste his energy. The Florida heat and humidity were taking its toll on him. Perspiration covered Elias' body. His shirt and shorts were soaked.

When they burst out of the woods at the end of their run and into the compound, Newton slowed to a walk. He turned to Elias as they walked toward the house. "Take ten minutes. Get hydrated and cool down. Then, meet me at the barn." He pointed to a two-story structure with a metal roof. "I know you're recovering from a pretty major head injury but I don't have a lot of time to get you retrained. Push yourself."

Elias nodded his head and crossed the back porch where Fat Freddy was seated under the rotating blades of an old ceiling fan. The blades squeaked as they turned. Fat Freddy held another cold beer in his hand. The sides of the can were sweating.

"Manny, want a beer?"

Elias shook his head negatively. "Nope. Water for me."

"Have it your way."

"I'm in training."

"Yeah, me too. I'm training to see how fast I can walk to the fridge to get another cold beer," Fat Freddy chuckled.

Elias entered the house. It was then he realized there was no air conditioning. He walked to the kitchen sink and turned on the cold water, then splashed it over himself to bring cooling relief. Next, he opened the fridge and took out two bottles of ice-cold water. He walked out onto the porch where he doused himself with the contents of one of the water bottles.

Then, he dropped into a chair next to Fat Freddy and began drinking from the remaining bottle as he enjoyed the respite from the heat. His break wouldn't last long.

"How did your run go?" Fat Freddy asked.

"Tough. I'm out of shape, a lot," Elias answered.

"You'll get there. This guy is supposed to be real good." Fat Freddy leaned toward Elias. "How's the head feeling?"

"Other than a headache, fine."

"Good." Fat Freddy sat back in his chair. "Did your jogging jog your memory?" Fat Freddy laughed softly at his own joke.

"Nothing. At least not yet."

"I'm sorry to hear that," Fat Freddy said with feigned concern.

Elias took a long swig of the cold water. "You know, you could join us."

Fat Freddy was quick to respond. "Not me. I don't run for anyone. Plus, I got a back problem."

Elias smiled. He didn't believe Fat Freddy. "I didn't know you had a bad back."

"Yeah. Yeah. I took a bullet in my side during a job," he explained.

"Hey, you slacking off already?" Newton shouted at Elias from the open barn door.

"I better go," Elias said as he rose and began walking toward the barn.

"Yeah. Get yourself in shape," Fat Freddy said as he lifted the beer bottle to his lips. "And remember another thing, I once was an Olympic gold medalist – in twelve-ounce curls! Yeah, you get in shape there, boy."

Elias had already left the house while Freddy was still talking. He entered the barn and was stunned by what he saw. A number of built-in and secure storage units had their doors open to reveal a wide assortment of weaponry.

"You've got quite a collection here!" Elias said as he admired the display of weapons.

"Comes in handy," Newton said as he handed Elias a .22 caliber handgun with a noise suppressor.

"What's this?"

"My assignment is to be sure you're proficient in using it. We'll be shooting some of the other guns, but this is the one that you'll go to bed with, always."

"Why a .22?"

"It's the hitman's weapon of choice."

"Why?"

"Most of your work will be done at close quarters. A .22 with a suppressor can be fired inside a building and it won't be heard outside. Helps you with a clean getaway."

"Does she do a lot of damage?"

"Does she ever! She creates wound channels throughout the brain. The round flies wildly around inside the brain like a pinball in a pinball game."

"I see," Elias said as he looked at the weapon.

"Learn to love her. Your life will depend on her," Newton said coolly as he tossed a clip to Elias and picked up a .22. He inserted a clip into it as Elias watched and mimicked the action. Newton said, "Let's go out back to start some close-in training."

They walked through the rear of the barn and to a shooting

range. Multiple targets had been set up. They were six-inch-square steel plates mounted on pipes protruding five feet from the ground.

"Why the steel plates?" Elias asked when he spotted them.

"We could set up silhouettes, but your most effective shooting is going to be within an area which is six inches by six inches. Think of a person's head or their chest area. We're going to concentrate on building your muscle memory and conditioning your brain."

"How's that?"

"By you being able to see and hear the rounds hitting the targets."

"Let's see what you can do. You've shot before?"

"Jimmy said I did. I don't remember," Elias replied.

"Good. You sound like you're raw, like a hard drive with nothing installed. You're ripe for learning."

"What do you mean?"

"I don't have to unlearn you from prior bad shooting habits. We're starting with a clean slate," Newton smiled. "Let's see how you'd position yourself."

Elias squared up to the first target as he held the .22 outstretched in one hand, pointed at the target. His left eye was closed.

"That's not going to work," Newton said as he positioned Elias sideways to the target. "You want to present a small profile in case fire is returned to you."

"I see."

"You're holding the .22 wrong, too. Here, look at how I hold mine." He swung up his .22 and pointed it down range. Both of his hands were gripping the .22. "This is called a clamshell hold." Newton adjusted his hands. "This is better. It's a 60/40 grip."

His thumbs were on the side of the weapon, pointing in the direction he was aiming. "You want forty percent of the pressure in your right hand if you're right-handed. Then, you want sixty percent of the pressure in your left hand. Your thumbs help in aiming when you point them in the direction you're firing."

Newton lowered his weapon. "Go ahead. Show me what you learned."

Elias raised his weapon again. This time he was using the 60/40 grip as he stood sideways to the target.

"Hold it. I forgot to tell you one more thing. Are you closing your left eye?"

"Yes."

"Don't do that."

"I thought it'd help me aim."

"It might, but you're limiting your peripheral vision. What if an adversary pops up on your left side? You wouldn't see him right away! You just lost a few critical seconds in seeing him because you're not using your entire field of vision."

"Got it," Elias said as he realigned himself and kept both eyes open as he imitated Newton's tactical position.

"Flick off the safety and try a couple of rounds."

Elias flicked off the safety and looked down range. He took aim and fired off two shots. The first one missed wide left, but the second one caught a corner of the metal.

"Not a bad start," Newton said as he suddenly turned and fired two shots, hitting near the center of the farthest target. "That's what we're going to train you to do."

"Nice," Elias said with admiration.

"Comes with practice," he said. "One advantage you have with the .22 is that she's incredibly stable. She doesn't have the kick some of the others do. So you don't lose time re-aiming at your target. The .22 will stay steady in your hand and you can fire off several rounds quickly."

"That makes sense," Elias agreed.

"This suppressor adds balance to the weapon and also helps her stay steady on the target," Newton added.

"Why are we so close to the targets?"

"The average gunfight takes place at twenty-one feet. So, we're going to do a lot of training at close quarters and with target recognition unless you don't care who you kill. I'm adverse to killing kids."

"As I would be," Elias echoed quickly. "Will I be shooting any other weapons?"

A large smile crossed Newton's face. "You can count on it. You need to know how to shoot a variety of weapons. What if yours jammed and you have a chance to pick up the target's weapon? What if you have to shoot your target from a distance, although I don't think that will be the case. You'll be learning how to shoot a number of the calibers, some of the sniper weapons and the McMillian .50 caliber BMG. That one you can use on armored vehicles.

"We'll spend time with explosives in case you need to blow someone up, hand-to-hand combat and medical training so that you can temporarily plug any holes you might get. It could save your life."

"Sounds like a full slate."

"And don't forget the physical conditioning. We get up early tomorrow for a run."

Elias groaned before he redirected his attention as Newton began coaching him on upgrading his shooting skills.

After two hours at the range, they returned to the barn and Newton returned his .22 to the storage unit. When Elias started to place his .22 in the unit, Newton stopped him.

"What do you think you're doing?"

"Putting it away," Elias responded.

"I told you that it stays with you all the time. I wasn't kidding." The tone in his voice meant business.

"I remember now," Elias said as he slipped the weapon in the waistband of his shorts. He thought to himself, I wish I could remember a lot more.

The two returned to the main house where a grousing Fat Freddy greeted them.

"I made dinner for you guys. But you got one problem here, Newt."

"What's that?"

"You don't have anything Italian here."

"Yes, I do," Newton said as he walked to the fridge and opened it. When he turned around, he held a bottle of Italian dressing in his hand. "See?"

Fat Freddy waved his hand at Newton. "Like that counts. You got to take me to town so I can buy us some groceries. Then I can make real Italian food for dinner. All this waiting around all day works up my appetite."

"Now, Fat Freddy, I've got a lot of healthy food in the fridge. You can help yourself to carrots and celery and any of the fruit."

"The only healthy food I saw in there was the beer. And I did help myself. Just be sure you don't run out."

Newton smiled and raised his eyebrows as he looked at Elias, who chuckled softly at the exchange as he joined Newton in sitting at the kitchen table. Fat Freddy had prepared a dinner of fresh tossed salad and ham sandwiches.

"Hope this didn't put you out," Newton said as he started in on the salad.

"I did have to cut the lettuce up. Back where I come from, they sell the lettuce in bags and it's already cut up for you," Fat Freddy said as he continued to whine.

After dinner, Newton returned to the barn and Fat Freddy and Elias sat on the back porch, sipping beers.

Elias turned to Fat Freddy, "This is really the first time that we've been alone."

Raising his eyebrows, Fat Freddy looked at Elias. "You're not going to hit on me, are you?"

"No, no. I just wanted to ask you some questions."

Relaxing, Fat Freddy said, "Oh good, you had me worried. I do want you to remember that you're not one of those 'light in the loafer' guys. You like girls. You do remember that, don't you?"

Smiling, Elias placed his hand on Fat Freddy's right arm and caressed it, causing Fat Freddy to jerk it away.

"Hey, cut that out!" Fat Freddy said, raising his voice.

Elias chuckled. It was the first time he had chuckled since he regained consciousness in the clinic. "I was just kidding."

"Yeah, well don't go kidding and come walking into my bedroom in the middle of the night. I sleep with my gun under my pillow."

"Is it a big gun?" Elias teased.

"Stop it! Stop it! Just ask your question, Manny."

"Tell me about myself," Elias asked.

Taking a deep breath, Fat Freddy thought back to the background that Diamonds and he had concocted in the time between their visit with Elias at the clinic and his release the next day. "You're the Babe Ruth of contract killers. You could snuff your targets and get away scot-free. Everyone was afraid of you. Everyone but Jimmy."

Nodding his head, Elias interrupted. "Okay, but tell me about my personal life."

"Like Jimmy told you in the clinic. You're an orphan. You kicked around in foster homes in Detroit for a while. Got in trouble for stealing cars for joy rides. You spent some time in the juvenile detention center. Then, you joined the army when you were eighteen. You remember any of this?" Fat Freddy asked as he paused to take a sip of his beer and eye Elias carefully for any reaction.

"No."

"It'll come back to you. After you got out of the army, you went back to boosting cars. It was during one of those boosts that the owner surprised you and came after you with a .38. You fought with him and ended up shooting and killing him. The police showed up and you did time for ten years in upstate Michigan."

Pausing again to drink his beer, Fat Freddy glanced at Elias and saw that he was listening intently.

"When you got out, one of your cellmates had you contact a guy in St. Louis. At the time, he was one of the top hitmen in the U.S. even though he was a sociopath. The guy liked you so much that he trained you and that's where you got your skills in killing people."

"How did I start working for Jimmy?" Elias asked.

"Jimmy had a problem with a guy across town. His name was Johnny Nubs. It used to be Johnny Fingers until Jimmy figured out he was skimming money. Jimmy had the fingers cut off his left hand as a warning. Some guys just don't learn.

"When Jimmy found out Johnny Nubs was skimming again, he decided it was time to off him. But Johnny Nubs was being real careful and not letting anyone get close to him. Somehow, he knew that Jimmy was on to him. Johnny knew all of Jimmy's people, so this was going to be difficult to pull off.

"That's where you came in. Jimmy wanted an outsider. He figured he needed somebody fresh. We'd heard about you and he had me track you down in St. Louis. You came to Detroit for the job. You've been with Jimmy ever since. You really sent a message with killing that guy back then."

"How's that?" Elias asked.

Leaning toward Elias, Fat Freddy responded, "You sneaked over to his house one night. It still beats me how you got by his guards, but you were able to open the kitchen window enough so that you could dump a ton of ants onto the sink and counter. Then, you left.

"The next morning, you waited around the corner until you saw an exterminator's van approaching and you flagged him down. You found out that he was going to Jimmy's house to get rid of the ants. You took the guy's shirt and cap and marched him into the bushes where you killed him. You put on his uniform and drove right up to Johnny Nubs' house in broad daylight.

"His two bodyguards didn't hesitate in greeting you and opening the front door. You walked into the hallway and turned around and shot them with your silenced gun as they closed the door. Johnny Nubs was in the kitchen grumbling when you walked in. He was still in his bathrobe. Didn't expect anything until he saw you raise your gun and point it at him. You put three shots into his chest. Then you walked over and shot him once in the head. But that wasn't the best part."

"Oh?"

"For style points, I guess, you stuffed a bunch of one dollar bills in his mouth and butt crack to let everyone know that he was killed for being too greedy. We all loved it!" A huge smile crossed

Fat Freddy's face as he finished the story, which was based on a hit he had made in the past.

"Don't you remember any of that?"

"No, I just don't," Elias said, frustrated by his lack of recall. "And I don't like that I killed the exterminator guy. He was innocent in all this."

"Don't feel bad about that. Part of the job. You never left a witness alive. As for your memory, like I told you, it'll be back. But you be sure to tell me when you start remembering, okay?"

"You can count on that," Elias said as he looked toward the barn.

The early evening dusk was slowly disappearing as the night began creeping in. The lively chatter of the birds had quieted and was replaced by the night sounds of crickets chirping and frogs croaking in the nearby swamp.

"Kind of peaceful here," Elias observed.

"Yeah, if you like this kind of lifestyle. For me, I'd rather hear the sounds of passing cars and the sirens of police cars or ambulances. I'm a city boy. Always was. Always will be," Fat Freddy commented. "Here, take a big breath."

Elias did as he was instructed.

"Now, let it go."

Exhaling, Elias asked, "What was that about?"

"No fumes. I gotta have some fumes to breathe," the ornery Fat Freddy said.

Newton returned from the barn and joined them on the porch. Looking at his watch, Newton advised, "Elias, you may want to hit the hay. We've got an early morning tomorrow."

"What does that mean?"

"Rise and shine at six o'clock for a quick run. Then we grab a quick breakfast and head to the firing range," Newton said, walking inside and toward his bedroom.

Groaning, Elias responded, "I'll be ready."

"Want to join us, Fat Freddy?" Newton called. "You could use the exercise."

"I don't believe in it," he yelled.

Newton stared at Fat Freddy's massive girth. "I've got some bending exercises that could help you get over that."

Fat Freddy saw that Newton was staring at his belly. "Listen, Newt. If God wanted me to bend over, he'd have put diamonds on the floor for me to bend over and pick up," Fat Freddy snickered at his own joke.

Elias moaned again.

Moving closer to Elias, Fat Freddy asked, "So, how's the memory doing? Any of it coming back?"

"No. I'm still drawing a blank," Elias responded.

"Ahh, that's a shame," Fat Freddy responded, faking concern.

An evil look appeared on Elias' face. "You keep asking about it and I told you I'd let you know if I remember anything. What's it to you anyways?" he snarled.

Fat Freddy recognized the change in personality as something the doctor had told them to expect from time to time. Fat Freddy stood and walked over to Elias. "Easy there, Manny. I'm just concerned." Fat Freddy placed his hand on Elias' shoulder.

Elias glared at Fat Freddy. He felt ready to snap. For some reason, he wanted to punch out Fat Freddy and release his pent-up emotions.

"You go on down and get your rest. I'm going to have a smoke on the porch first." Fat Freddy walked toward the porch.

Elias' mood shifted and he became morose. His head looked toward the floor and he didn't comment. Turning, he walked to his bedroom.

"Hey, Elias!" Fat Freddy called.

"What?" Elias yelled.

"Don't interrupt my beauty sleep when you get up in the morning." Fat Freddy opened the screen door and entered the porch. He walked to a corner and pulled his cell phone from his pocket. Quickly punching in a number, he waited for the call to be answered.

"It's about time you called," Diamonds said with an irritated tone. "You think you're on vacation?"

"Hey, give me a break. We had to get settled in and start training."

"I'm just busting your chops," Diamonds chuckled softly. "How are things going there? And remember leave out names in case someone is eavesdropping on our conversation."

"I get it. It's going good. He's off to a good start with his training. Running and target practice."

"What about his memory? Any signs of it coming back?"

"No. Nothing there. I'm keeping an eye on that. I asked him a couple of times." Fat Freddy decided he wouldn't tell Diamonds about the edginess he had briefly observed in Elias.

"Good. That could wreck our plans if his memory comes back too soon."

"How are things with you?"

"Good. I'm visiting with my cousins in Chicago," Diamonds answered, referring to his mob contacts there.

"Going to start a business there?"

"No, but they are advising me on another location where I can get established. I'll tell you more when I can."

"Okay."

"You just keep a close eye on our friend and make sure he's learning everything he needs to learn. Got me?"

"I'm on it."

They ended their call and Fat Freddy re-entered the house and waddled to his bedroom. He turned on the overhead fan and a box fan he had found in another bedroom. It was going to be a stinking hot night and he wasn't looking forward to trying to sleep in the humid heat that hung over the house like a heavy blanket. He stripped to his boxers and lay on his double bed. Finally, he drifted off to a fitful sleep.

In the room next to him, Elias was awake. He couldn't sleep. It wasn't the heat that was blocking his sleep. It was his growing frustration with his memory loss. He was trying to remember his past and becoming angrier that he could not. His memory simply had vanished.

He sat up and swung his legs over the edge of his bed. "Why can't I remember my life?" he wondered aloud. It was driving him crazy.

Suddenly, Elias bounded out of his bed. He kicked open the door to his room, waking the house's other two occupants. Screaming irrationally, Elias walked briskly into the kitchen. He picked up one of the chairs that was set around the kitchen table and swung it against one of the walls, shattering the chair into pieces. Still screaming, he reached for another chair. Before he could grab it, a body flew across the room and tackled him. Elias rolled and began trying to free himself from the arms that bound him.

"Easy does it, Manny. Everything's okay." Newton said as he wrestled with Elias. He continued controlling Elias as Fat Freddy watched. Finally, the pent-up tension in Elias ran its course and his body relaxed. When it did, Newton let go and moved to a sitting position on the floor. "You okay?" he asked.

Sweating profusely, Elias responded, "Yeah. Sorry, I don't know what came over me."

"Sounds like a little post traumatic stress syndrome to me," Newton said as he turned to look at Fat Freddy. "Everything's okay now, go back to bed."

"Yeah, whatever. You two looked like Roman wrestlers the way you were wrestling around. Lucky for all of us that neither of you lost your briefs," Fat Freddy cracked.

Newton just stared quietly at Fat Freddy.

Seeing that there was no appreciation for his humor, Fat Freddy shut his mouth and extended a hand to help Elias to his feet. "His doctor told us that stuff like this would happen." He turned to Elias, "Come now. You need to go back to your room and get some rest. You going to be okay, Manny?"

"Yeah," Elias replied. He looked at Newton and said, "Sorry about the chair. I'll replace it."

Standing, Newton commented, "Not a problem. Just don't get in the habit of doing this kind of stuff."

"I'll try not to," Elias said as he headed back to his bedroom, followed by Newton and Fat Freddy.

The next morning, Elias was awakened by Newton pounding on his door. His dreams were tormented with flashbacks that he didn't recognize. It was a restless sleep. He was tired.

"What?" Elias groaned in response to the intrusion into his early morning sleep.

"Rise and shine," Newton called.

"Not yet," Elias moaned as he rolled over and covered his head with his pillow.

"Get up! Time to run!"

"I'll be there in fifteen minutes," Elias said irritated.

"You've got five," Newton called.

"Cool it," Elias yelled from beneath his pillow.

"If you're not out here in five, I'll open your door and throw a rattlesnake on your bed."

Hearing the very real threat, Elias bounded out of his bed. "I'm up." Five minutes later he joined Newton on the back porch.

"Grab that backpack," Newton commanded as he pointed to a backpack he had left out for Elias.

"Why do I need this?"

"You'll see. You have the .22?"

"Yes." Elias pointed to his waistband.

"Grab that pack," Newton again directed as he turned and started quickly walking away.

Elias did as instructed and grabbed the backpack as he followed Newton out the door. As they walked, Newton asked, "How are you feeling this morning?"

"Fine."

Carefully examining Elias' face, Newton asked, "Any bad feelings from last night lingering?"

"No, I'm fine. I don't know what came over me. I just wanted to punch out the walls."

"Yeah, I know the feeling. I get like that when I take prednisone."

"What's that?"

"A steroid. It makes me punchy just like you were last night."

"Like I said, I'm sorry," Elias apologized again. "Maybe you can get me a punching bag or something so I don't tear up your house."

"No problem," Newton said as he walked to the beginning of one of the trails leading through the swamp. Newton stopped next to a pile of rocks.

"Start filling your backpack with rocks," he said as he pointed at the pile.

"What for?" Elias asked as he knelt next to the pile and started to reach for one of the rocks.

"You need about thirty pounds in that backpack. Then, you're going to wear it while we run every day. Builds up your endurance." Newton said as he watched a frown appear on Elias' face.

"One other thing," Newton said as he watched.

"What's that?" a less than happy Elias asked.

"Watch where you're reaching. Poisonous snakes like to hide in these rock piles," he said with a mischievous smile.

Elias suddenly slowed down as he carefully picked up the medium-sized rocks and stuffed them in his pack. He was watching intently for any movement.

Shortly thereafter, Newton commented, "That's enough. Throw the backpack on your back and let's go. We're burning daylight." Newton turned on his heels and started to jog down the path.

Heaving the rock-filled backpack onto his shoulders, Elias followed.

An hour later, Newton was working in the kitchen. A pot of

chicory coffee was brewing. The smell of coffee and the noise of dishes clattering woke Fat Freddy and he ambled down the hallway.

"You making breakfast?" he asked as he began to salivate at the tantalizing aroma.

"Today only. From now on, you'll be doing the chow preparation."

By the tone of Newton's voice, Fat Freddy knew that he better not push the issue. "I can do that," he agreed. "I'm quite the cook."

"Just make sure that you're making healthy meals for us and limit the sandwiches. Fruits, vegetables and meat. That's what we need."

"And pasta!" Fat Freddy added.

Newton glared at Fat Freddy for a moment and then relaxed his facial muscles. "A couple of times a week," he relented.

"Are you two arguing again?" Elias asked from the doorway.

Newton and Fat Freddy turned to look in his direction and saw a perspiring Elias leaning against the wooden door frame. As he dropped the backpack, Newton handed him a plastic bottle of cold water. "Here's a water. Go grab a quick shower to cool down and we'll eat."

After gulping half of the icy water, Elias lowered the bottle from his mouth and asked, "Are we running every day?"

"No."

"Good."

"We're running twice a day," he said with a serious smile.

Elias groaned, and then asked, "Do I wear the pack both times?"

"Yes. It's called conditioning. Grab your shower before the food gets cold."

Elias trudged down the hall as Fat Freddy called after him. "Be sure you wash behind the ears. You smell," he said as the stench from Elias' sweat blocked out the smell of the coffee and eggs.

After breakfast, Elias and Newton started to leave the house when Fat Freddy asked, "Newt, you mind if I have a few words alone with Manny?"

"No. You've got two minutes," he said without turning his head or breaking his stride. "Elias, bring your backpack out to the barn when you come."

"Will do," Elias said.

"Thanks. It'll be just a sec," Fat Freddy said as he looked at Elias. "How's the memory thing working this morning?"

Shaking his head from side to side, Elias responded, "Nothing. You don't have to ask me every five minutes. I just don't remember my personal stuff. My memory is missing and you don't need to keep reminding me."

"Okay, okay. How did you sleep last night?"

"After I finally got to sleep, I had nightmares," Elias admitted.

"Yeah, the doc said that you'd have those. With all the running you're doing, how does your head feel?"

"It feels fine. A few headaches. It's the rest of my body that aches." Elias cast his eyes toward the barn. "I'd better get going.

Newt is a stickler about wasting time."

"Yeah, I know. Time is precious. That's why I try to waste it wisely," Fat Freddy said with a slight chuckle as Elias headed for the barn.

When Elias reached the barn, he walked through it and out to the firing range where Newton was waiting for him.

"More target practice?" Elias asked.

"Yeah. Line up and fire away only at the blue-painted targets."

Of the four shots Elias fired, two nicked the target.

"You're firing wide. You have to confidently and skillfully aim and fire," Newton cautioned.

"I'll do better next try."

"You'd better. Otherwise, you're going to be very tired. Give me one hundred!"

With a blank look on his face, Elias asked, "What?"

"Strap on your backpack and run as fast as you can to that post and back. It's a hundred yards round trip.

"Why?"

"That's how I teach you to focus on the task at hand. If you don't want to run, then be more accurate on the firing range. I have a low tolerance for unfocused rookies or whiners. Now, start running."

Bending over, Elias picked up the backpack and threw it over his shoulders. He started to run with the bright sun overhead. It was going to be another hot day.

"Faster," Newton yelled.

Picking up speed, Elias grimaced as he ran to the post and back. When he returned, he was sweating as he dropped the backpack to the ground.

"Think you can focus now?"

"I better. I don't like this extra running thing," Elias responded as he used the back of his hand to wipe sweat from his brow.

They spent the rest of the day firing at the targets as Newton honed Elias' skills with his .22. They broke for a quick lunch before returning to the firing range. The afternoon was peppered with 100-yard runs when Elias' shooting was not to the skill level Newton expected.

After their late afternoon run and dinner, Newton drove Elias and Fat Freddy into Cedar Key so that Fat Freddy could pick up some groceries from the limited selection at the small island market. When they were done, they drove back to the house as a vociferous Fat Freddy complained about the lack of selection at the store and how it would affect his cooking style. Newton and Elias allowed him to ramble the entire drive as they sat in silence.

The next morning, they repeated their routine from the previous day with the early morning run and training. Fat Freddy cooked the meals as they settled into a daily pattern.

After lunch, Newton and Elias returned to the firing range. As he looked over the targets, Newton turned to Elias and asked, "So, I understand you've lost your memory."

"Yes. I don't remember anything."

"That's tough."

"Nothing at all. Not from my personal life. I remember some things. You know, the basics, like how to drive a car. But I don't remember my past life."

"How about geography?"

Elias grinned. "Like the fifty states?" He didn't wait for Newton to answer. "Yeah, I remember my way around for the most part. I don't remember where I lived in Detroit or St. Louis. That's still in a fog for me."

"I've seen people with memory loss due to brain injuries. Funny thing is that you can snap out of it at any time. It can be a short period of time or a long period. And in some cases, I have to warn you, it can be permanent."

"With my luck, that'll be my case," Elias said sullenly.

"Cheer up, at least you're still alive. Let's start shooting!"

After dinner, Elias found a couple of deflated punch balls on an elastic string. He blew up one of the balls and began bouncing it like a paddle ball on elastic. Then he spotted the back of Fat Freddy's head poking above the top of the chair he was sitting on while he had a conversation with Newton on the back porch.

Elias walked onto the back porch and began bouncing the ball off the back of Fat Freddy's head. Without interrupting his conversation, Fat Freddy reached in his pocket and pulled out a pocketknife, which he quickly opened. When the ball hit his head again, he quickly slashed upward, popping the ball like a balloon.

"I'm impressed!" Newton said. "That's the fastest I've seen you move since we've been here."

"But like I told you, I could put you guys to shame if I wanted to," Fat Freddy said without turning to look at Elias as he returned the knife to his pocket.

"Aw, that wasn't anything. You should have heard him move down the hall to the bathroom the other night. Did you have the runs, Freddy?" Elias asked.

"Ha-ha!" Fat Freddy replied. "I think I've been eating too much green stuff. It ran right through me," Fat Freddy replied as he squinted at Newton.

Newton chuckled at Fat Freddy's response.

Elias didn't chuckle as his uncontrollable mood began to turn negative. He glared at Fat Freddy for ruining his fun by puncturing the ball. Slowly, he walked back into the kitchen and tossed the burst ball into the trash. He then picked up the other ball and held it under the kitchen faucet. He filled it with about a quart of cold water and then shut off the faucet. He then blew up the ball and began punching it as he returned to the porch where Fat Freddy was sitting.

Hearing the noise from the approaching punch ball, Fat Freddy leaned toward Newton. "Some people just don't learn," he annoyingly said as he retrieved the knife from his pocket and waited.

When the ball hit his head the second time, Fat Freddy slashed upward and punctured the ball like he did before. The water inside the ball showered him when it burst, much to the delight of Elias and Newton, laughing at his wet predicament.

"Go ahead and laugh. I'm the guy who just got cooled off. It didn't bother me one bit," Fat Freddy said as he placed the knife in his pocket. He had learned long ago to control his temper.

"Be glad that I didn't put acid in the ball. You'd be in a fine mess if I had," Elias said with a surly tone.

Fat Freddy turned halfway in his chair. "Manny, you know there's nothing like payback. I'd sleep with one eye open if I were you."

"I always do," Elias said with a sardonic grin.

"Good on you," Newton chimed in. "Very creative. There's hope for you, Elias."

Still sullen from his mood swing, Elias retreated to the quiet solace of his room.

Later that night, Newton was by himself in the barn when his cell phone rang. He reached for it and answered, "Yeah?"

"Newt, it's Jimmy."

"Yes?"

"I wanted to check in with you and see how my friends are doing."

"Bert and Ernie are doing fine," Newton said with a touch of sarcasm.

"And the training?"

"Going good."

"Is he picking it up?"

"Yeah. He's making very good progress."

"So, you're pleased with his progress?"

"I'd say so."

"Good. Any problems?"

"None."

"Good. I'll check back next week."

"Okay."

When Newton finished in the barn, he returned to the house. It was late. No lights were on. Assuming that Fat Freddy and Elias had called it a night, Newton walked to his room and turned in for a restful sleep.

Contrary to the peaceful sleep Newton was experiencing, Elias tossed and turned as flashbacks and nightmares filled his dreams. He woke twice in a cold sweat. He was frustrated at not being able to identify reality from figments of his imagination.

End of the Week
Newton's Training Grounds

"It's been a productive week. We're going to town for dinner. It's on me," Newton said to Elias as they walked toward the house.

As they approached it, they saw Fat Freddy reclining in a chair, catching some rays. He was quite a sight. Short hairy legs. Bright red Speedos. His large hairy belly, upper torso and big head were trying to match the color of his Speedos. His sunglasses were askew on his face. Noisy snores greeted the two as they neared him. Seeing him like this, it was hard to believe he was a brutal mobster.

The two couldn't resist laughing at the sight, waking Fat Freddy in the process.

Fat Freddy stood up from his chair as he grabbed at his sunglasses. "What are you guys laughing at?"

"You look like you belong on the cover of GQ!" Newton kidded.

"I use to model in my younger days," Fat Freddy retorted.

"Wouldn't surprise me one bit." Newton began to push further, but decided to let it go. "We're going to town for dinner," he announced.

"Good, I've been working up an appetite," Fat Freddy said.

"Not you. You haven't done anything this week," Newton said as he saw that Fat Freddy wanted to tag along.

"Hey, I've been working on my tan. Look how dark I got," Fat Freddy beamed. He threw them a wink. "Look how attractive I made myself for the ladies tonight," he said as he whirled around to show off his "tanned" body.

"You look more like a redskin potato to me," Newton teased.

"I'm golden-baked!" Fat Freddy countered.

Elias looked at Newton. "Let him come with us."

"Yeah. I'm a ton of fun!" Fat Freddy added.

"You're a ton all right. But I'm thinking something other than fun!" Newton retorted. He thought a moment and decided to relent.

"Grab a shirt. You go in topless and you'll scare everyone away."

"Just more for the girls to love," Fat Freddy replied as he ambled down the hall to grab a fresh shirt and change into shorts. The other two went to their rooms to clean up and change.

Fifteen minutes later, the three men left the house and drove into town. As they drove along Dock Street, the large pier over the water on which several restaurants were located, they saw rows of chromed motorcycles parked along the street.

Newton commented, "Must be Biker Week."

"Yeah. Look at all the bikes!" Fat Freddy said as they drove past the parked shiny Harley-Davidson and other custom motorcycles. "And you know what bikes mean!"

"What's that, Freddy?" Elias asked from the back seat.

"Biker chicks! I like them biker babes." Fat Freddy was already beginning to drool.

"Rein it in," Newton warned. "We don't need any trouble."

"I know. I know, but women just find me so irresistible. I'm a real chick magnet."

"Sure you are, Fat Freddy," Newton smirked.

"You just watch how they're attracted to me," Fat Freddy said with an air of false confidence. "They can smell money and power on a man."

Newton found a parking spot in the marina parking lot and they walked back to the first restaurant and bar, Seabreezes. It was a large two-story wooden structure with a restaurant on the second floor and a bar with music and pool tables on the first floor.

"Hey, I need to buy one of those T-shirts!" Fat Freddy said as he pointed to a T-shirt. It read "Some do! Some don't! I might!"

"I think the last line should be along the lines of 'I don't fit'!" Newton teased. "Not sure that they have a shirt big enough for you, Freddy," Newton laughed softly.

"Real funny!" Fat Freddy said as he turned away from the T-shirt rack.

Elias and Fat Freddy followed Newton to the second floor with its large beams and rafters where they were seated next to a window overlooking the Gulf of Mexico.

It was then that Newton noticed Fat Freddy's face. "What do you have on your face?"

"What do you mean?" Fat Freddy asked as he looked up from his menu.

Newton and Elias peered closely at Fat Freddy's face.

"You've got sparkles on your face!" Newton said as he sat back and began laughing. "Why did you put sparkles on your face?"

Elias was now laughing, too. "You do, Freddy. What did you do?"

"I didn't do nothing," he said as he pushed away from the table and walked to the restroom on the first floor. Within minutes, he returned. His red face now highlighted his sparkles. "Must have been the suntan lotion I used. I thought there was something gritty in it," he said as he plopped in the chair. "I tried washing it off, but I couldn't get it all. Does it look better?"

"No," Elias grinned as he inspected Fat Freddy.

"We'll just have to call you 'Sparkles' tonight," Newton chuckled.

"Hey, can you lower your voice?" Fat Freddy asked as he looked at the bikers and their women in the restaurant.

"Oh yeah. With a name like Sparkles, we don't want to give anyone any ideas, do we?" Newton laughed again. "By the way, did you get hit on in the restroom, Sparkles?" he teased.

"Cool it. Just cool it!" Fat Freddy steamed quietly.

When the waitress arrived at their table, Fat Freddy noticed her eye-watering neckline. "Well, hello darling," he greeted her.

The waitress smiled. She knew the type and played along. "Hi, handsome!" she joked back. "I like your sparkles," she added as she took in the remaining glitter on his face.

Fat Freddy ignored her second comment and said, "Give us drafts all around, okay, sweetie?"

"Okay. Would you like to order now?"

"Oh, baby, would I like to place an order!" Fat Freddy said as he seductively raised his eyebrows. It may have looked seductive on other men, but it was just not working when Fat Freddy did it.

"What would you like?" she asked, already guessing the nature of his response.

"You on my lap for starters," Fat Freddy teased.

"How about that for dessert?" she teased back, although Fat Freddy thought she was serious. His head pulled back and a large smile filled his cherubic face.

"Now, you're talking," he said as his eyes twinkled as bright as the sparkles on his face. "You do that, baby, and I'll sing to you."

Elias interrupted. "Let me warn you that he sings like a cat being strangled," he kidded.

"Oh, my!" the waitress squealed as she looked from Elias back to Fat Freddy.

"I do not!" Fat Freddy stormed. Then softening his tone, he said, "It's like the voice of a nightingale."

"Right," Newton said sarcastically. Then he added, "In your dreams. And that would be nightmares for us."

"Can you give us a few minutes?" Elias asked as he glanced up from his menu.

"Sure. I'll be back with your drinks."

When she walked away, Fat Freddy said. "She likes me. I'm such a pretty boy, sparkles or no sparkles. The girls just can't resist me."

The three focused their attention on the menus and the waitress returned with the beers that she set down in front of them.

"Are you having a good day or a bad day?" Fat Freddy asked as he raised his beer glass and looked at the waitress.

"Kind of a bad day," she said.

"Do you want to be a bad girl?" Fat Freddy asked with a glint in his eyes. "If you do, I can turn your day around to be good. Real good."

Before she could answer, Elias spoke. "Cool your jets, Freddy."

"Hey, I'm just being friendly," Fat Freddy protested.

The three gave her their food orders and as she walked away, Fat Freddy said to her, "My favorite toast is 'bottoms up'." He had a salacious grin on his face.

She smiled at them but, as she turned, she rolled her eyes on her way to the kitchen. The men continued their banter and devoured their meals when she presented them fifteen minutes later.

As they finished eating, Fat Freddy threw several bills on the table. "You two settle up with the waitress. I'll be downstairs by the pool table, waiting for you. Might be some chicks looking for a good-looking guy like me." He pushed back from the table, stood and walked downstairs as Newton and Elias chuckled at his audacity.

Fat Freddy entered the crowded bar area and saw a woman bent over the pool table as she lined up a shot. He raced to the other side of the table and lowered his head so that he could see the angle from the opposite side. He was also eyeballing her ample cleavage as her low top gaped open. Pointing to the ball she was targeting, he said, "You'll want to hit it lightly on the side and she'll drop right in the side pocket, baby cakes."

The blonde glared at Fat Freddy. "Did you hear me ask for any help?"

"Listen, baby cakes, I can always spot a damsel in distress. And here I am, your white knight to the rescue," he grinned. "Now, do as I say and I can make you a real winner!"

"Bite me!"

"That would be my pleasure and yours," Fat Freddy cracked.

The woman glared evilly at Fat Freddy.

"Hey, don't go pre-menstrual on me!" Fat Freddy retorted in response to her look.

Before she could respond, her biker boyfriend saddled up next to Fat Freddy. "Buzz off, little man," he said coldly.

"Worried I'm going to help the little lady beat you?" Fat Freddy asked as he ignored the comment and touched the targeted ball. "Just hit it right here."

"Keep your hands off her balls!" the boyfriend said as he towered over Fat Freddy.

"Oh, excuse me; I didn't know she was that kind of girl. She's got balls?" Fat Freddy smirked.

The boyfriend swung his fist and knocked Fat Freddy to the floor.

"You really shouldn't have done that," Fat Freddy said as he got on all fours and stood up. In his hand, he now held his handgun and it was pointed at the boyfriend.

The boyfriend backed up as Fat Freddy advanced. But Fat Freddy didn't see another biker moving quickly toward him. The biker grabbed Fat Freddy's gun arm and firmly wrested the weapon away from him. Then, he and another biker restrained Fat Freddy between them as the boyfriend advanced.

Looking closely at Fat Freddy, the boyfriend began to laugh.

"Isn't this sweet? Look, everyone. He has glitter on his face."

Fat Freddy was steaming as he tried to break the iron grip the two bikers had on him.

"Maybe you're the only one here with no balls!" the boyfriend laughed as his friends joined him. "We'll just have to check."

The crowd of bikers roared and egged on the biker to depant Fat Freddy.

Fat Freddy stopped struggling. He became serious as he looked at the boyfriend. "I'm warning you. You have no idea who I am. You had better let me go."

The boyfriend leaned toward Fat Freddy. "Or you'll do what?"

"I'll use my secret weapon, Cinderella."

The boyfriend laughed again. "And what is that? Are you going to do a ballet for us?"

"Newt," Fat Freddy called. "Show them."

The bikers turned to look in the direction where Fat Freddy was staring. Newton and Elias stood in the doorway.

"I'll handle this. You stay here," Newton said before he took two steps into the room. "Apparently my wayward friend has gotten himself into a little trouble. He's just a harmless, big flirt. Would you folks be willing to let bygones be bygones and release him to me?"

"What are you smoking?" the boyfriend asked indignantly as he glanced at Newton.

Ignoring the question, Newton took two more steps toward the group. "I'm kindly asking you to release my friend."

Fat Freddy's eyes widened in surprise at Newton's use of the word "friend" to describe him.

"Not going to happen. He needs to pay for insulting my woman," the boyfriend said.

"You know I can't let that happen."

"Your choice then."

Newton looked around the room. "I count three of you. Are there any others?"

Three more bikers stepped forward as the others stepped back.

"Good. Six of you. That should make it more fair." No sooner had the last words left Newton's mouth than he rocketed across the room and grabbed the boyfriend's arm, bringing it down sharply across his raised knee and allowing a large crack to fill the room as the arm broke. He tossed the boyfriend toward the wall as he spun around to face three advancing bikers.

The three bull-rushed Newton, who first targeted the one on the left edge. He gave him a strong jab to the chin, driving the chin inward and knocking out the attacker. At the same time, Newton swung on his left leg and lifted his right foot with a sharp kick into the groin of the middle rusher, dropping him to the ground.

The third rusher grabbed at Newton's arm and began to pull him around. As Newton spun, he allowed his momentum to carry him and the rusher toward the floor-to-ceiling windows overlooking the Gulf. Grabbing the rusher with both of his hands Newton threw him through the window, shattering the glass. The rusher landed ten feet below in the water.

Newton turned to face the two bikers who were still restraining Fat Freddy.

Elias called from the doorway. "Need some help?"

Newton smiled. "Nope. Just getting warmed up." Next he asked, "You two want to let go of my friend, Sparkles?"

From the side of the room, the boyfriend yelled, "Take him!"

The two bikers let go of Fat Freddy and warily advanced on Newton. One approached him from the left. The other approached him from the right. Suddenly, they rushed Newton, who immediately struck the first with a kick to the left knee, dropping him to the ground. As he spun around, the second one tackled Newton and they fell to the ground where they grappled. Newton was able to position himself so that he placed a chokehold on the man. He held the man tightly as he struggled until he became unconscious.

Then Newton stood to his feet. As he surveyed the bodies strewn around the room, he heard a gunshot. He spun to face the door where Elias was standing with his .22. Newton then turned and saw that the boyfriend was gripping his bleeding shoulder. At his feet was a 9mm weapon. A couple of seconds earlier, it had been in the boyfriend's hand.

Newton smiled at Elias. "You're learning well."

"It looks like it," Elias smiled back. He was proud of his accuracy. It looked like the training was paying off.

Suddenly they heard Fat Freddy yell. "Oh, no you don't!"

The biker chick who Fat Freddy had accosted was approaching Newton with an upraised pool stick. Fat Freddy pushed her through the broken window and she splashed into the water below.

"You're first up for the wet T-shirt contest," Fat Freddy chortled as he looked at the woman below.

"Picking on girls, Freddy?" Elias asked as he saw Fat Freddy retrieve his weapon from the pool table.

"Not sure that she was one!" Fat Freddy quipped.

"We better go. With that gunshot, the police will be right here," Newton said as he pushed Fat Freddy and Elias out the door and onto the sidewalk. They hurried to the parked Jeep.

"Thanks for rescuing me, Newt," Fat Freddy said from the passenger side of the front seat as they drove away.

"I had to do something, Mr. Smooth. You were screaming like a girl," Newton teased.

"I was not!" Fat Freddy replied with indignation.

"You owe me," Newton replied.

"Yeah, I do," he said as he fumbled in his pocket and extracted a small pill container. He twisted off the lid and popped a small white pill into his mouth.

"You okay? I don't need you dying on me or anything. Jimmy wouldn't be happy," Newton said as he watched Fat Freddy slump in the front seat.

"It's nothing. Just a little too much excitement. Got to watch my ticker if you know what I mean," Fat Freddy responded.

"Nitro?" Newton asked as Elias leaned forward from the back seat and looked at Fat Freddy.

"No, it's Viagra," he countered. When he saw the grim look of concern on Elias' face, Fat Freddy decided to go ahead and tell him. "Yeah. Nitroglycerin pills. I'll be fine."

"You sure, Freddy?" Elias asked.

"Yeah. Yeah. This happens once in a while. I'll be fine," he said as he straightened up in the seat. "Mind if I roll down the window and get some fresh air?"

"Go ahead," Newton said as they drove quickly along Route 24 and out of town. As the fresh air filled the car and Fat Freddy relaxed, Newton looked in his rear view mirror at Elias. "You did well tonight."

"Thanks. So did you. Six of them against one," Elias said. "Impressive."

"I've been in worse. I'll give you some pointers in street fighting in case you get into a situation like that. Shooting your way out isn't always the right option," Newton advised.

Within minutes, they arrived at Newton's place and bedded down for the night.

Back at Seabreezes, the police arrived and couldn't find anyone willing to talk to them. Apparently, everyone was in the bar area and didn't see what happened in the pool room or know how the window was broken. Likewise, no one knew anything about a gunshot. Nothing at all.

Two Weeks Later
Newton's Training Grounds

Only one more week to go and his training would be over, Elias thought to himself as he and Newton walked toward the house for dinner. Elias was still struggling with the nightmares, but he had made tremendous progress in his conditioning and killing skills.

As the two neared the house, they spotted Fat Freddy. He was wearing short shorts and a T-shirt. A slab of his belly bulged over the top of his shorts. His two feet were stuck in a wash-tub filled with water and ice. In his hand, he held a steaming cup of coffee.

"What are you doing there, Freddy?" Elias asked with a puzzled look on his face.

"I had to have my hot coffee and it's too hot of a day for that so I decided to put myself in the Goldilocks zone," Fat Freddy responded as he took another sip of his coffee.

"What are you talking about? Goldilocks zone?" Newton asked.

"Yeah. You know, Newt. Not too hot and not too cold," Fat Freddy smirked before taking another sip of his brew.

Newton shook his head and looked at Elias. "If you and I were in a bar, we'd be doing belly shots. Fat Freddy, on the other hand, would be doing butt shots," he teased Fat Freddy.

"Funny. Real funny, Newt!" Fat Freddy said as he watched Newton and Elias laughing.

Later that evening, Newton was working in the barn. Fat Freddy and Elias were relaxing in two of the rocking chairs on the back porch.

Listening to the sounds of the early evening, Elias commented, "I like this time of the day. Everything is winding down."

Swatting a mosquito that had landed on his arm, Fat Freddy quipped, "Not everything is winding down. Them mosquitoes are winding up for a feast."

"Especially when they see you," Elias snickered.

"Ha-ha. Real funny." Fat Freddy looked toward the barn, then spoke. "I miss city life. Can't wait to get outta here. This is too slow-paced for me, Manny."

"It doesn't have to be that way. You could always join us in the training."

"No. Not for me," he said as he reached for his cold beer. It had been sitting with two other beer cans in a stew pot filled with ice.

Elias leaned toward Fat Freddy. "Tell me, Freddy. Is Jimmy as bad as you've hinted these last two weeks?"

"Worse." Fat Freddy took a long sip of his beer. "There was one guy he took out in St. Clair Township. The guy was a competitor. So we kidnapped him one night, then killed him. Jimmy cut the body in pieces and we put the body parts in garbage bags. Then we dumped the bags in several places."

"Why didn't you bury the body?"

Allowing a small smile to cross his face before responding, Fat Freddy said, "There are some bodies you want found and some you don't. This one we wanted found to send a message. The police found everything except for the guy's eyes."

"What happened to his eyes?"

"Jimmy mailed them to the guy's brother in Kansas City. He didn't like the brother, either."

"Did Jimmy kill the brother?"

"No. Last we heard, he closed his business and moved to the West Coast."

"There was another time when Jimmy invited another mob boss to have a sit down dinner together to settle their differences. They each had a bodyguard. I'm Jimmy's and the other guy has one. We stand behind them to make sure that nothing bad happens.

"While they're eating, the other guy asks Jimmy to pass him the salt. Jimmy gives the guy the salt and watches him sprinkle it on his food. The guy devours the steak and the two keep talking. Suddenly the guy starts having trouble breathing. Next thing you know, he passes out and falls out of his chair onto the floor."

"Heart attack?"

"You might think that, but it wasn't. His bodyguard kneels down to him and starts talking to him. He can't figure out what's going on. I call 911 so he knows that Jimmy and I are trying to help."

"If it wasn't a heart attack, what was it?"

"Potassium cyanide."

"In the steak?"

"No, the salt shaker. It was filled with a lethal compound. Five minutes after you pass out, the brain starts to die. Then your heart muscles start to die and the heart stops beating while your body starts to have seizures. You vomit and your skin turns cherry red. The guy was dead before the ambulance arrived."

"And the bodyguard?"

"What was he going to do? He didn't know about the cyanide

until the autopsy. By then, Jimmy had taken control of the guy's organization."

"Did the bodyguard join Jimmy's organization?"

"No, he ended up disappearing." Fat Freddy smiled. "Jimmy took care of him after the funeral."

"I've got one better to tell you about." Without waiting to see if Elias wanted to hear it, Fat Freddy continued. "There was this guy. His name was Teritina. He'd been giving Jimmy fits with running the numbers racket. Jimmy caught him skimming some of the profits. So, it was payback time.

"After a meeting at Jimmy's warehouse one night, Parella and I grab this guy before he leaves. We take his weapon and Jimmy has us tie the guy to a table downstairs in the basement. The guy can't move. Then Jimmy takes this small metal container he had built and has us strap it to the guy's belly. It's all wire mesh and no bottom. It's got a wire that you plug into the wall so you can heat up the container.

"The guy's lying there and Jimmy walks over. He's carrying a rat in a cage. This rat looks mean and hungry. Jimmy reached down and opens a little door on the mesh container, then dumps the rat into it. He closed the door and plugs in the wire. The container on the guy's stomach starts to heat up. The rat doesn't like the heat and neither does the guy because it's burning his skin. The guy starts to twist and turn. The rat can't find a way out because the container is hot. There's only one thing for it to do."

"The stomach?" Elias guessed with a look of revulsion on his face.

"Exactly. The rat starts to burrow out through the stomach and intestines. Jimmy just stands there and laughs. He can be such a sick freak at times."

"That's gross!"

After finishing off his beer, Fat Freddy reached for another, popped the tab and took a drink. "I'm telling you. Never mess with Jimmy. Now, I will warn you about another guy in our organization. You've got to keep an eye out for Tony Parella."

"Why?"

"He's crazy. He wants my job as Jimmy's right-hand man. The guy's a loony wannabe. I think he's a nut case. Probably clinically insane. Don't ever turn your back on him. He'd stick you without thinking twice."

"Why does Jimmy put up with him?" Elias asked.

"Jimmy likes a little competition in our organization. Keeps people on their toes." Fat Freddy lowered his arm, holding the beer can. "But Parella likes to torture dogs. People sometimes deserve it, but animals don't. No, don't trust anyone who does stuff like that to animals. They're a whack job!"

"I'll be careful around him."

"You do that. And keep an eye out for Jimmy wannabes. Sometimes, I think he has wannabe successors lined up like planes waiting to land at Chicago O'Hare," Fat Freddy quipped. Then he chuckled.

Oak Point State Park
Put-in-Bay

It was among the rarest of Lake Erie island days with no wind present, not even a tiny hint of a breeze. Every scrap of sail on every boat docked along the waterfront and at the mooring buoys hung limp. Pedestrian traffic droned mindlessly along the streets under the sweltering heat. Boaters and deep-tanned, bikinied women lay on the boat decks as sweat rolled off their well-oiled bodies.

The memorial service for Emerson Moore had just concluded. It took place mid-morning as the warming sun cast its rays across the tranquil bay. Oak Point State Park had been one of Moore's favorite spots on South Bass Island. The small peninsula jutted out into the bay like a finger, pointing toward Gibraltar Island.

It was here under the massive oak trees that Moore would park his uncle's 1929 Model A Ford truck and walk over to one of the picnic tables scattered about the tiny park. He often would sit quietly alone and just mindlessly stare across the bay and watch the activity on the water. He could see over to Perry's Monument and his aunt's house on East Point, on the far side of the bay. It was home.

It had been four weeks since Moore had vanished and the authorities now presumed that he was dead. No one could find a trace of Emerson Moore or Jimmy Diamonds. It was believed by Detroit investigators that Moore had likely been killed in some fashion and his body buried in some forgotten field or perhaps weighted down and tossed overboard somewhere.

After weeks of anguish and forlorn hope that the local celebrity reporter was still alive, Aunt Anne decided to hold the memorial service. There had not been one response, either, to a reward offer of $25,000 put up by Moore's newspaper, and an even larger $50,000 reward offered by an anonymous benefactor, for information on his whereabouts.

A large open-air tent had been erected near the point and rows of chairs had been set up, facing a small podium. Moore's Aunt Anne sat in the front row. On one side of her was Mike "Mad Dog" Adams. On the other side was Moore's former Navy SEAL buddy, Sam Duncan. Both had to comfort Aunt Anne on several occasions as she broke down in tears at the loss of her nephew. John Sedler, Moore's editor from *The Washington Post*, had flown in to the island and sat next to Duncan.

Aunt Anne's friends from the OWLS, the Old Women's Literary Society, occupied the rest of the seats in the first row. Many members from the entertainment community attended – Scott Alan the Island Doctor, Westside Steve Simmons, Ray Fogg, Bob Gatewood, Alex Bevan, Tim Goldrainer and the Menus, and Pat Dailey.

Others in the community filled the chairs, including Tim Niese, Bob and Judy Bransome, Maggie Beckford, Billy Market, Jeff and Kendra Koehler, Marv and Eric Booker, Richard Warren, and Dana and Bill Blumensaadt. Many stood outside the tent as they listened to several speak about their adventures with Moore. "Mad Dog" Adams, Sam Duncan and John Sedler were the final speakers.

After the memorial service concluded and the attendees headed over to the Crew's Nest for a memorial meal, Adams, Duncan and Sedler purposefully huddled together. They seemed to have a plan in mind and watched as the OWLS herded Aunt Anne onto the Put-in-Bay tram with several others. The three men turned and looked at the bay in an added moment of silence and reverence for their fallen comrade in joviality and adventure.

Adams and Duncan started to talk at the same time, then stopped.

"Are you thinking what I'm thinking?" Duncan asked. The thirty-nine-year-old former Navy SEAL was powerfully built and blonde-haired. He had known Moore for years and the two had escaped death on more than one occasion in their adventures together. Duncan's normally cocky attitude had been replaced with one of genuine and deep concern.

"I hope so. I'm thinking that Emerson somehow is still alive. With all the stuff he's been through in his life, my gut tells me he's alive," Adams said optimistically. "I think I'd feel it if he was really gone."

"Amen to that," Sedler offered. "He's like a cat with nine lives and always lands on his feet – always comes back with incredible tales of adventure. Some of those, we could never publish in the paper, mind you."

"He does have more lives than a cat," Duncan commented. "He and I have been through too much for him to just disappear like this. He's alive somewhere, somehow."

"John," said Adams, "we tried to talk Aunt Anne out of doing this memorial crap, but she wouldn't listen to us."

"I bet. I stayed at the house last night and she was a mess, emotionally," Sedler observed as he looked around. "She's a practical woman, and this makes sense to her. But to me, I finally make a trip to Put-in-Bay and it's for the wrong reason."

"That's for sure," Duncan responded.

Looking around before he spoke, Sedler said, "I see why Emerson wanted to use Put-in-Bay as his base of operations.

This island is a delight."

"Yeah. It's beautiful here," Adams agreed. "That's part of the reason I've been playing here for over thirty-five years."

"I'd like to have played here for thirty-five-years," Duncan said as he eyed two bikini-clad bodies walking along the dock, then looked back at Adams. "I guess that's not the type of playing you meant," he teased with a twinkle in his eye to break the sullen mood among the three men.

"A gentleman never tells," Adams kidded.

"And when did you become a gentleman?" Duncan asked as he took another look at the two attractive women.

"Okay, you two," Sedler said as he redirected the banter. "Do either of you have any insight as to what really happened?"

"Not me. I just got back in the country," Duncan answered.

Adams had heard in the past that Moore was suspicious about some of Duncan's clandestine assignments, suggesting that they were covert for a variety of governmental agencies. Adams turned to Sedler. "John, have you heard anything?"

"Actually, I have. I've been burning the phone lines with the guy at the Organized Crime Section for the Detroit P.D. Emerson had told me that he was meeting with him."

"Did he give you any hope?" Adams intently asked.

"No, he hemmed and hawed. Said that Jimmy Diamonds more than likely killed Emerson for payback because of the whole court thing. They did trace the getaway gang to the Grosse Ile Yacht Club. They had reports that a van was waiting for Diamonds and company. A body, which I assume was Emerson's, was seen being carried from a getaway boat to a van."

"Was he alive?" Duncan asked.

"The two yacht club members couldn't tell if he was, or if in fact it even was Emerson who was being carried away."

"What about the van, John? Did they track it down?" Adams probed.

"No. It completely vanished, too. Not a single trace."

"Didn't anyone get the plate number?"

"They did, but they were stolen plates."

"So, the trail's gone cold?" Adams asked.

"That's what the police said. They also suggested we may never find Emerson's body. Diamonds would have cut it up, burned it and dumped the ashes down the toilet or spread them in a field."

"Or in the Detroit River," Adams mused. Then Adams looked hopefully at Duncan. "But why would they go to all that trouble transferring a dead body from a boat to a van? Why not just dump it in the water? Dead is dead, and I don't think Emerson is. I think we start with finding Jimmy Diamonds."

"Yep. We find Diamonds first and then I have ways of making him talk. Trust me," Duncan said with a confident look in his eyes.

"I bet you do," Adams said seriously.

"Let me start by talking with some of my agency friends," Duncan offered.

"Okay and let me know what I can do to help," Adams said. He also was a former Navy SEAL and ready for whatever it would take to track down Diamonds. He and Duncan hadn't worked together on anything since their gun-toting days with Moore. A couple of years earlier, they broke up a Jamaican drug lord's drug trafficking ring in the Cayman Islands. Adams was itching for action, and this was, after all, for Emerson.

"And I'll see what I can dig up with my contacts in D.C. when I return this afternoon," Sedler said. "Diamonds still has to do business, even if he is laying low right now, so somebody knows something. It's a matter of getting people to talk."

Adams looked toward the Crew's Nest. "We better get moving and join the folks at the memorial lunch. Then, I've got a two o'clock show at The Round House."

The three men walked over to a golf cart and drove it to the Crew's Nest.

Newton's Training Camp
Cedar Key, Florida

"Fat Freddy still sleeping?" Newton asked as he entered the kitchen where Elias was pouring himself a cup of freshly made coffee.

"Of course," Elias grinned. "He finished off that beer last night. He won't be up for a while."

"He's wasting his time. He should be working out with us even if it's on a limited basis."

"Yes, he should," Elias agreed. "But he won't."

"Can't force him to," Newton uncaringly said as he reached for the coffee that Elias had poured for him. "Besides, my contract is only for you."

"Too bad," Elias quipped as he looked out the kitchen window at the rising sun working its magic with the morning's shadows. "Another beautiful day," Elias commented. "So tranquil."

"It is. That's why I like living here," Newton said as he reached for an orange and peeled it. Before biting a slice of the juicy fruit, he said, "I think we'll take a little break this morning."

"How's that?"

"I'll take you on a boat ride."

A puzzled look appeared on Elias' face. "I didn't see a boat around here."

"No, it's back in the woods, pulled ashore. It's a bit of a walk, but I think you might enjoy it."

"Sure, why not?" Elias responded eagerly. He could use the break.

An hour later, they emerged from the woods and found Newton's boat at the edge. It was a 12-foot long rowboat. Two oars and two life vests were aboard and a long pole jutted from the stern.

"No motor?"

"No. I like to enjoy the natural and quiet solitude of being on the water."

Elias noticed several fishing poles and nets on the deck. "We going fishing?"

"No, I'm going to take you to one of my favorite spots out here. Just a little R & R," Newton said as pulled off his shoes and began to push the boat into the water. "Give me a hand."

Elias quickly pulled off his own shoes and helped.

"Hold her for a second."

While Elias held on, Newton tossed their shoes into the boat along with a small cooler of beer they had carried with them. "Climb in," he said to Elias.

Once Elias climbed aboard, Newton pushed the boat out a little farther in the water, then climbed in the bow and carefully stepped to the stern. He picked up the pole and while standing aft, began poling the boat through the backcountry. "Pay attention," he demanded. "You're poling us back."

"I'm going to relax and imagine I'm in Venice in a gondola." Elias smiled, pleased that he remembered the canals in Venice.

Newton laughed. "I'd take this any day over Venice," he said as he poled them through the marshes. "They call this wet area the Gulf Hammock Wilderness. There are thousands of acres here. There's no landside access to the preserve other than boat ramps at Yankeetown or Cedar Key."

"No wonder you don't see anyone."

"Yeah. It's pretty remote. It's filled with cypress trees, salt marshes and tidal creeks. Makes it great for saltwater fishing, crabbing and shell fishing. When you fish this backcountry, you can catch redfish, trout, mango snapper and black drum."

Elias nodded his head as he looked around. A movement along the water's edge caught his attention as he saw an alligator slip into the water from the shore. "There's an alligator," he pointed.

"Plenty of gators around," Newton acknowledged. "And that's not all. Sometimes you'll see manatees and black bears, too."

"I'd prefer not to run into one of the bears."

"They don't bother you unless you bother them."

A flock of birds launched skyward out of the water as they poled past.

"I enjoy watching the birds. They seem to have so much freedom," Elias said as he thought about his own lack of freedom.

"Got them, too. You'll see great egrets, herons, bald eagles and white pelicans. You already saw some gulls," Newton said. "For years, the Gulf Hammock provided Cedar Key with its livelihood."

"Fishing?"

"That's today, but it used to be the cedar for making pencils and palm trees for the fiber factory. That's where they made brooms."

"I didn't know that or maybe I did and just don't remember now," Elias said forlornly, moderately frustrated with his ongoing memory loss.

"In the late 1800's, two New York pencil companies had mills here. They harvested the cedar into slats and shipped them to New York where they made them into pencils."

"And what was so special about cedar lumber?"

"It didn't splinter. Perfect for pencils."

Elias nodded in understanding. "What about the brooms?"

"The area is filled with cabbage palms. The palms were cut and used for dock pilings and the fronds were used for brush fibers. They processed them and made whisk brooms. Shipped them all over the world in the 1900's."

"I had no idea."

"You wouldn't know it today, but Cedar Key was the major population center in Florida in the early days. People would ship goods down the Mississippi River to New Orleans, then it came here to a deep-water port. They'd load goods on railcars and haul them over to the East Coast and then up to the Northeast."

"Why wouldn't they just sail around the tip of Florida?" Elias asked, pleased that his partial memory recalled the layout of Florida.

"They wanted to avoid hurricanes. In fact, that's what ruined Cedar Key."

"A hurricane?"

"Yep. In the late 1800's, it wiped out the town. The only thing that remained was the cemetery."

"They rebuilt it?"

"No, they moved the town," Newton smiled.

"What?"

"Yeah. The town was originally on Atsena Otie Island. They used barges to move whatever buildings survived across the channel. They reestablished the town on Way Key."

"What happened to the pencil companies?"

"They didn't rebuild here. Moved somewhere else," Newton said.

"But they did get the broom factory here in the new Cedar Key?"

"Yeah, that helped. But they had another problem. When the new owner of the railroad tried to purchase the railhead at Cedar Key, the folks here wouldn't sell it. The owner decided to show them and moved his railroad business about 100 miles south of here to a little village called Tampa."

"And now I know the rest of the story."

"Boy, it sure seems like that memory of yours is working again," Newton grinned.

"Not like I wish it would though," Elias said with much disappointment.

The rowboat emerged to the open pristine water of Waccasassa Bay and across the flats that stretched out to the Gulf of Mexico.

"Where are we heading?" Elias curiously asked as he saw a number of nearby small islands.

"R & R like I told you," Newton answered as he looked around the bay. "We're in the Waccasassa Bay Preserve. It's a state park that runs from Cedar Key down to Yankeetown."

"Relaxing," Elias said as he took in the peaceful solitude, interrupted occasionally by the cawing of sea gulls.

Within minutes, the boat nudged ashore on one of the small

islands. Both men jumped out and Newton took the free end of a line from the bow and secured it around a rock.

"Grab the beer cooler," Newton said before Elias could wade too far from the boat. Elias returned to the boat and grabbed the cooler, carrying it ashore.

"We've got a short hike through the palms to the other side. Wait until you see this."

"See what?"

"Patience," Newton said.

Soon, they emerged from the palms onto a pristine white sand beach.

"This is beautiful!" Elias said as he took in the quiet splendor.

Taking the cooler from Elias, Newton set it in the shade of a palm tree. He then pulled off his shirt and dropped his shorts. "I'm hot from the poling. Nothing like a quick dip," he said as he ran naked into the water. In seconds, he dove under and his head emerged.

"Come on in. It's refreshing."

"Sounds like a good idea," Elias said as he stripped off his shorts and T-shirt and joined Newton in the water. When he surfaced ten feet away, he said, "This is so refreshing."

"You deserved a break, Manny. You've done a good job with your conditioning," Newton said as he floated on his back for a few minutes. Newton felt sorry for his student. "I'm ready for a beer." He swam back to the beach and walked over to the cooler. He grabbed a beer, opened it and took a long drink, allowing the cold liquid to cool him further.

Meanwhile, Elias too, had emerged from the water and slipped back into his shorts, then joined Newton in throwing down a brew.

Newton retrieved his shorts and slipped them on. He grabbed another beer before sitting on the beach and allowing the sun and breeze to dry him.

Elias joined him, dropping to the sand near Newton.

Newton turned to Elias. "You took a chance today coming out here with me."

"How's that?"

"What if I had orders to kill you today? No one would know that you're missing," Newton said.

Elias' body shifted into a defensive posture.

Newton grinned. "Relax. That's not on the agenda, but you have to be careful. You don't know who to trust."

"I'm gathering that," Elias replied. "But really, nobody knows I'm missing now. They said I don't have any family. Nobody knows I'm missing – or cares."

"So, you really don't have your memory back?"

Shaking his head from side to side, Elias answered, "No, I can't remember anything about my past life. I remember basic stuff like how to drive, brush my teeth and how to cook some stuff. But I don't remember my personal life at all."

"Got any strange dreams? Flashbacks?"

"Oh yeah. All the time. I wake up. The problem is that I can't tell what the difference is between dreams and my past life."

"That's tough. Memory is a strange thing. It can come back when you have the right emotional stimulus. Or it could be a traumatic event."

"I hope that it does come back," Elias said. "I'd like to remember things everyone takes for granted. My mom. Her face. My dad. What I did as a kid – sports or whatever. Any women I've loved. Any pets. Home. Simple stuff like that."

"And I hope, for your sake, that it's a memory filled with good things," Newton said.

"From what Freddy has told me, I don't think that will be the case. He made it sound like I had a dark past. But somewhere in the past, I must've had some good things. Everyone does."

"Yeah, your past could be dark, but I sense something different in you, Manny. You're not like the typical people I train."

"Oh?"

"There's something inherently good about you. That's what I sense."

"Thanks, but I think you're wrong, according to Freddy."

"Time will tell."

The men continued to converse over the next two hours about Newton's background and training and life in Cedar Key.

Looking at the length of the shadows from the palm trees, Newton stood.

"We better head back." He donned his shirt. "Whoa," he said as he noticed that he was tipsy. "Good thing you're poling us back."

Elias, who had slipped on his shirt, was picking up the empty beer cans and tossing them into the cooler. "As long as you can keep me pointed in the right direction, especially when we enter the marshes."

"No problem," Newton said as he walked toward the path, followed by Elias who was carrying the cooler.

They returned to the boat and Elias poled them back to Newton's property. Once there, they pulled the boat ashore and began walking back to the house. "Thanks, Newt," Elias said sincerely. "I enjoyed the break from the training."

"Don't get soft on me! This was only a morning break! This afternoon, we're back at it!"

"Yeah. I didn't think this was going to last," Elias chuckled.

The Landing Strip
Cedar Key

The thirty days had passed quickly for Elias. Newton had driven them to the landing strip where a chartered plane was waiting for them. Fat Freddy had finished with his good-byes and was stuffing his bulky frame inside the plane. Elias had held back.

"Thanks for the training, Newt."

"Glad to help out. You'll do just fine. You did well in relearning how to kill people. You did real well with your shooting skills."

"I guess that I have a natural aptitude for it. That's why I've been such a good contract killer in the past. At least, that's what Freddy told me."

"You'll do just fine," Newton assured him.

"I have to admit that I feel like I'm in great shape physically. I just wish that I could remember my past," Elias commented as he picked up his duffel bag.

"I'm sure it'll come back sometime," Newton said.

"Thanks again," Elias said as he turned and started to walk to the plane.

"Two more things, Manny," Newton called.

"Yeah?" Elias paused and turned to face Newton.

"Remember. Watch your back and don't trust anyone. Nobody."

"Got it!" Elias said as he walked to the plane and climbed aboard.

Within minutes, the plane was taxiing down the runway and taking off.

"Good luck, Manny," Newton said softly. He had grown to like the troubled killer and was worried about his longevity. He was running with a tough crowd without conscience. But Manny had conscience, that he knew for sure. Newton turned and walked back to his Jeep. He started it and drove back to his training grounds.

As the twin-engine plane banked over the Gulf of Mexico, Elias leaned forward and asked Fat Freddy, who was seated next to the pilot, "Where to now?"

"Wooster, Ohio."

"I thought we were headed back to Detroit," Elias said, confused.

"Too hot for us in Detroit," Fat Freddy answered. "Just sit back and enjoy the flight." He didn't want to say too much in front of the pilot, even though the pilot worked for a lot of the guys in organized crime. You never got in trouble for being quiet.

Wayne County Airport
Wooster, Ohio

After the two men exited the plane, the pilot took off for his next assignment. He had barely spoken to his two passengers during the flight. His business explicitly was to mind his own business.

"That's our guy," Fat Freddy said as he recognized the driver of an approaching SUV.

The tan-colored vehicle pulled to a stop in front of Fat Freddy and Elias. It was driven by Tony Parella.

"Hey, Fats!" Parella called as he leaned out the driver's window.

"Knock it off, Parella! I told you not to call me that," Fat Freddy warned.

"Yeah, that's so much worse than Fat Freddy, huh? Sensitive still, Doublewide? I thought being away from me would make you miss me," Parella smirked, then pursed his lips together in a kissing fashion toward Freddy.

"Missed you like a hemorrhoid!" Fat Freddy retorted as Parella now glared at him while they threw their duffel bags in the rear of the vehicle and climbed in.

Driving away, Parella turned right onto Honeytown Road and drove south to Smithville Western Road where he turned right again. The vehicle followed the road down into several valleys until it turned right onto an old unpaved farm lane.

"Oh, this looks interesting," Fat Freddy said as the vehicle followed the lane for a half mile through clumps of trees, pastures and fields before pulling up in front of an old farmhouse and parking.

It was a two-story structure, badly in need of repair, and set in a small clearing. Two large oak trees provided shade for the porch on the south side of the house. To the right of the house and a hundred feet away was an old red barn that overlooked a small pond and fields filled with weeds. The lane continued past the house and disappeared into the woods.

Not what Fat Freddy was expecting after spending a month at the Cedar Key training camp. "You pick this, Parella?"

Gloating, Parella replied, "That I did. Nothing but the best for you, Fats!"

Fat Freddy whirled around in his seat and stared at Parella. "Knock it off!" he warned in a serious tone. One of these days he was going to get even with Parella. He never liked him.

As Fat Freddy and Elias exited the vehicle and grabbed their gear from the rear of the SUV, a figure with long silver-colored hair and a neatly trimmed beard appeared on the porch and greeted them. It was Jimmy Diamonds.

"It's about time you got here!" he growled.

Overlooking the snarly reception, Fat Freddy opened by saying, "Look at you! You've grown a beard and let the hair grow."

"Part of the disguise, Fat Freddy. Everyone under the sun is still looking for me." He reached into his pocket and pulled out a pair of cheap sunglasses that he slipped on. "Can't tell it's me, can you?"

"Nope."

"Good, it's working." Diamonds turned his attention to Elias. "I see you copied my look," he said as he evaluated the bearded and long-haired Elias.

"Just like you said, Jimmy," Elias commented.

Leaning toward Elias, he asked, "And how's that memory doing?"

Frowning with continual frustration, Elias answered, "Still not good, Jimmy. Not good at all."

Doing his best to hide a smile, Diamonds said, "That's too bad, Manny. It'll be back one of these days."

"You staying with us?" Fat Freddy asked.

"Nope, I got a place up in North Royalton, southwest of Cleveland," Diamonds replied. "I'm using it to set up operations in Cleveland. The guys in Chicago want me to control this area next."

Looking around the old farm, Fat Freddy asked, "And Elias and I are staying here?"

"Right. You're not too far from I-71, just west of here. Keeps you both hidden."

Crinkling his nose as he sniffed the air, Fat Freddy asked, "This place got an outhouse or indoor plumbing?" Fat Freddy wasn't happy that he was still out in the boondocks after spending thirty days in Cedar Key.

Laughing, Diamonds responded, "Indoor. It's not that bad. You're in the middle of farm and dairy country."

"Yeah, I got a whiff of the cow manure on the drive here," Fat Freddy disparagingly remarked. "I thought we'd at least be near civilization."

Diamonds tossed Fat Freddy a set of car keys. "There's a car parked in the barn that you can use if you decide to go to the store or eat at one of the town's restaurants."

"Isn't that dangerous, Jimmy? Aren't people looking for us?" Fat Freddy asked as he held the keys in his hand.

"They're looking all over Michigan, not here. Besides, you two look different with your facial hair."

"Okay," Fat Freddy said with a hesitant tone.

"Seriously, no one should know you two are here and I want you to keep a very low profile."

"How long do we have to stay here?" Fat Freddy asked.

"Until I tell you otherwise. We got some people to pay back so I'm counting on you two to take them out." Diamonds handed a cell phone to Fat Freddy. "Take this. I'll call you when I need something. Probably sooner than later."

"Is your number in here?" Fat Freddy asked.

"Yeah, I programmed it in. It's under Dad," he snickered.

"What about me? Do I get a phone?" Elias asked.

"What do you need a phone for? You can't remember anyone to call anyways. We're your family, Manny. That's the way it's been for some time. If you need to talk to me, just ask Freddy if you can call dear ole Dad." He chuckled at his own joke.

Elias wasn't happy. He felt agitated at being handled like a two-year-old.

Diamonds looked Elias up and down. "Manny, you're in good shape now. I want you to stay that way. You'll need it. There are plenty of trails to run on and there are several weapons in the barn for you both to practice with. And stay away from the girls' camp," Diamonds warned.

"Girls' camp?" Fat Freddy perked up.

Shaking his head, Diamonds replied, "Yeah. It's some halfway camp for young women. This farm's property abuts it in the back over by the lake."

"That sounds interesting!" Fat Freddy said as Elias listened.

"I'm warning you!" Diamonds cautioned Fat Freddy. "We don't need no trouble. Don't need anybody sniffing around here."

"I get it, Jimmy. No problem."

"Bring your stuff in the house," Diamonds said as he turned and entered the front door.

When the two walked in, Diamonds faced Elias. It was time to test him. "Manny, I'm wondering if you still have blind obedience to me?"

"I do, sir" Elias replied.

"You armed?"

"Yes sir, I am."

"Let me see your piece."

Extracting his .22 from the waistband of his slacks, Elias handed it to Diamonds.

"A .22 - just like you used to shoot," Diamonds lied as he strode out onto the porch where he fired the weapon.

"And it's loaded," he smiled confidently when he walked back inside.

"You never know when you might need to use it," Elias explained.

"That's right, Manny," Diamonds said as he handed the pistol back to Elias.

Before Elias could return the weapon to his waistband, Diamonds surprised Elias with his next comment.

"Kill Fat Freddy. Now!"

Without hesitation, Elias turned and pointed the .22 at Fat Freddy, whose eyes immediately bulged with deathly fear as he opened his mouth to protest. But he couldn't speak. Calmly, Elias pulled the trigger. It clicked harmlessly as Fat Freddy visibly wet his pants.

Diamonds had a broad smile on his face. "That's what I like,

Manny. Blind obedience." Diamonds tossed the clip to Elias. "Better put that back in."

Elias reinserted the clip in the .22 and returned it to his waistband.

"Jimmy, I didn't do anything to deserve that!" Fat Freddy said as he mopped his brow that was covered with beads of sweat and stared down at his urine-soaked pants.

"Sorry, Fat Freddy, but I had to test him. He did well. If he hadn't I'd have emptied my own gun in his face, then probably yours," Diamonds said in a sinister tone.

"Better change your pants, Fats," Parella laughed from the doorway. "You're probably still a bed wetter, too!" he mocked.

"I'm warning you, Parella," Fat Freddy said angrily as he took a couple of steps forward before Diamonds jerked Fat Freddy by the shoulder backwards.

"Settle down, boys. Go back to the SUV Tony. I'll be right there." Diamonds looked at Elias. "Store your stuff upstairs. First bedroom on the right."

Grabbing his duffel bag, Elias dutifully walked up the stairs as Diamonds turned his attention to Fat Freddy. "I didn't mean anything by it, but I needed to know. You should know I wouldn't snuff you out unless you did something to double-cross me. I'm satisfied. He's the one."

"Gee, Jimmy. Don't ever pull crap like that on me," Fat Freddy quietly stormed.

"Now you make sure to keep a close watch on Elias. If you see any changes in his memory, you call me right away. No delays, capisce?"

"Like I wouldn't, Jimmy? Got it."

"Make sure he keeps his skills sharpened and don't leave the farm. I'll be calling you with a hit. I owe some people and we're going to have Elias do the killing."

"Got it."

"And keep him away from newspapers and the Internet, too," Diamonds directed as he slowly walked down the steps and headed out the front door to the waiting SUV where Parella was sitting with the engine running.

"Will do, Jimmy," Fat Freddy said as Diamonds climbed into the vehicle and it drove away.

Hearing a noise behind him, Fat Freddy walked back into the house to find Elias had returned to the first floor. Elias was wearing his running gear. Fat Freddy walked up to Elias and slapped him across the face.

"You crazy putz! Why would you aim and shoot at me?" he shouted angrily.

"I knew it wasn't loaded," Elias replied as he rubbed his red cheek.

"You knew it wasn't loaded!" Fat Freddy repeated. "How would you know something like that?"

"As much time as I spent on the range, I can tell by the weight when there's no clip."

"Oh yeah? And what if he had left a round in the chamber?"

"That was a chance I was willing to take," Elias spoke quietly.

"A chance on my life!" Fat Freddy said, irritated.

Elias looked around the room and said, "Like he said, if I didn't, we'd both be dead. I think I'll go for a jog."

"Stay away from that girls' camp!" Fat Freddy warned.

"Of course," Elias called as he walked out the front door, bounded down the steps and jogged down the lane. At the same time, Fat Freddy grabbed his gear and headed to his room to change his wet pants. He was swearing softly to himself.

As Elias ran northward through the valley, he enjoyed the beautiful countryside. The lane cut through groves of leafy trees and open pastures. As he emerged from a thickly wooded area, he spotted the lake that the property shared with the girls' camp. Elias gradually stopped running and leaned with mild exhaustion against a tree to take a short breather.

As he wiped the sweat from his face with the sleeve of his gray T-shirt, he spotted a woman in the distance standing near the lake. She was struggling to remove a small tire pump from her bicycle. It looked like the bike had a flat tire.

Making a quick decision, Elias jogged over to the woman to see if he could assist.

"Hi, could you use a little help there?"

Startled by the unexpected intrusion in an otherwise tranquil setting, the woman jumped back, knocking over her bicycle in the process. She seemed to Elias to react like a scared little rabbit.

"I'm sorry. I didn't mean to surprise you," he said as he bent over and stood up the bicycle. "I just wanted to help."

Being closer, Elias was able to see the woman's features more clearly and he very much liked what he saw. She looked to be in her late thirties and was five-foot-eight-inches tall with blonde hair down to her shoulders. She had bright, emerald-green eyes, full lips and two dimples on her cheeks. She was wearing a white polo shirt with the girls' camp logo, blue shorts and pink tennis shoes.

"Are you okay?"

The woman shrank away from Elias.

"Listen, I'm sorry. I didn't mean to spook you," he said as he turned his attention to the bike's front tire so that she could compose herself. Pulling off the tire pump, he attached it to the tire. "Let's see if you were just low or you have a flat."

Pumping quickly, Elias inflated the tire and laid the pump on the ground. "Let's see what happens here," he said as he turned back to face the attractive woman.

"Thank you," she stammered.

"Glad to help. I'm Manny," he said without thinking. "I just moved into the farmhouse today," he added as he pointed over his shoulder toward the farm.

"I'm Desiree," she replied as she assessed the handsome jogger. "You just caught me off guard. It's not often I meet strange men in the woods. In fact, never."

"No problem. And I'm only a little strange," he said, surprised by his own lightheartedness. The fresh air, free of Florida's suffocating humidity, seemed to be good for his mood.

"Looks like the tire is holding air," he continued as he squeezed the front tire. "It should be good enough for you to ride back to your camp." Elias reattached the pump to the bike and held the bike out to her. "Guess I better get on with my jogging."

"Thank you," she said as she took the bike from Elias and mounted it.

"Nice meeting you," Elias said as he started to jog away with a little added spring in his gait.

Desiree didn't respond as she started to pedal away toward the camp.

"Maybe I'll see you again," he called out to her as the distance between them widened.

Elias couldn't see her face as she rode away, but it had a large, telling smile. She pedaled away and Elias continued his run. Elias was smiling, too, but for a different reason. He hoped he'd soon run into her again. As he jogged away he decided not to tell Fat Freddy about his encounter. He hadn't gone to the girls' camp, so it's not like he broke any rules. Still, he didn't think Fat Freddy and Jimmy would like his encounter with Desiree. Not at all.

Two Days Later
The Farm

Since they had moved into the farmhouse, Elias had started a daily routine of working out in the barn, firing weapons with Fat Freddy behind the barn and helping with the household chores. He also ran twice a day, once in the early morning and once in the afternoon.

Even though he had kept an eye out for the blonde at the lake, he didn't encounter her again. He did occasionally see several other young women frolicking in the cool lake water and tanning, but didn't spot the pretty one with the bike. His nights continued to be filled with nightmares and flashbacks, although he had hoped those were left behind in Florida.

Late one morning, Elias was walking toward the barn when he heard the sounds of a vehicle driving up the long lane to the farmhouse. As it rounded a curve, Elias recognized the SUV as the one Tony Parella had driven two days earlier.

"Freddy!" he called. "We've got company."

"Yeah, I know. Jimmy called and said he'd be stopping by today," Fat Freddy said as he walked onto the porch and watched the SUV pull to a stop in front of the farmhouse. The doors opened and three people exited the vehicle – Diamonds, his blonde girlfriend, Veronica, and the driver, Parella.

Taking a deep breath of the fresh country air, Diamonds instructed Parella to stay by the SUV. He and Veronica walked toward the farmhouse. As they walked, Diamonds dutifully warned her. "Nothing. Don't you say nothing to him about who he really is."

"For crying out loud, Jimmy. Why would I ever mess up your plans? I know better," she responded. She remembered meeting the "former" Emerson Moore when he interviewed Diamonds at his Grosse Ile home. She also remembered how nice looking he was and she was anxious to see the quasi-Frankenstein Diamonds had now created.

"Don't slip. I'm warning you."

Before Diamonds could say anything more, Fat Freddy greeted them.

"Morning," Fat Freddy called as he stepped back and held the door open for them to enter the farmhouse.

"You got coffee?" Diamonds gruffly asked, as he walked into the kitchen and looked around.

"Yeah. Over here, Jimmy," Fat Freddy said as he rushed to grab a cup and fill it for the boss.

"Morning, Jimmy," Elias said.

Diamonds was followed by Veronica, who was taking in the sight of the now hard-bodied, bearded and long-haired Elias. She was very impressed by the physical transformation, although she recalled that the earlier version of Moore had also looked quite good. But now, he looked like a muscular stud.

As Diamonds reached for the cup that Fat Freddy was handing him, he returned the greeting. "Morning, Manny."

"Aren't you going to say hello to me, Manny?" Veronica asked as she looked at Elias with a little pout on her face.

"I apologize," Elias stammered. "I just don't remember," he said as he eyed the beautiful blonde. He was frustrated that he'd forget someone as striking as her.

"Manny, that's Veronica," Diamonds spoke as he walked to the kitchen table and sat in one of the chairs. "And there's one important thing to remember about her," he said as he noticed Elias' eyes checking her out.

"What's that, Jimmy?"

"She's my girlfriend. That means she's off limits to you," Diamonds warned.

"And that's just too bad, isn't it, Manny?" Veronica seductively cooed. "Manny is a very good name for you. Manly Manny."

Diamonds shot a warning look at Veronica before continuing. "So, Manny, why don't you take her for a little walk around the buildings? I need to talk to Fat Freddy for a few minutes."

"Sure, I can do that," Elias said as he politely held open the door for her. He'd enjoy spending some time with a woman for a change since he had been so isolated from society. He followed Veronica onto the porch and started toward the barn. "You've got to see this barn. It's the coolest place."

"I'd love to," Veronica said as she firmly grabbed onto Elias' muscular arm. When Elias started to pull away, she tightened her grip. "It's okay. Jimmy won't mind if I hold onto you. You wouldn't want me to fall since I'm wearing heels, would you now, stud?"

Smiling bashfully, Elias relaxed and allowed her to maintain her firm grip as they slowly walked to the barn. Parella followed them from a distance to look out for Diamonds' best interests. If he could catch them doing something inappropriate, it would be a real feather in his cap.

Out of the corner of his eye, Elias saw Parella shadowing them. "Don't look behind us, but we're being watched."

"Tony?" she asked with no surprise.

"Yep."

"He doesn't trust me. He doesn't trust anyone."

"Why's that?" Elias asked as they entered the barn and sought relief from the hot sun.

"He'll do whatever he can to get close to Jimmy. He gives me the creeps the way he looks at me." They stopped in the middle of the barn. "You, on the other hand, Mister Tall, Dark and Handsome, have quite the opposite effect on me," she warmly said as she still gripped his arm tightly and moved her shapely body closer to him.

Elias defensively pulled away. As he did, Parella stepped inside the barn door. "Everything okay in here?" he asked, half-hoping that he'd catch the two in a compromising situation.

"We're fine. Tony, can you quit following me?" Veronica glared at him. "One word from me to Jimmy and you're back to running numbers."

Parella scowled, "Yeah. I guess I'd better get back to the car."

When Parella disappeared, Elias asked, "So, why does he think he'd catch us doing something?"

"He thinks I'm loose. Besides, Tony is interested in me and mad that I won't return his attention."

"Have you told Jimmy?"

"No, Jimmy would whack him. He don't want any guy flirting with me, let alone hitting on me the way Parella has. I'm not the kind of person who'd wish ill against anyone. I get mad at him a lot but I've never ratted on him."

"So, how did you meet Jimmy?" Elias inquisitively asked as they reached the other end of the barn. There was a momentary pause as they stood together in the open doorway and looked toward a shaded pond where several ducks were swimming.

"I met him a few years ago. I was dancing in a club and he was a very generous tipper."

"You were a stripper?"

"Yeah. I didn't have any skills. Quit high school and got involved with drugs. Always ended up with the wrong men. I had this attraction to the bad boys, if you know what I mean."

Elias nodded his head in acknowledgment.

"And Jimmy was a real gentleman when we met. He wined and dined me. Spent all kinds of money on me. Took me on nice vacations. He can be charming when he wants to be. Can fool a lot of people."

Elias sensed where this was going and nodded.

"Oh yeah, I see his bad side," she sighed. "He has a temper, that one."

"I bet he does," Elias said.

"I've seen him go ballistic with his guys. I've heard rumors about stuff that happened to his enemies, but I try to distance myself from that side of him."

"Did he ever harm you?"

She didn't respond right away. She was looking through the open barn door. After a few seconds, she said, "Those ducks look so peaceful in that pond. Not a care in the world."

Looking at her closely, Elias noted, "You didn't answer my question."

Raising her hand, Veronica softly stroked Elias' bearded cheek.

"I bet you're not the kind of guy who would hit a woman."

Pulling away as he realized that she wasn't going to answer his question, Elias said, "I don't think so. I hope not. I'm not quite sure who I am. I just don't remember. My memory is missing."

"Oh, I'm sure it'll come back to you at some point, Manny," she said as she turned. She just missed seeing that Parella had been watching them in the near distance and again had headed toward the SUV. "Let's get back to the house, okay?"

"Sure."

Meanwhile, Diamonds and Fat Freddy had been talking about the move to the Cleveland area.

"Why Cleveland, Jimmy?" Fat Freddy asked.

"The Chicago family is dissatisfied with the family running the Cleveland business. They want me to take it over."

"And what do the Cleveland boys say about that?"

"They don't know. That's why I'm using our associates, Elias and Santoro."

"You brought in Santoro?" Fat Freddy knew about the feared assassination specialist from the West Coast.

"Yeah. Two weeks ago."

"I thought the whole reason that you had Elias get trained was so that he'd become your killing machine," Fat Freddy commented, obviously perplexed.

"Santoro is the backup. You don't know when Elias' memory is going to return. When it does, poof! I've lost my top enforcer. You know I always have a backup. "

Diamonds wasn't telling Fat Freddy that Santoro would be his insurance policy in case Elias turned against him. If that happened, Santoro would snuff Elias. That was the agreement. And, he wanted Santoro to keep an eye on Elias. Diamonds always played his cards wisely. It never hurt to have a few aces up his sleeve.

"I don't like what I've heard about Santoro," said Fat Freddy. "If we have Santoro, why do we need Elias? Why did we go through all this?"

"Turning Mr. Boy Scout into a killer? That's revenge, Fat Freddy. But he could be a loose cannon, and we don't really know how good of a killer he is yet. With Santoro, I know what I'm getting. Santoro can do a clean kill or leave a real mess to send a message. I think I've got a real one-two punch with the two of them to take over Cleveland. It'll be just like the old days when the Donardos and Porrellos ruled Cleveland crime!"

Diamonds was referring to the 1920s when the two Sicilian immigrant families controlled organized crime in Cleveland. The Donardos' dominance continued through the early 1970s, despite the alleged Depression-era elimination of many of the older Mustache Petes such as Joe "the Boss" Masseria, Salvatore Maranzano, Joseph "Iron Man"Ardizzone and Joseph Siragus.

"I'm going to be the reincarnation of Danny Greene and the Mayfield Road gang," Diamonds smiled as he recalled two of Cleveland's infamous crime organizations. Greene, the self-styled Celtic Club mobster in the 1970s, was assassinated in Lyndhurst when a car bomb, planted by rival mobsters, exploded next to him.

Fat Freddy just nodded his head. He didn't know the history of

Cleveland's organized crime, but he liked to appease Diamonds with feigned awe.

"And who are the cousins in Cleveland?"

"A couple of young Turks! The Caniglia Brothers. We're …"

The sound of the door opening caused Diamonds to stop in midsentence as both men swiveled their heads to see Elias and Veronica entering the farmhouse.

Diamonds changed topics. "Veronica?"

"Yes, Jimmy?"

"Why don't you do me a favor and go back outside and sit on the porch? I need to talk business with these two meatheads."

"Sure, Jimmy," she said obediently as she went outside and took a seat in one of the chairs on the porch.

"Sit down, Manny," Diamonds said after she walked out and Parella entered the house.

"Sure."

"You ready for your first hit as the new Manny?" Diamonds asked.

"Whatever you say, Jimmy. You're the boss."

Diamonds convincingly smiled. This was going to be a test to see if all the training paid off and if Elias was certain that he had always been a contract hitman. "Good. I want you and Fat Freddy to drive up to Detroit. You're going to snuff that little Colombian prick, Ramos."

"The guy who testified against you during your trial?" Fat Freddy asked.

"Yeah, the lying S.O.B. He made all of that up," Diamonds growled. He was sure that Ramos had been working for Diaz and planned to cut out Diamonds so that he could take over the Detroit territory.

"Where are we going to hit him?" Fat Freddy asked.

"Show them, Tony," Diamonds said as he sat back in his chair and lit a cigarette.

Parella took the map that he held in his hand and spread it outward across the table. "Here in Mexicantown. We know that Ramos has a girlfriend. She lives in an apartment building here." He pointed to a circled area of the map. "You can take him out when he comes out in the morning, usually around eight o'clock."

"Can we have the map? I need to study it," Elias asked.

Parella looked at Diamonds for permission.

Before Diamonds could comment, Elias explained, "Jimmy, I'm sorry, but I just don't remember that area."

"Yeah, you can have it. Fat Freddy probably knows where it is, but you should know your way too, in case he goes liquid stupid on us."

"I wouldn't do that, Jimmy!" Fat Freddy protested.

Ignoring his protestation, Diamonds continued. "Make it a clean hit, Manny, and be sure to tell him it's from Jimmy Diamonds."

Elias nodded his head. "I'll do that."

"Don't blow it," Parella warned as he gave Elias an icy stare.

"Don't you be giving my boy orders. He don't work for you, slimeball," Fat Freddy scolded as he stood from his chair and gave Parella a menacing look.

"Cool it!" Diamonds directed before the situation escalated. "Tony, go on out. Get Veronica and take her to the car. I'll be right there," Diamonds said as he exhaled cigarette smoke into the air.

Parella shot Fat Freddy an evil glance before walking out of the farmhouse.

"One of these days," Fat Freddy started as he stared at the departing Parella.

"Easy does it. Tony's not perfect and neither are you, Fat Freddy." Diamonds stood and looked at Elias. "Manny, it's going to be good to see you use your skills again. Nobody can do a hit like you can," Diamonds encouraged Elias. He was anxious to see if Emerson Moore would pull the trigger and actually kill someone in cold blood.

"Thanks, Jimmy. I'm looking forward to shaking off the cob-webs."

"There you go, Manny," Diamonds said, patting Manny on the shoulder. Diamonds looked at his watch. "You can drive up tonight so you're in position for tomorrow morning."

"No problem, Jimmy," Fat Freddy said as the three men walked out of the farmhouse and onto the porch. "What about the Caniglia Brothers?"

"Let's get this one out of the way first, then we'll worry about taking them out," Diamonds said as he reached into his pocket and pulled out a pack of playing cards. "Take these with you," he said as he handed them to Fat Freddy.

"What are these for?"

"The pack contains aces of diamonds. When you pull off a hit, I want you two to leave one," Diamonds beamed. "It's my new calling card. Kind of cryptic. We'll see who figures out what's going on."

"Yeah, we can do that, Jimmy."

"The cards are clean. No fingerprints on them, so make sure you're wearing gloves or use a tissue. We'll keep everyone guessing," Diamonds smiled.

"Sure, Jimmy," Fat Freddy happily agreed.

"Let me know how it goes," Diamonds said as he walked down the steps and entered the waiting vehicle.

Diamonds smiled as they drove away. What he didn't tell Fat Freddy or Elias was that he was having Santoro shadow them. If they didn't follow through and kill Ramos, Santoro would kill Ramos, then Fat Freddy.

As for Elias, Santoro had been instructed to capture him and immediately take him to a small farm near Findlay, off of I-75. There, Diamonds would torture Elias before killing him – and maybe even give him the real backstory to make it all the sweeter.

The Next Day
Ohio Turnpike

After driving north on I-71, the tan 2007 Chevrolet Malibu driven by Fat Freddy picked up the Ohio Turnpike and drove west toward Toledo where they'd take I-280 north into Detroit.

After about forty-five minutes on the turnpike, Fat Freddy noticed Elias staring at an approaching exit sign. It read "Port Clinton and Put-in-Bay Next Exit."

"See something interesting?" Fat Freddy probed.

"Not really, although that Put-in-Bay name seems somewhat familiar," Elias said with slight puzzlement as he settled back in his seat.

Silently, Fat Freddy was cursing himself for not taking U.S. Route 30 west from Wooster and then north on I-75 toward Detroit. He didn't need any signs near Lake Erie triggering Elias' memory. He glanced at Elias. "You okay?"

"Yes."

"How's that memory working for you? Anything come back yet?" It was part of his daily questioning, but now he needed to be unerringly certain. He was dreading the day that it returned because he knew that Diamonds would kill Elias. As much as he fought it, Fat Freddy had grown to like Elias and despised what they were doing to him. But, he wouldn't disobey Diamonds.

"Still nothing." Elias answered in a monotone.

Later, as they drove on I-280 across the Skyway Bridge over the

Maumee River, Fat Freddy noticed that Elias again was looking around at their surroundings.

"See anything you recognize?" Fat Freddy asked tensely.

"Not really! But it seems like I've been here before," he answered. "Especially those two cranes along the river bank." Fat Freddy had no way of knowing that Elias once had broken a story on human trafficking in Toledo and had worked undercover in the warehouses near those cranes.

"Maybe you did some enforcement work for Jimmy here," Fat Freddy said as casually as he could.

"Probably. I just don't know," Elias said with an air of growing frustration. He again sat back in his seat and forcefully tried to work his memory, but it was to no avail.

They picked up I-75 on the north side of Toledo and shortly drove across the Michigan state line. "We'll grab a room in Taylor. It's right off of I-75 and not too far from where we need to make our hit tomorrow."

As they drove farther north, past the I-275 Detroit bypass, Elias soon noticed another exit sign, "Grosse Ile." He stared intently at it. Fat Freddy noticed.

"See something there that's helping your memory?" Fat Freddy suspiciously asked.

"Grosse Ile. That seems a little familiar."

Fat Freddy quickly recovered. "It should. That's where Jimmy used to live. You used to hang out with us there. Remember now?"

Elias shook his head. "Nope. Can't remember that, but that

must be why it seems kind of familiar."

Relieved, Fat Freddy focused his attention on the road.

They found a hotel and grabbed dinner at a nearby restaurant. Then, they returned to their shared room. Diamonds had instructed Fat Freddy that he wanted them in the same room when they went out so that Fat Freddy could monitor what Elias did and saw. They went over their plans and the map for the next day before getting ready for bed.

"Want to watch TV?" Elias asked as he sat on the edge of his bed.

Diamonds didn't want Elias watching anything. "What's come over you? Don't you remember you don't like watching TV? You always said how stupid it was."

"Oh," Elias said sheepishly. "I don't remember." He lay on his bed and tried to get comfortable.

After switching the lights out, Fat Freddy pounded his pillow a couple times with his fist and then relaxed. "Manny?"

"Yes?"

"So, are you ready for your big day tomorrow?"

"I guess."

Hearing a touch of hesitancy in Elias' voice, Fat Freddy tried to encourage him. "You'll do just fine. Once you pull the trigger, you'll be back in the swing of killing. Just like you used to be," he lied.

"I certainly have had the training for it."

"Yeah, yeah," Fat Freddy said quickly. He decided to change the topic to take Elias' mind off any apprehension he was having. "It's nice being back in the Detroit area. You know what I did for fun when I was in my teens?"

"What?"

"My buddy and me used to walk through the neighborhood and jump on cars so that the alarms would go off. Then, we'd hide behind some cars and wait. They didn't have very good remote key fobs, so the owners would have to get out of bed and come outside to turn off the alarm. Once they turned them off and went back inside, we'd go over and set them off again."

"Wouldn't they call the police?"

"Sure, if you did it too much. We'd only do it a couple of times, then go over to another street. Sometimes, one of us would hide by the door and when the owner walked out, we'd run into the house with flashlights and grab something valuable and run out the back door. Sort of like a smash and grab," he chuckled as he recalled his unremarkable youth.

"Freddy, did you tell me that you were married?"

"Oh yeah. She was a real piece of work, that one. Thought the world owed her and that she was smoking hot." Fat Freddy sounded irritated.

"Was she?"

"I told her that the only way she'd be smoking hot is the day they cremated her." He chuckled again.

"What happened to her?"

"She died in a car wreck." Fat Freddy quickly added, "For real. I had nothing to do with it."

That comment about a car wreck sounded familiar, but Elias couldn't place where he had heard it. If his memory as Emerson Moore had returned, he would have remembered that he had also lost his wife and son in an auto wreck.

"Anyone since then?" Elias asked, trying to keep his mind off of having to kill someone soon. He wasn't sure he was ready – not mentally, anyway.

"Yeah, but I didn't remarry," Fat Freddy said wistfully. "I had to fight off the broads back in the day. It used to be that the ladies wanted me for my body. Now they want me for the body heat I give off on a cold night. They say I'm like a furnace."

"Hey, what's that noise?" Elias asked.

They both listened. The noise was coming through the wall behind their headboards.

Fat Freddy chuckled. "Sounds like two people getting it on." Fat Freddy sat up in bed. "Time for a little fun," he grinned as he swung his legs over the edge of the bed and stood up.

"What are you doing?"

"I'm going to interrupt them. You stay here." Fat Freddy walked over to the door and opened it. After peering down the hall, he cautiously stepped out and walked over to the door to the room next to theirs. Suddenly, he knocked hard three times on the door and scurried back to his room, closing his door quietly behind him.

Through the wall, they heard someone swear and the noise

from the passionate couple ceased. They heard the door to the adjacent room open and then slam shut.

Fat Freddy also was laughing quietly. "Nothing like a little coitus interruptus!" he chuckled softly as he held up his hand for Elias to remain quiet.

A few minutes later, the sounds of passion began anew. Fat Freddy repeated his earlier actions. When he returned to the room, they heard a man's voice cursing in the adjacent room. The man ran to his door and swung it open. He stepped naked into the hallway and screamed at the top of his lungs at being interrupted. Slamming the door, he returned to bed. The couple's passionate mood disappeared for the evening.

Meanwhile, a snickering Fat Freddy had returned to his bed. "Nothing like causing a little aggravation," he smiled.

"You ruined their evening!" Elias said.

"Well, they ruined mine. I'll be having dreams all night about what they were doing in the next room."

"Better than the nightmares I have," Elias said.

"Enough chit-chat. We got a big day ahead of us." Fat Freddy rolled over on his side and started to fall asleep. It wasn't too much later that Elias also drifted off to sleep.

Around two o'clock in the morning, Elias woke up. He was sweating despite the air conditioner running noisily beneath the window. He'd been having nightmares and flashbacks again. Nothing made sense.

He stood and walked into the bathroom where he turned on the faucet and ran cold water. He bent over and splashed it on his face and then grabbed one of the towels to dry off.

"You okay?"

Elias turned and saw Fat Freddy standing there in a tank top and his blue boxer shorts.

"I was until I saw your boxers. Are those smiley faces on there?"

"Yeah, yeah. Seriously, are you okay?"

"Just nightmares."

"Anything from your past?"

"I don't know. I don't know the difference between dreams and reality any more."

"I know what you mean. I met this girl one time. She was a real looker. I told her that holding her in my arms was like holding a dream." Fat Freddy smiled as he recalled holding her. "You know, holding a dream in your arms is not an everyday event."

"I bet. I wish I remembered how it felt to hold a woman."

"Yeah, well, me, too. It's been a long while. Now, you get back to bed. I've got to take a leak."

Elias returned to his bed and tried to fall back asleep. It was thirty minutes after Fat Freddy returned to his bed that Elias finally fell asleep. He slept deeply despite the loud snores coming from Fat Freddy's direction.

The alarm buzzed at five o'clock, awakening them. They got ready quickly and went next door to Waffle House for a hot breakfast before they checked out of their room. Afterward, they drove over to Lincoln Park and parked behind a donut shop. They were wearing black ball caps and dark sunglasses to hide their identities.

"Prime place to steal a car," Fat Freddy said as the two pulled on plastic gloves.

"How's that?"

"Donut shops are short-handed. They're making donuts and serving the customers. They don't have time to come out and check their cars. Come on," Fat Freddy said as he stepped out of the Chevrolet.

There were two cars parked behind the donut shop. One was a Volkswagen; the other was a Mercury Milan.

"Pick one," Fat Freddy said as Elias caught up to him.

"Mercury."

"You stand watch," Fat Freddy said as he approached the driver's side of the car with his slim jim, a lock picking tool. He slipped it between the window and the rubber seal, catching the rods that connected to the lock mechanism. Carefully, he manipulated the rods and unlocked the door.

"Still clear?" he asked as he slid behind the wheel.

"So far."

Inside the vehicle, Fat Freddy moved rapidly to remove the plastic cover from the steering column. He identified the bundle of wires leading to the battery, ignition and starter. He stripped away the insulation from the battery wires and twisted them together so he'd have electricity for the ignition components. He connected the ignition on/off wire to the battery wire and saw the electrical components on the dashboard come to life.

He pumped the accelerator a couple of times before touching the end of the starter wire to the connected battery wires, sparking it to start. Next, he broke the steering wheel lock and yelled softly to Elias.

"Follow me in the Chevy."

Elias returned to the Chevy Malibu and followed Fat Freddy as he exited the rear of the parking lot and headed towards Mexicantown on the southwest side of downtown Detroit. They found an old building and drove behind it to park. Fat Freddy motioned for Elias to leave the Chevy and get into the stolen Mercury.

"Why did you pick this one?"

"I didn't think you wanted the Volkswagen," Elias replied.

"I've been in golf carts that go faster than this," Fat Freddy groused, as the car's engine coughed and he drove it back onto the street.

In a few minutes, the car was coughing its way along West Vernor, the main street in Mexicantown. The car made a couple of turns and parked in front of an apartment building.

"That's Ramos' car over there," Fat Freddy pointed to a late model Ford, parked two cars ahead of theirs.

Glancing a little hesitantly at his watch, Elias said, "It's seven forty-five."

"Won't be long now," Fat Freddy said as he kept the engine idling.

"And he won't be expecting us, right?" Elias asked.

"Shouldn't be. We've gone underground for about two months now. He shouldn't be looking out for us," Fat Freddy responded confidently.

Slipping the silencer onto his .22, Elias then flipped off the safety. Fat Freddy was the backup and duplicated the same procedures.

"Time to set up," Fat Freddy said as he released the hood and the two men exited the vehicle. Both walked to the front where Fat Freddy raised the Mercury's hood. Each acted as if they were working together on the engine.

Hearing a door shut, they both glanced toward the apartment where a Hispanic man was walking down the sidewalk.

"That's not him."

The man walked by them without giving them a second look.

Within two minutes, the apartment door banged shut again.

"That's him," Fat Freddy anxiously said as he looked over the top of his shades.

Elias waited until Ramos was ten feet from his car. "Excuse me. Could you give us a hand?" he asked in a calm voice.

Ramos paused for a second and turned toward the car where he saw Elias raising his .22 and taking aim at him.

"Jimmy Diamonds says 'hello'," Elias solemnly stated.

Fat Freddy slammed the hood down and turned to watch. His gun, too, was now at his side.

Elias had his .22 pointed squarely at Ramos' chest, but he couldn't fire. He was having a mental block about killing someone in cold blood. Ramos, however, quickly took care of that issue by producing a .45 semi-auto handgun and aiming it at his assassin.

"Shoot him for crying out loud!" Fat Freddy screamed.

It was kill or be killed time. Elias pulled the trigger twice, catching Ramos in the chest with two deadly kill shots. Shocked at what he had done, Elias was staring at Ramos' bloody body on the ground while Fat Freddy was racing around the stolen Mercury and jumping in behind its steering wheel.

"Come on! Get in the car, stupid!" Fat Freddy yelled.

Breaking out of his trance, Elias turned and started for the car.

"The card. The card!" Fat Freddy screamed.

Remembering, Elias whirled around and ran over to Ramos' body. Elias then reached inside his pocket and withdrew from it an ace of diamonds. Elias tossed the card on the body and raced back to the vehicle. He leapt in before it pulled onto the street and sped out of sight.

As the stolen car sped away, Fat Freddy lambasted Elias. "What was that all about? Why didn't you shoot him?"

"I, I don't know. I just froze."

"You let him get his weapon out. He could have killed you – or me!" Fat Freddy ranted. He also imagined what would have happened to him if he had to complete the kill himself and then tell Diamonds that Elias had been killed. His job was to keep Elias alive until Diamonds was ready to personally off Elias. If he failed, he was as good as dead.

"I don't know. I couldn't do it for some reason," Elias said nervously.

"Listen, we're not going to tell Jimmy that you got cold feet and gave Ramos time to almost take you out. Our story is that it was a clean kill. You did as you were told," Fat Freddy coached. "You're a hitman, Manny! That's your claim to fame!"

"I'm sure I'll do better next time," Elias said. "I must be a little rusty, that's all."

"You better. You're creeping me out, Manny. You're going to cause me to have a heart attack, I swear you are. You can't allow them to get the drop on you. Especially Ramos. And don't go feeling bad about taking him out. Look at the bright side. You did what Jimmy wanted. You did the Detroit police a favor by taking out a bad guy, too." Fat Freddy was beginning to wonder if Emerson Moore's morals were so ingrained that they were the true reason Elias hesitated in pulling the trigger.

Back at the murder scene, there was another car parked nearby – a unique car. Its solitary occupant had in fact been parked there since seven o'clock to observe the hit. Santoro stretched, started the car and casually drove away.

The hit had been pulled off successfully as far as Santoro could tell from where Santoro's car had been parked. There was no need for Santoro to follow through with the backup plan that Diamonds had earlier installed. Fat Freddy and Elias would live another day. Santoro called Diamonds to let him know that the trial mission was successfully completed.

When Fat Freddy and Elias arrived back at the vacant building where they earlier had left their Chevy Malibu, they removed several containers of gasoline from the car's trunk and doused the stolen Mercury. Elias set an explosive charge with a timer. Within five minutes, the car went up in flames.

They got back into the Chevy, departed the area and drove south toward I-75 bound for Toledo. This time Fat Freddy decided to take I-75 down past Findlay to Route 30 and then drive east back to the farmhouse near Wooster. He chose this route so that he could avoid the Put-in-Bay signs. No need to drive by anything that could potentially stimulate Elias' mind. They already were lucky he didn't remember anything yet. No need to push that luck.

The Farm
Near Wooster, Ohio

Along the drive back, Fat Freddy had pulled into a truck stop where he called Diamonds and told him that their mission had been successfully accomplished. Diamonds already had the news from Santoro and was extremely pleased. He suggested a celebratory dinner.

The four-hour ride home with a brief stop at a drive-through restaurant for lunch had been quiet. When they returned, Elias told Fat Freddy that he needed to go for a run and went into his room where he changed clothes. Shortly afterwards, he emerged in his running gear and ran out of the farmhouse.

He ran through the countryside and back to the lake with hopes of seeing Desiree, but she wasn't there. He was disappointed and wanted desperately to talk with someone.

Elias gazed upon and soulfully embraced the scene around the lake. It seemed to be rather bucolic and pastoral, he thought. It was peaceful, almost spiritual. There wasn't a ripple on the water.

The leaves on the oaks, maples and white birch trees around the lake were perfectly calm as there was no breeze. Peace. Seclusion. Escape. These thoughts ran through Elias' tormented mind as he sat down on the lush grass by the water's edge, thinking about killing Ramos and recounting Fat Freddy's comments afterward. He knew that he was supposed to be this special hitman, but was stymied as to why he had such bad feelings about killing Ramos, even if he somehow deserved it. Something about actually killing people was very disquieting and unsettling to Elias.

After not reaching a satisfactory resolution to his conflicted feelings, Elias gradually stood and took one last look at the lake as the late afternoon shadows stretched across its surface. Turning away, he jogged back to the house where Fat Freddy greeted him on the porch. He had been sitting in one of the rockers, sipping a beer.

"Feeling more like yourself, Manny?" he asked.

"I guess. I've got a terrible headache."

"Go on and take a nap or something. There's aspirin in the bathroom if you need it."

"That might help," Elias said as he walked from the porch into the house.

"I'll wake you around six o'clock so we can go into Wooster for dinner tonight," Fat Freddy yelled.

"Not sure I'm hungry," Elias shouted back as he walked into the bathroom and rummaged through the medicine cabinet for the aspirin. His insides were still seething. When they had gone through the drive-through restaurant earlier, he had passed on the food. The kill was not sitting well with him at all.

Not hearing a response from Elias, Fat Freddy shrugged his shoulders and took a swig from the beer bottle in his hand.

When Elias emerged from the bathroom, Fat Freddy spoke. "And Jimmy pays us for the kills. He deposits money for us in an account."

Heading to his bedroom, Elias didn't respond to the comment. Money was the least of his worries.

An hour later, Fat Freddy knocked on the door of Elias' bedroom. "Rise and shine Sleeping Beauty," he called.

They were soon in the Chevy, driving toward Wooster.

"Where are we going?" Elias asked.

"To jail," Fat Freddy replied nonchalantly.

"No, seriously. Where are we going?" Elias was in no mood for jokes.

"I am serious. We're going to jail."

Frowning, Elias looked at Fat Freddy. "Come on. Tell me what this is all about."

"We're going to the Olde Jaol Steakhouse and Tavern. It just sounds cool. I found it on the Internet."

"You have a computer!" Elias exclaimed, stunned by the revelation.

Fat Freddy swore. "Yeah, it's locked in my bedroom and off limits to you."

"But we've been in such a news blackout. First in Florida and now here."

"Believe me, it's for your own good," Fat Freddy cautioned. "Plus, you probably don't remember how to use one."

"I remember how to drive. Why wouldn't I remember how to use a computer? Can I try it and see what I can do? It might help my memory."

"Nah. Jimmy doesn't want you on it. Remember, blind obedience. With this memory blackout, you have to build his trust."

"Yeah, I guess," Elias said as he sat back to enjoy the drive.

Wooster is set in the rolling countryside off of Route 30, about thirty minutes west of the intersection with I-71, the Ohio interstate running north to Cleveland and south through Columbus. It was a perfect location for what Jimmy Diamonds had in mind.

The city has a population of about 26,000. Its main street, Liberty Street, runs in an east-west direction. Picturesque structures line its streets and add to its appeal.

"You're going to like this restaurant. It's two restaurants in one. There's a grill on street level, but next door is where we'll eat. It's the old jail and it was converted into the restaurant. Pretty nice place based on the reviews I read."

"Sounds interesting."

"And I'm interested in eating some good food," Fat Freddy said as he wheeled the Chevrolet into a parking spot in front of the two-story structure located at the northeast corner of Walnut Street and North Street.

The two men walked into the building and down the stairs where the restaurant's owner, Jerry Baker, greeted them.

"Welcome, gents! Two for dinner?" the affable owner asked. He was in his fifties and known as a tireless promoter for the community. And being single and good-looking made him naturally attractive to the area's women.

"Yeah," Fat Freddy said as he looked around at the brickwork. "Heard you have good steaks here."

"The best," Baker smiled as he picked up two menus and handed them to his business partner, Tim DeRhodes. "Tim will show you to your table."

Fat Freddy and Elias followed DeRhodes through one of the brick archways and into an area that had previously been a cell – except the iron bars had been removed.

As they sat, Fat Freddy commented, "Manny, this is how they should treat you when you're in jail. No bars other than the one that serves drinks and steak dinners!"

DeRhodes smiled. "Can I take your drink order?"

"Yeah. I'll take a double Manhattan. I haven't had a stiff drink in so long I was thinking about drinking that lava lamp back at the house."

DeRhodes chuckled. "And you, sir?"

"Rum and Coke."

"Make that a double for him. He needs to grow some more hair on his chest!" Fat Freddy offered.

DeRhodes looked at Elias, who shrugged and nodded his head affirmatively.

Elias smiled as he picked up his menu and looked through the selections. When a waitress returned with their drinks, Fat Freddy ordered the shrimp scampi as an appetizer and the 14-ounce Delmonico steak. Elias ordered the fried Lake Erie yellow perch dinner.

"Fish?"

"Yeah. I enjoyed the fish we ate in Florida," Elias replied. "Plus, I still don't have my appetite back." But there was more to his answers that he didn't feel like sharing. There was something familiar about Lake Erie yellow perch, but he couldn't precisely remember what.

"No appetizer?"

"I'm in training, remember?" Elias responded as the waitress disappeared.

"Yeah. Yeah. Here's to our success," Fat Freddy said as he raised his glass in a toast that was returned by Elias.

He mimicked the large gulp that Fat Freddy took and twitched as the drink went down his throat. He coughed a couple of times.

"Whoa, that twitch hit the Richter scale! You okay?"

"Yeah. It's just been awhile," Elias said as he looked at the beverage in his glass. He pushed it aside. "You can have it if you want. I don't think I'm in the mood."

"Sure. No sense in letting good stuff go to waste," Fat Freddy said as he grabbed the glass and set it next to his.

When their meal was served, Fat Freddy gobbled down his steak while Elias ate one of the perches on his plate. After dinner,

Fat Freddy suggested they walk down to Liberty Street, a couple of blocks away, and take in the city sights.

As they turned the corner onto Liberty Street, they heard a band playing through the open door of The First Amendment restaurant, located across the street. The Zydeco Kings band was playing lively Cajun music.

"I love that music, especially the squeeze box," Fat Freddy commented with a smile as he suddenly surprised Elias by breaking into a few dance moves.

"I didn't know you could dance like that," Elias noted, stupefied by his nimbleness.

"In my day Manny, you'd have been shocked how the women flocked to me when I strutted onto the dance floor," Fat Freddy bragged. "I'm not kidding."

"Were you holding twenty dollar bills in your hand to entice them?" Elias chuckled.

"Not funny," Fat Freddy said as he stopped dancing and wiped sweat from his brow with the back of his hand. Looking across the street at the band playing in the restaurant's front window, he said, "That sax player is good, too." Fat Freddy closed his eyes for a moment and swayed to the music.

"Just so you know, I'm not going to dance with you," Elias teased as they resumed their after-dinner stroll.

They walked down to Bever Street, passing the historic courthouse building, Ride On Wooster bike shop, Muddy Waters Café, Broken Rocks, and the Everything Rubbermaid store. Then they turned around and walked back to the main intersection with Market Street near the Gazebo.

As they walked, Fat Freddy spotted an ice cream shop. "Want an ice cream cone? I haven't had one in ages."

"I guess," Elias answered.

As they closed the distance to the shop, Fat Freddy asked, "Manny, do you know where ice cream goes to school?"

Sighing with exasperation at the lack of sensitivity Fat Freddy had for the way he was feeling, Elias replied, "No. I don't have a clue. Where?"

"Sundae school. Get it? Sundae like in ice cream sundae," he snickered at his joke.

Elias didn't comment. His frustration was steadily growing.

"Let's go in and see if sundae school is in session," Fat Freddy chuckled as he swung open the door and the two walked inside and up to the counter where they waited for a tall, husky server to take their order.

The server looked to be about twenty-years-old with red hair and a pasty complexion. He blended in well with the stark white interior of the shop. He was busy texting and looked up in disdain at the two customers who were going to interrupt him.

"What do you want?" he finally asked in a tone that clearly conveyed his irritation at being interrupted.

Grabbing Fat Freddy by the arm, Elias said, "Let's go. Don't need to give him our business."

Fat Freddy pulled his arm away. "No, I want an ice cream cone." Fat Freddy wasn't going to walk away from a tasty ice cream, no matter how rude the kid was. He loved ice cream. He looked at the server and said, "I'll take a chocolate mocha in one of them big waffle cones."

The young man set down his cell phone and placed several scoops in the waffle cone and then handed it to Fat Freddy.

"Thanks," Fat Freddy said as he took a big lick of the cone. "You go ahead and pay. I'll be outside enjoying this monstrosity before it melts." Before Elias could comment, Fat Freddy disappeared through the door. Elias turned back to the server. He didn't like him and the feeling was mutual.

"What do you want?" the irritated red-head asked abruptly as a beep signaled an incoming text.

"A small vanilla in a regular cone."

"Our special today is chocolate fudge," the server said as he decided to ignore Elias' request.

"I don't like chocolate fudge. I want vanilla," Elias responded firmly, but calmly.

"But it's our special," the server said as he placed two scoops in a cone and handed it with a smirk on his face to Elias.

Elias took the cone and smashed it on the counter. "I told you a small vanilla. Don't jerk me around, kid!" Elias said sternly as he glared sharply at the server. He wasn't about to let some snot-nosed kid play games with him.

The server saw the look on his face and realized that he had better back off. He placed the scoops of vanilla in the cone and handed it to Elias. "That'll be $11.50."

Scanning the prices on the sign affixed to the wall, Elias grumbled,

"You charged me for three cones."

"Of course, I gave you two guys three cones."

"I didn't order the first cone you handed me. Your mistake, not mine."

The server felt emboldened. "Listen, pal, you'll pay me for three because I handed you two three cones."

Elias' eyes narrowed. He suddenly reached across the counter and grabbed the server by the front of his shirt. "I'm paying for two cones. Got it?"

The young man pulled away. "You don't have to get so pissy about it. I can give you a break and charge you for two cones," he said with a tone of sarcasm as his cell phone beeped again with an incoming text.

"You'll do it because it's the right thing to do," Elias countered.

"Fine. It's $9.25," the boy responded.

Elias handed over the exact amount and turned. As he walked toward the door, the server called, "No tip?" and laughed.

Elias ignored the comment. He held the door open for an older lady who was bringing her young granddaughter for an ice cream treat. Rather than walking out, Elias turned to watch how she was going to be treated.

The server ignored her as he went back to texting.

"Young man, could you help us?" the lady asked after a brief period of time.

The server released a deep sigh of frustration at being interrupted again. He set his cell phone on the counter and asked, "What do you want, you old bag?"

If the server had been more aware, he would have seen Elias standing by the entrance door, listening. It could have saved him a lot of grief.

Elias threw his cone in the trashcan and raced behind the counter where he grabbed the server by the back of the neck and squeezed tightly. "I apologize for my associate's behavior. He'd be more than happy to scoop up whatever your little one would like. Wouldn't you?" he asked as he tightened his grip on the young man's neck.

With eyes bulging, the server said, "That's right."

"Apologize!" Elias ordered.

"And I'm sorry for being rude to you, ma'am. What can I get you?"

"Say please!" Elias squeezed again.

"What can I please get you, ma'am?"

The lady got over her initial shock of what was transpiring in front of her and ordered two small cones, one for herself and one for her granddaughter.

"Give them extra scoops," Elias ordered.

"Oh no, I can't afford it," the lady protested.

"Tell her it's her lucky day. She gets her order free. You'll pay for it. It's today's special."

"I can't do that!" the weasel argued.

Elias tightened his grip again.

The server spoke quickly to the lady. "Yes, that's right, ma'am. There's no charge for your order." He quickly filled the two cones and handed them to the woman and her granddaughter.

"Thank you." The lady's comments weren't directed to the server. Elias nodded his head in acknowledgement and smiled as he watched the two customers leave the shop with their ice cream cones.

Releasing his grip on the server, Elias spun him around to face him. "Now, I don't want to hear any more stories about you treating people like that. My friend and I will be checking in from time to time. We know people in this town and we will have them tell us if you're mistreating your customers," Elias lied. "And if your boss won't do anything about it, we will. Understand?"

Realizing that this was someone who could get very nasty, the server agreed quickly. "Yes. Yes, I'll do better."

"You'll do better, what?

"I'll do better, sir."

"Good, I'm glad now we have that understanding." Elias walked over and picked up the server's cell phone. "Is this yours?"

"Yes."

Elias dropped it in the sink full of soapy water. "And no more texting! Got it?"

"Got it! Yes. Thank you, sir."

Walking toward the door, Elias called, "Remember, I'll be back if I hear that you're not treating people right."

"I will," the server said as he watched Elias walk out the door and his body began to shake from the encounter.

"Eat your cone already?" Fat Freddy asked as Elias caught up to him walking on the sidewalk.

"Lost my appetite," Elias responded as he looked at Fat Freddy's shirt, which had splotches of chocolate ice cream stains on the front. "Gee, Freddy, get a bib, why don't ya?"

Reading the tension in Elias, Fat Freddy asked, "What's eating you?"

"Nothing. Let's just head back to the farmhouse. I'm ready to call it a day."

"Okay. We can do that," Fat Freddy said as he stuffed the remaining piece of his waffle cone in his mouth.

The two returned to their vehicle and drove to the farmhouse where Elias spent a restless night. The Ramos killing replayed in his mind throughout the night, and he tossed and turned from the memory of it all.

The Farm
Next Day

The cool morning air felt fresh on Elias' face as he ran down the lane. He again was hoping that he'd encounter Desiree at the lake.

It had been awhile and he wanted to talk to someone other than Fat Freddy.

As he neared the lake, he saw the white bicycle with the aqua blue rims. He smiled to himself, knowing Desiree would be nearby. He slowed to a walk and allowed a wide smile to cross his face in anticipation of greeting her.

When he reached the bike, he heard splashing in the lake and realized that she must be taking an early morning swim. He made his way through the brush and toward the water's edge. That's when he saw her shorts, T-shirt and bra hanging on a shrub.

His smile again broadened as he walked into an opening and saw her up to her neck in the water, skinny dipping. "Good morning!"

Desiree spun around to face him. She had a look of surprise on her face, which faded as she recognized the bearded intruder. "I guess this, perhaps, is a little awkward," she smiled demurely as she turned her back to him.

Laughing, Elias commented, "Oh, I don't mind."

"I'm sure you don't. Now you be a good boy and turn your back, Manny. This water is crystal clear."

Elias did as he was instructed. "I noticed," he smiled.

"I'm sure you did! You bad boy sneaking up on an unsuspecting woman!" she teased.

"Sorry. I thought you may need help with your tire again." He didn't know why, but he was enjoying the conversation with this woman. Part of it was her beauty. Another part was her easy nature. He liked it.

"I'm sure that was it. I'm going to come out of the water now. No peeking," she said as she emerged naked.

Elias began taking off his T-shirt.

"What are you doing?" she asked, concerned by his action.

Without turning, he held out his shirt behind his back, offering it to her. "I noticed you didn't have a towel. You can use this. I haven't worked up a sweat yet, so it should be okay."

"My, you are a gentleman," she said thankfully as she took the T-shirt and quickly dried off. She hung it on a small tree branch nearby and dressed quickly.

"I do my best," he smiled.

"You can turn around now."

"You have rosy cheeks," he admiringly said.

"It is a little brisk in there. You out for a morning run?" she asked as she sat down and patted the ground next to her, signaling him to sit.

"Yes. Got to stay in shape."

"Looks like you're doing a pretty good job of it," she replied as she glanced at his chiseled chest.

"I try."

"And why do you work out? Is it for pleasure or your job?"

"Both." Elias didn't want to talk about himself in case questions came up about his past and he couldn't answer them. "How are things going at the camp?"

"Good."

"So, what kind of camp is that?"

"It's a step-up program. We work with a halfway house in Toledo. They help women who have been victims of human trafficking. Once the women go through their programs, they have the option to join us here. We try to provide them with a safe shelter and educational programs in a peaceful setting."

"I bet they've gone through a lot." Elias remembered Fat Freddy talking to him about human trafficking and how involved Jimmy Diamonds had been in trafficking women.

"Yes, they have. They're emotionally fragile and we want them to feel loved. We help restore their feelings of self-worth."

"That's admirable."

"I'm not sure about that. It's important, though," Desiree noted.

"What do you do exactly?"

"I'm one of the counselors. I try to be there for them and encourage them through the next part of their recovery journey."

Elias looked at the fresh-faced blonde. "I bet you do a great job."

Glancing at her watch and standing, she replied, "I do my best. I just noticed the time. I have to get back to the camp." She retrieved his still damp T-shirt and handed it to him as he stood. "Sorry, it's still wet." She smiled, turned and began slowly walking away.

Following her to her bike, Elias said, "No problem. I enjoyed our conversation."

Throwing one leg over the bike and kicking up the kickstand, she smiled at Elias. Her green eyes were sparkling. "Maybe I'll see you here again."

"That would be nice."

"Next time, you can tell me what you do," she smiled as she pedaled away.

Elias watched her until she disappeared around a bend. He was going to have to create some sort of backstory to tell her. He really liked the woman. Holding his soggy T-shirt in his hand, he jogged away.

In the woods on one of the slightly distant hills overlooking the lake, a solitary figure had been watching the encounter. He withdrew silently into the woods.

When Elias emerged from the woods near the farmhouse, he saw Fat Freddy relaxing on the porch in one of the rocking chairs. "Out for an early jog?"

"Yeah," Elias answered as he used the T-shirt in his hand to wipe away the sweat.

"I know why you were jogging," Fat Freddy said.

"Yeah, to keep in shape." Elias worried for a moment that somehow Fat Freddy was aware of his visits with the woman at the lake.

"Oh. I guess I was wrong."

"What did you think, Freddy?" Elias asked, perplexed.

"I thought you were trying to jog your memory!" he cracked with a chuckle.

"Funny. Ha-ha!" Elias said as he climbed the two steps to the porch. He was relieved that Fat Freddy wasn't aware of his visits with Desiree.

"You might want to get yourself cleaned up."

"Why's that?"

"Jimmy's on his way. I think he has another job for us."

Elias frowned.

"Why the frown? You and me, we're working stiffs for the guy. When we were doing all that training in Florida…"

"We?" Elias interrupted.

"Okay, so I made an overstatement. Jimmy's been spending his time redoing his organization and making a list of people he owes. It's payback time and I'm not talking about money."

"Another Ramos?" Elias asked.

"You just go get ready. Jimmy will tell us about it when he gets here." Fat Freddy motioned his hand for Elias to get moving.

Elias had a grim look on his face as he entered the farmhouse and hurried to clean up. Within fifteen minutes, Elias had cleaned up and returned to the front porch. As he did, he saw Parella drive up in the SUV and park it. Diamonds and Parella exited the vehicle. Elias looked beyond them, hoping to see Veronica, but she wasn't with them.

Diamonds was scowling as he smoked a cigarette and walked up the steps. "Inside," he said as he walked past the two men on the porch.

Once they joined him at the kitchen table, Fat Freddy asked, "What's up, Jimmy?"

"Listen," Diamonds started. "One of my crews knocked off a jewelry salesman after he left a trade show in Los Angeles. He had $3.7 million in gems in the trunk of his car."

"That sounds good," Elias said.

"Nice haul," Fat Freddy chimed in.

"Not so good," Diamonds said as he took a draw on his cigarette before continuing. "Another crew from Los Angeles apparently was waiting outside the same restaurant for the same guy. When my crew pulled off the heist, this second crew sat back and watched. Then, they came out of their cars and heisted the diamonds from my guys. Only one of my guys survived it. The other crew wasted the jewelry salesman, too."

"That's not so good."

"No, it ain't. We can get twenty cents on the dollar by fencing the gems. The crew that took out my crew sometimes plays in our backyard. Last year, we think they did about a dozen diamond heists in the Midwest. That was about $15 million. I've got to stop that and that's where you come in," Diamonds said as he looked at Elias.

"He's your guy," Fat Freddy said.

"You both are doing this one. Manny, you're the shooter. Fat Freddy drives the getaway car."

"Sure, I can do that," Fat Freddy said as a wry smile crossed his face. "What's the deal?"

"A snitch got word to me that Connors, the guy who heads this crew, is going to be down in Columbus."

"Lou Connors?" Fat Freddy asked.

"Yeah. He's been a thorn in my keister for years. It's time to get rid of him."

Elias nodded his head as he continued to listen.

"Connors is meeting with a couple of fences at a Columbus hotel in a few days. I want you both there."

"Yeah, we can do that," Fat Freddy said eagerly as he tried to please his boss.

"Do they have a parking deck?" Elias asked.

"That's what I like about you, Manny. You're always planning," Diamonds grinned as he reached over and slapped Elias on the shoulder. "To answer your question, it does."

"If we can figure where he parks and where the fences park, we can get the diamonds and the cash," Elias said as his mind calculated the plan.

"You're reading my mind," Diamonds beamed. "The snitch can find out where they park. You take them all out. They're bad guys, anyhow."

"Can do," Elias said with a confident air. "It may be difficult if they park on different levels in the parking deck, but we can find a way to make it work." Elias was surprised at himself at how he had effortlessly contributed to the plan. He didn't realize that he was going through another emotional wave that suppressed his earlier guilt feeling of taking another's life.

"From my past experience, no one walks out at the same time. That increases their odds at making a clean getaway and no double-crossing," Diamonds said.

The three continued to talk and plan for the next hour. When they were finished, Diamonds walked off the porch and climbed back into the SUV. As Parella drove the SUV away, Diamonds had a broad smile on his face. He was very pleased with the way Elias' mind worked in helping plan the heist. Perhaps, this was going to work out better than what he had previously thought.

On a wooded hill overlooking the farmhouse, a figure watched as Diamonds' SUV pulled away. The figure disappeared into the woods.

The Crew's Nest
Put-in-Bay

Mike "Mad Dog" Adams was enjoying a Lake Erie yellow perch sandwich before he headed for his two o'clock show at the Round House Bar. He was seated on the patio next to the white picket fence overlooking Bayview Avenue and the bay. Across the table from him was another island entertainer, Westside Steve Simmons, who sang at The Keys complex.

They had been enjoying lunch at the popular private club as well as views of the marina and bay. A large green umbrella, sprouting from the middle of their table, shaded them from the strong rays of the sun.

Adams' cell phone rang, interrupting their chatter.

"You've got the Dog here," Adams answered.

"Mike, it's Sam," Duncan said as he identified himself.

"Turn up anything?"

"Not much. I did get an interesting call from a guy at the Detroit PD's Organized Crime Section this morning."

"Oh?"

"Apparently, somebody shot and killed a mobster named Ramos when he walked out of his girlfriend's apartment."

"Jealous husband?" Adams couldn't help himself.

Chuckling, Duncan responded, "No."

"What's the connection to Jimmy Diamonds?"

"Ramos was the guy who testified against him at the trial."

"So, it would seem that Mr. Douche Bag is still alive."

"That's what they're thinking in Detroit. And they're thinking it's payback time."

"Wouldn't doubt it."

"They're setting up surveillance on a number of mobsters whom Diamonds may want to hit."

"They think he's that stupid enough to go back into Detroit with everyone looking for him?"

"No, it wouldn't be Diamonds. They think he's got a new hitman working for him, so he doesn't have to set foot in Michigan, although they're not sure where he is. Could be in upper Michigan, Chicago, New York, Los Angeles or Miami. Who knows?"

"They're still looking for him, right?"

"Oh yeah. They've got a number of the agencies involved. It may take some time, but they'll track him down. He's laying low but knowing him, he can't stay low for long. He's too much of a peacock."

"Unless we can get to him first and find out what he did with Emerson," Adams said.

"You and I are on the same page, Mike," Duncan agreed. "I'm still working my sources."

"It might be good if we can get a lead on this new hitman. He could take us to Diamonds."

"I'm with you on that. I'll see what I can stir up, but wanted to let you know the latest development."

"Thanks, Sam. I called a couple of my bad-ass friends in Detroit to see what they learned. I'll get back in touch with them and let them know about this new hitman. See if they can help us, too."

"Be careful who you talk to."

"Oh, I am. When you wrestle with pigs, you've got to get dirty, too," Adams opined. "But my dirt will wash off faster than theirs. Theirs is ingrained."

"You be careful," Duncan warned.

"Hey, it's just like being a Girl Scout selling cookies and knocking on Death's Door. That's the one door you don't want answered early on," Adams stated philosophically.

"Like I said, you be careful. Talk more later," Duncan said as he ended the call.

Adams returned the cell phone to his pocket and looked at Westside Steve. "Nothing really new on finding Emerson."

"That's too bad," the long-haired, red-headed singer replied. "I heard that you didn't think he was dead."

"I don't. You know we're good friends."

"Yeah," Westside Steve agreed.

"Good friends are like bras," Adams said with a twinkle in his eyes.

Westside Steve's eyes lit up. "How's that?"

"Supportive, hard to find and close to the heart," Adams chuckled.

"Like bosom buddies," Westside Steve quipped.

Adams grinned. "Spot on." He turned his head and looked across the bay. "I really think Emerson is alive."

Escapade Lounge
Columbus, Ohio

After they checked into an inexpensive motel room off Morse Road, and ate a quick dinner at Texas de Brazil's meat palace at Easton Town Center, Fat Freddy persuaded Elias to stop at the Escapade Lounge for a nightcap. Fat Freddy's style had been cramped for over thirty days and he wanted to have an evening out.

They found a table in the dimly lit lounge and sat down to listen to the solitary saxophone player on the postage stamp-sized stage. He was softly playing blues and contemporary jazz tunes. Twenty minutes later, a statuesque blonde, wearing a clinging, white sweater dress and four-inch heels, walked through the lounge and took a seat nearby at the bar.

Fat Freddy leaned back in his chair as he lustfully eyed the woman. "What do you think?"

"Nice," Elias answered. "Be careful. Remember what happened last time, Sparkles," he cautioned.

Fat Freddy ignored the warning. "I think she's a high-class hooker."

Elias shrugged his shoulders.

"Go find out," Fat Freddy urged him. "She can ride me like a new pony!"

Elias shook his head from side to side. "Not interested."

"What do you mean, not interested? You weird or something?

Go find out."

"Not my type."

"What? You like boys?" Fat Freddy asked, perplexed.

The woman stood up and leaned toward the bartender. Her skirt stretched tightly over the curves of her derriere.

"You going to pass up a chick like that? Come on, Manny. Go get her." Fat Freddy was like a deer in rut – the deer-mating season.

The woman turned and began to walk toward their table.

"She wants you, Manny. I'm telling you that she wants you. Or me. Here she comes," Fat Freddy panted.

Twenty feet. Fifteen feet. Ten feet. Five feet. Three feet.

Fat Freddy saw that she was going to walk by their table. He was wrong. He couldn't help himself. "Hey, how are you, good-looking?"

She stopped and looked at Fat Freddy and then Elias. She gave Elias a small smile and looked back at Fat Freddy. "I'm very well, thank you."

"Want to join me and my friend here for a drink?" Fat Freddy asked as he stole a glance at her large chest.

"I was on my way to the bathroom. Give me five minutes and I'll be right back."

"Go ahead. Go ahead. Take your time. Pretty yourself up for us," Fat Freddy suggested.

The woman continued her walk to the bathroom as Fat Freddy swiveled in his chair to watch her. "That my friend, is what I call 100 percent, Grade A-certified. We do this right and one of us will get lucky tonight. And I'm planning on it being me." He swiveled back to face Elias as she entered the bathroom.

"Be my guest," Elias said.

"I'll have to be careful and time it right, then I'll ask her how much she charges." Fat Freddy thought that Elias' memory loss probably damaged Elias' recollection on how to snare a woman. "You just watch me and I'll show you how it's done," he salivated.

Elias didn't comment. He just smiled. He was going to get a kick out of watching Fat Freddy showcase his moves.

Fat Freddy harangued Elias until he heard the woman's foot-steps on the tile floor, signaling her return.

Jumping to his feet, Fat Freddy pulled out a chair. "Here you go, sweetheart. Sit that delicious body right here."

She smiled at the compliment even though it was rather crude. As she sat, she said, "Thank you."

"You got a name or what?" Fat Freddy asked.

"You can call me, Jade," she coolly responded.

"What's that? Your stage name?" Fat Freddy asked. Not letting her respond, he continued in a rat-a-tat-tat manner. "I'm Freddy. This is my pal, Manny. Say hello to Jade, Manny. Don't sit there like a dufus."

Elias looked at Jade as she smiled all-knowingly. "Nice to meet you, Jade." Elias decided to have a little fun. "His name's actually

Fat Freddy."

"Gheesh! Why did you have to go ahead and tell her that?" Fat Freddy stormed.

"I think it's cute. You remind me of a big teddy bear!" she commented as she tried to ease the painful blow to Fat Freddy's ego.

His demeanor changed quickly and it was his turn to smile at her warm comment. "Yeah, that's what all the women say. They want to take me to bed and cuddle me," he beamed, as he baited her. He was still miffed at Elias for revealing his nickname.

"I certainly can understand why," she said as she reached a hand out to Fat Freddy's face and ran her fingers slowly down the side of his chubby cheek.

"Aw, there you go, sweetheart. I'm nothing more than a teddy bear at heart," he grinned sheepishly. "But a tiger in bed. Rawwwr!"

"Would you like a drink?" Elias asked, trying to overcome his embarrassment at Fat Freddy's desperate come-on to the lady.

"Yes, I would. Thank you. I'll take an Appletini," she said as she flashed a smile at Elias.

"I'll go get it," Elias said as he rose and walked to the bar.

"So, what kind of work do you do?" Fat Freddy asked.

"I'm a sex therapist."

Fat Freddy's face lit up. "You are?"

"No, I'm just kidding, Sugar," she said in a seductive tone.

"I got a question I'd like to ask you," Fat Freddy began as he decided to ask her how much she charged. "How much …"

He didn't get to finish his question as she interrupted, stood up and waved before sitting down again. "Honey, I'm over here."

Fat Freddy turned to see whom she was addressing. A man had entered the lounge and was heading toward their table. He was massive at six-foot-six-inches tall and two hundred-fifty pounds of muscle. Not the kind of guy you'd want to run into in a dark alley – unless he was walking with you.

"Freddy, this is my boyfriend, Hugo."

Fat Freddy popped out of his seat and shook Hugo's hand. With his other hand he was mopping the beads of sweat that had suddenly appeared on his brow. "Hi there, big fella. We were just keeping your girlfriend company until you got here," Fat Freddy explained nervously.

"Hello," Elias said as he returned with her drink and handed it to her.

"Manny, meet Hugo. This is Jade's boyfriend," Fat Freddy said, nervously emphasizing the word "boyfriend."

Shaking Hugo's hand, Elias said, "Nice to meet you."

Before the conversation continued, Fat Freddy said, "Well, we better go. We have to be up early tomorrow for work." He had his hand on Elias' back as he pushed him in the direction of the door. "Love to talk more, but business calls. Enjoy your drink. Bye-bye," he said, as he moved quickly to the door and pushed Elias outside.

"What was that all about? I thought you were going to show me the ropes?" Elias asked.

"Let that guy have her. While you were at the bar, I decided that she wasn't that interesting after all," Fat Freddy lied, glad that he had avoided a public confrontation. The last thing he needed to do was to cause any disturbance that could have interfered with their assignment for the next day. Diamonds would have killed him for screwing up.

The Grand Palace Hotel
Columbus, Ohio

The elevator doors on the seventh floor level of the parking garage opened and fifty-two-year-old Lou Connors stepped out. He was of average height and build with dark brown hair. He was pulling his once diamond-filled suitcase on wheels behind him. It was now filled with crisp one hundred dollar bills. He paused to survey the garage for any potential threats. While he looked around, he listened carefully for any sounds that could alert him to danger. Nothing seemed out of place.

Satisfied, he walked to his car. It was in the third parking space. As he approached, he saw that a commercial van was parked next to his Mercedes. The lettering on the side showed that it belonged to Roth Roofing. Unknown to Connors was that it had been stolen an hour earlier and parked in the garage.

Connors walked to the rear of his car and looked around one more time before depressing the key fob to pop open the trunk. He lifted the trunk lid and threw the suitcase inside. Before he could close the trunk, he heard the sliding door on the van open.

Connors turned his head to face the potential threat. He also withdrew his .38-caliber handgun from the waistband of his slacks and brought it up to point at the van. He didn't like to take chances and was known for killing first, then asking questions. That reputation was working against him this morning.

As Connors pointed at the man jumping out of the van, the assailant, who was wearing a ball cap pulled down tight on his head, fired two shots from his silenced weapon. They thudded into Connors' chest, killing him instantly. His gun fell from his hand and hit the concrete deck. It was followed quickly by Connors' body.

"I'd call that self-defense," Elias reasoned as he looked down at the body and reached into the trunk to retrieve the cash-filled suitcase.

At the same time, a Chrysler 300, which Fat Freddy had stolen from the parking lot at the Polaris Fashion Mall just north of Columbus, pulled out of a parking space across from the van and stopped next to Elias.

"Nice job, Manny."

"Thanks."

"Time for step two. The snitch said the fence's car is parked two decks below us. Let's move it."

Elias jumped into the car and Fat Freddy drove it down two levels.

"He said it was a blue, late model Ford Explorer and near the elevator doors."

They drove close to the elevator doors and Fat Freddy immediately spotted the Explorer.

"That's it."

He backed into a parking spot next to the elevator. Elias then stepped out of the Chrysler and spotted a large concrete support to hide behind and wait for the fences.

"I'll flash my lights when they come out," Fat Freddy said as he placed his .45 handgun on the seat next to him.

Hurrying, Elias walked to his designated spot between the support post and a parked car. He was partially hidden from the view of anyone exiting the elevator.

While he waited, he heard another vehicle drive behind him and pull into a space across from Fat Freddy's vehicle. He saw that the driver was an attractive woman in a business jacket and turned his attention back to the elevator door.

After parking her car, the woman stepped out and walked to the rear where she opened the trunk. As she bent over to retrieve a briefcase, Fat Freddy eyeballed her figure and her long legs as her short skirt rode up and exposed her shapely, well-toned thighs. Fat Freddy forgot his assignment.

When he turned back to look in the direction of the elevator doors, he saw that one of the fences, who was carrying a brief-case, was walking to the Explorer. Fat Freddy couldn't see that the fence's partner was standing in the open elevator door with another briefcase. As the woman disappeared into the stairwell, Fat Freddy flashed his headlights.

Seeing the signal, Elias walked over to the fence, who was in process of placing his briefcase in the trunk of his car. He laid the muzzle of his silenced .22 handgun against the back of the man's neck.

"I'll take that," Elias said as he reached for the briefcase.

"I don't think so," a voice called from near the elevator door. The second man had taken six steps out of the elevator. He had a weapon pointed at Elias. "Drop the briefcase and your weapon."

Without waiting for further conversation, Fat Freddy stuck his .45 out of his open car window and fired off three rounds, dropping and killing the second man. At the same time, the first man produced a weapon in his hand and turned to shoot Elias, who was distracted by the second man. Sensing danger, Elias's head whipped around as the man raised his weapon. Elias' training paid off. He was quicker and fired two shots into the man's chest, killing him instantly.

Picking up the briefcase, Elias ran to the second man and secured his briefcase. He was surprised that Fat Freddy hadn't pulled out to pick him up. When he looked toward the Chrysler, he didn't see Fat Freddy at the steering wheel.

"Now where did he go?" Elias muttered angrily to himself.

Elias ran to the car and looked through the open driver's window. He saw Fat Freddy bent over the seat and reaching for something on the floor. He was breathing heavily.

"What are you doing, Freddy? We've get to get out of here," Elias stormed.

"My pills! My pills! I dropped them on the floor," Fat Freddy wheezed.

"What?"

"My nitro pills. I dropped the container and they're on the floor on your side!" Fat Freddy said urgently. His skin had a pasty pallor to it.

Looking around and seeing no one, Elias raced around the car and pulled opened the passenger door. Reaching in to pick up several of the pills, he shouted, "How many do you need?"

"One," Fat Freddy said weakly.

"Here," Elias said as he shoved the pill into Fat Freddy's outstretched palm.

Fat Freddy threw the pill into his mouth and then was surprised when Elias grabbed him and pulled him across the console.

"You sit over here. You're in no condition to drive," Elias said as he settled Fat Freddy into the passenger seat and shut the door. He then ran around the car, picked up the two briefcases and threw them onto the back seat.

This was taking too much time, Elias thought to himself. He knew that any delay increased the risk of being caught.

He jumped into the car and started the engine. Putting the car in drive, he drove it down and through the exit onto North High Street. He was thankful that this was a free parking garage.

"How you feeling?" he asked Fat Freddy as the car headed north.

"Better," Fat Freddy said. The color was slowly beginning to return to his face.

"Listen. Don't tell Jimmy about my little episode," Fat Freddy pleaded.

"Your secret is safe with me," Elias said to assure Fat Freddy as he wheeled the car around a corner and drove quickly down the next street.

"Jimmy knows I have a bit of a heart problem, but doesn't know that I can have an incident like that. He wouldn't like it if I was in a situation and went through something where I couldn't function."

"Not a problem," Elias said as he stopped at a red light. "Tell me. Why did you let that second guy get the drop on me? You were supposed to flash the lights when I was to come around the post."

Fat Freddy didn't respond.

"Tell me," Elias urged.

"It's kind of embarrassing, Manny."

"Something to do with that woman parking her car?" Elias probed.

"How'd you guess?"

"You were looking at her and not focused on the job we had to do?"

"Oh, for crying out loud, I was just taking a quick peek at that babe," Fat Freddy whined.

"You almost got me killed," Elias said firmly. "If you ever want to work with me again, you have to promise me that you'll focus on the job," Elias warned. Newton's warning at the Cedar Key landing strip to watch his back now echoed in the back of his mind.

"Okay. Just don't tell Jimmy any of this. He'd go crazy nuts! He'll kill me."

Nodding, Elias concentrated on driving to the empty warehouse in Worthington, a northern Columbus suburb where they had left their vehicle. When they arrived, they transferred the suitcase and two briefcases to their vehicle. Elias also transferred four containers of gasoline to the stolen vehicle and set them in the front and back seats. He next set the timer for three minutes on an explosive device and set it between two of the containers on the front seat.

"Let's go," he said as he walked away, which was unnecessary because Fat Freddy was already sitting behind the wheel of their vehicle.

"You did a nice job today, Manny," Fat Freddy said as he started the engine and they drove away. Within several minutes, they were driving east on I-270 toward the I-71 interchange. They were sufficiently away from the warehouse when the explosive device detonated and the stolen car went up in flames.

Four Days Later
The Farm

It was a daily routine for Elias – getting up and jogging out to the lake to see if he could spot Desiree. She hadn't been around the previous three days and he was hoping to see her this morning. He wouldn't be disappointed.

When he burst through the clump of trees into the open pasture, Elias spotted her sitting under a giant oak tree that overlooked the lake. Her bike was leaning against the tree and she had a small picnic basket on the ground.

"Hi, stranger," he called as he slowed.

"Hi," she smiled back.

"I haven't seen you in a few days," he said as he sat on the ground near her.

"I know. I've been so busy with the girls. A new group arrived and we had to take them through orientation." She looked at Elias whose long hair was pulled back and tied. "You've been looking for me, then?" she asked, already knowing the answer and pleased by his interest.

"Yes, I have," Elias grinned at the beautiful woman. "I enjoy our chats."

"Me, too." She turned to the picnic basket and opened it. "I brought you a treat to make up for me not being available the last few days."

"Oh?" he asked, with raised eyebrows.

"Something sweet for you, Manny."

"Being with you is sweet and a treat," he said.

"Charmer," she teased, handing him a cinnamon roll. "I made these this morning."

"Hmmm. Delicious," he said, as he bit into the roll. "Nice and light."

"Thank you," she said as she took a bite and stared at the placid lake waters. "You owe me something, by the way."

"I do?" He knew what she was going to want, but he wanted her to tell him.

"Yes. I told you a little about my background and now it's your turn."

Elias used the napkin that she had also handed him to wipe sweat from his forehead. He began to tell her the story, a fabrication he created based upon what he had heard Newton tell him during his Cedar Key training.

"There's not much to tell. I was in the military. In special forces."

"Oh, the hush-hush stuff?"

"Yes. So, there's not a lot I can tell you about it."

"What do you do now?"

"I'm in protective services. I help keep important people safe," he lied.

"Sort of like a bodyguard?" she asked wide-eyed as she offered him another cinnamon roll.

"Yes," he said, as he accepted it and took a bite.

"You'll be the first I call if I ever need one," she said alluringly.

"I'd like that. And I'd do a good job for you."

"I bet you would. Is that why you try to stay in such good shape?"

"Yes."

The screams from a group of teenagers jumping into the lake nearby carried to their ears. Desiree stood up and walked down to the water's edge.

"There are some of my girls," she said as she waved at them. "I'd better be going."

"So soon?" he asked disappointedly.

"My job is calling." She walked over and began to pack up her picnic basket. "Would you like a couple of these to go?"

"Only if you have a 'to go' box big enough to put you in, too," he grinned, as he stood to face her.

Smiling affectionately, Desiree walked over to Elias with two cinnamon rolls wrapped in a napkin. "Aren't you sweet?" She stood up on her tiptoes and gave him a kiss on the cheek.

"That was nice. I had better start working on my lines for you," he smiled.

Securing her picnic basket on the bike's rear rack, she sat on the bike seat and began peddling away. "Don't do that! Just be real," she said as she rode away. "Hope I see you soon, Manny."

He waved. "I hope so, too." He watched as she disappeared around the bend in the lane and then began jogging back to the farmhouse. He was looking forward to bumping into her the next morning. He didn't know that Jimmy Diamonds had other plans.

On the hill overlooking the lake, a figure had been discreetly watching them. He had shaken his head negatively when he saw the blonde kiss Elias. Slowly, he turned and walked away.

When Elias broke through the clearing and jogged up to the farmhouse, he saw Fat Freddy sitting on the steps. "Anything new?" he called as he bounded up the steps.

"Nothing," Fat Freddy said as he glanced over at Elias. "You sure seem happy."

"Nothing like a good run through the woods," Elias quipped.

"Hey! Hold up one minute!" Fat Freddy called.

"What?"

"What do you have on your cheek?" Fat Freddy asked as he stood and peered at Elias' upper left cheek.

"Nothing."

"Nothing my keister!" Fat Freddy said as he rubbed his finger above Elias' beard line and looked at it. "That's lipstick! Where did you get that?" he asked, irritated.

Angry with himself for not thinking about Desiree's lipstick smudge, Elias offered, "I rescued a damsel in distress."

Fat Freddy slowly eyed Elias. "You lying to me, Manny? That's not a good thing if you're lying to me." He sniffed the air. "I smell stupid." He glared at Elias.

"Some lady had a problem with her bike over by the lake. I helped her fix it. No more. No less. You're reading too much into this," Elias said in a half-truth because that was how he had recently met Desiree.

"You can't be meeting people without me around," Fat Freddy warned.

"Why?"

"Because it's dangerous for you," Fat Freddy responded. Diamonds had told him to keep Elias on lockdown. No talking with anyone unless Fat Freddy was involved. If there was a chance that something could jog Elias' memory, Fat Freddy was to be on top of it.

Fat Freddy thought for a moment and decided to let Elias in on a secret to make sure that he knew how dangerous things were for him. "I'm going to tell you something, but you can't tell Jimmy. You understand?"

"Sure." Elias' interest was piqued.

"Walk with me," he said, as he went down the steps and headed for a small grove of trees. Elias followed on Freddy's heels.

"Why do we have to go over here?"

"I'm careful, Manny. That's why I've lasted as long as I have," he replied as they stood together in the shade of the trees.

"So, tell me," Elias urged.

Looking around before beginning to speak, Fat Freddy relaxed. "Do you recall hearing the name Santoro?"

"No, why?"

"That's a name you need to remember from this day forward," Fat Freddy cautioned.

"And the reason for that is?"

"Santoro is a lot like you. A hired assassin. Top hitman. Jimmy brought Santoro over here from the West Coast to keep an eye on you in case you went postal."

"Why would I go postal?" Elias had a look of clear bewilderment.

"You never know about how people will react when they've had a brain injury. It's Jimmy's insurance policy," Fat Freddy explained. "Just be careful."

"What does Santoro look like?"

"Nobody seems to know for sure," Fat Freddy lied. He had met Santoro on a couple of occasions. But he wasn't going to tell Elias. He wanted Elias alert all of the time.

"Sounds like a ghost!" Elias surmised.

"More like a shadow. A deadly shadow, my friend."

Recalling again what Newton had said, Elias wasn't trusting anyone. "I'll be careful."

"Don't just mouth the words. You do it!" he said as they began walking back to the house.

On the wooded hill above the farmhouse, a figure melted into the woods. It had been watching the two men talk through binoculars and trying to read their lips. But the distance was too great.

As they walked, Fat Freddy said, "We've got a project."

"Oh?"

"Parella dropped off some stuff from Jimmy while you were out doing your morning run."

"Another diamond deal?" Elias asked as they walked up the steps and to the kitchen table where a large opened envelope lay.

"No, this one is more serious. There are two guys in Cleveland hindering Jimmy's plan to move into the area. They're blocking him, so we have to take them out."

Elias frowned. He wasn't sure that he was going to ever get used to this killing business despite what they had told him about his past. "What's the deal?"

"Here's a photo of the two. Their street names are Smoke and Fire. They're basically inseparable. Where there's Smoke, there's Fire."

"I don't recognize them."

"Well, neither do I. So don't feel bad. From what Jimmy once told me about them, they're pretty cagey guys and hard to fool. It's like they have a sixth sense. It's kept them alive. That's where we come in."

"Oh?"

"Yeah, Jimmy outlined how we can get them. Let's take a look."

"When does he want this done?"

"Tomorrow night. And you don't leave the house until we roll out of here tomorrow night."

Grimacing at the thought of not seeing Desiree at the lake the next day, Elias focused on the task at hand.

The two bent over the open documents on the table to see how Jimmy wanted the kill carried out.

"Jimmy doesn't expect me to make myself that vulnerable, does he?"

"You did this once before and it worked," Fat Freddy lied. He knew it was risky, too. But if Elias didn't perform, he'd be dead anyway. Diamonds would take care of it.

After they finished going through the plan, Elias went out to practice shooting on the other side of the barn. He was nervous about the approach. It wasn't tight and was highly risky, in his opinion. Either Diamonds was a genius, or by midnight the next night, Elias would be dead after being set up by Diamonds. He didn't like it, but he knew that Diamonds expected blind obedience. Elias resigned himself to following Diamonds' plan.

Around nine o'clock the next evening, the two men drove the Chevrolet east to pick up Route 83. When they reached Lodi, they turned onto I-71 driving north to Cleveland. They drove to the Brunswick exit, just south of Cleveland, where they pulled in behind a Bob Evans restaurant. While Elias stood guard, Fat Freddy broke into an older Chevy Suburban while the owners were dining inside.

"It's all yours, Manny," Fat Freddy said as he jumped out of the running vehicle and returned to their car. "Follow me."

Elias sat behind the wheel of the stolen vehicle and followed Fat Freddy back onto I-71, north toward Cleveland. They exited at Bagley Road in Middleburg Heights and drove west of Olmsted Falls where they found an open field off a side road. Fat Freddy parked next to the road and jumped out of the car to direct Elias as he parked in the field.

He walked over to Elias' vehicle. "You ready to go through with this?"

"I guess so," Elias responded with a tinge of nervousness.

"Come on now. You've got cajones of steel!" Fat Freddy encouraged Elias even though he was also nervous about the outcome.

Pulling a bottle of artificial blood that had been included in the package from Diamonds, Fat Freddy poured it over the two bullet holes made earlier in the chest area of Elias' shirt. The shirttails hung over his slacks. Fat Freddy also splattered blood on the dashboard and seat.

"Picture time. Lay back and close your eyes," Fat Freddy said as he pulled a cell phone from his pocket and Elias bit on a blood pill that allowed artificial blood to drip from his mouth. He slumped with his head askew for the photo.

Fat Freddy clicked several photos and then e-mailed one to Smoke and Fire with the following message: *Jimmy Diamonds did you a favor tonight as a peace offering. He took out this hitman who was targeting you both.*

He then provided the location so that they could drive over from the nearby Cleveland suburb of Brooklyn.

"Okay, we've set the bait. Now, let's see if they go for it," Fat Freddy said.

After fifteen minutes, Fat Freddy pulled a plastic bag from his pocket. "It's time for you to take this."

He handed the bag to Elias, who opened it and withdrew a small syringe. It contained Xylazine that had been secured from Dr. Ranney. If taken in the correct dosage, it would induce a death-like state for a relatively short period of one to two hours. That would be enough time for Smoke and Fire to inspect the body and take it to their hideout while they tried to identify the dead hitman.

With skepticism, Elias looked at the syringe in his hand. "I'm a little nervous. You sure this is going to work?"

"Yeah. Yeah. Nothing to be nervous about! Remember, this

worked in Canada when you did it there. It'll work again," Fat Freddy lied.

Fat Freddy convinced Elias to take the risk as part of the blind obedience Diamonds expected and that Elias had previously displayed in his forgotten past. The bigger risk was that Smoke and Fire pump an extra couple of rounds in Elias' body and actually kill him, but Fat Freddy had developed a ruse which he hoped would deter that action.

"I hope so," Elias said reluctantly as he injected himself in the inside portion of his forearm and waited for it to take effect.

"I'll see you in a little while, Sleeping Beauty," Fat Freddy said with feigned confidence.

Within a couple of minutes, Elias sank into oblivion.

Fat Freddy walked back to his car after planting a small surveillance camera above the passenger's sun visor. He drove down the road and found a place to park and to watch the scene unfold.

Fifteen minutes later, two vehicles pulled into the field. The first vehicle, a van, drove up to Elias' stolen vehicle. The second contained Smoke and Fire and halted on the edge of the field.

The three occupants from the first vehicle exited and, with weapons drawn, warily scanned the area for any sign of possible trouble. Satisfied in not seeing any immediate threat, two of them approached Elias. They saw his lifeless eyes and then began to carefully search the vehicle for booby traps. Not seeing anything after inspecting it, they reached through the open window to release the hood and examine the engine compartment, as well. They looked underneath and didn't see anything there, either.

One of the men cautiously opened the door behind the driver and slipped into the seat. He leaned over Elias as he looked for anything that would show that the body was booby-trapped, but couldn't find anything.

"Looks clear," the man spoke somewhat cryptically into a walkie-talkie. "Took two in the chest. Got the red stuff all over."

The second vehicle drove over to where the first was parked, and Smoke and Fire exited the vehicle. They looked like two big-time wrestlers in their fifties, broad shoulders and a hint of the beginnings of pot bellies. Both of their heads were shaven. They walked over to look at the body while the others continued to scan the area for likely trouble.

"Know him?" Smoke asked.

"Never saw him before."

"West Coast?"

"Could be. Or New Orleans?" Fire asked as he withdrew a .45 caliber handgun from his waistband.

"What you doing there?" Smoke asked when he saw the weapon.

"I'm going to put a couple in his head before we go," he said, raising the weapon and pointing it toward Elias' head.

"Wait," Smoke said authoritatively. "We still don't know who this is. Nobody else seems to, either. You don't just off a top hit-man without anybody knowing who he is. It could be Diamonds' trash man for all we know. All a big story. Let's take the body with us and ID him before we make nice with Diamonds."

Fire leaned in the Suburban's window to grab Elias. That's when he saw something unusual out of the corner of his eye, something was out of place. He looked up and saw a camera pointing at him. "I thought you guys said we're clean."

"I did," the one henchman called out.

"Well, somebody almost got me on film shooting this guy," Fire shouted angrily as he pulled back. He walked around the vehicle to the passenger side, swearing as he walked. He jerked open the door and reached up in the visor, grabbing the camera. He spotted the switch and turned off the camera before dropping it on the ground and smashing it with his foot.

"What do you call this, stupid?" he asked as he straightened up and held the camera in his hand.

The henchman started hemming and hawing. "Sorry, Fire. I missed it." He knew he was in big trouble.

"There's more to this than what we can see," Fire bristled.

"Close," Smoke commented angrily, as he looked around the area to see if they had an audience.

"What the - ? What's Diamonds up to? Throw the body in the back of the van and torch the Suburban. Do it now. I'm sure your fingerprints are all over it."

"Yeah. We'll sort this out back at the warehouse."

"Jimmy either set us up," Fire said as he and Smoke returned to their vehicle, "or just wanted to prove that we saw his offering by filming it. Not sure what that snake is up to, but I'm sure it's no good."

They drove across the field and parked next to the road while two of the henchmen carried Elias. One had him by his feet, the other by his wrists. The third henchman opened the rear of the van so the two could throw Elias' body onto the floor. The third man returned to the Suburban with a can of gasoline, doused the interior then set it on fire. They drove away and followed Smoke and Fire back to the Brooklyn warehouse.

Meanwhile, Fat Freddy had finished downing a nitro pill as his heart reacted to the video. He wiped the sweat from his brow as he started the car and followed the two vehicles. A small tracking device had been planted in Elias' back pocket, and Fat Freddy could follow him by watching the monitor.

The vehicles traveled northward and picked up I-480, taking it to the Tiedeman Road exit in Brooklyn, a working class neighborhood with manufacturing and warehouses, just west of Cleveland.

After a couple of turns, they pulled into a warehouse drive. Smoke depressed the garage door opener to open the entrance door to the warehouse and the two vehicles drove inside. Fat Freddy drove slowly by as the door closed. He found a parking spot a short distance beyond the warehouse entrance and waited.

Smoke and Fire exited their vehicle and directed the three henchmen to transport the hitman's body to a vacant office. The two went into an adjacent office to talk.

The three men grabbed the body by its feet and hands, carried it into the designated office and laid it on top of a desk. Completing their task, they shut off the office light and closed the door behind them as they exited. One went to the front of the building where he stood watch near an entrance door. The other two joined Smoke and Fire in a conference room next to their private office.

Meanwhile, the effects of the injection were waning. Elias felt himself regaining consciousness, but he was groggy. He kept his eyes closed and didn't move his body. With heightened awareness, he listened in the dark room for any sounds that would indicate that he was not alone. Not hearing anything after a few minutes, he slowly opened his eyes and cautiously turned his head. He ascertained that he was alone and then stretched his body.

He gradually sat upright and allowed his blood flow to return to normal. After shaking his head from side to side to clear his mind, he reached into the crotch of his underwear to locate his .22. He breathed a sigh of relief when his hand grasped the gun, realizing that he had not been searched. It was one of the risks that Fat Freddy had mentioned. He quickly checked that there were still ten rounds in the clip and another in the chamber. He'd have to fire wisely since he had limited ammo and didn't know how many mobsters he'd be confronting.

He reached down to his shoes and pulled off the right shoe. Withdrawing a hidden pair of plastic gloves and pulling them on his hands, he replaced the shoe on his foot.

Standing quietly, he checked his back pocket and found the tracking device. He switched it off and on twice, signaling Fat Freddy that he was on the move. Before he could open the door, it swung open and a hand reached inside to switch on the light.

Moving like lightning, Elias grabbed the hand and pulled the startled man into the room, twisting him so that his back was against Elias and using him as a human shield. Seeing that the man was alone, Elias spun him to the floor while shoving the door shut.

He pulled one of the henchman's arms sharply behind his back, causing the man to grunt in pain.

"How many of you are there?" Elias asked as he pressed his weapon against the man's skull.

"Too many for you," the man snarled.

Realizing that he wasn't going to get any intelligence from the man, Elias clipped him on the temple with his weapon and knocked him unconscious. He ran his hands over the man's body and found a .45 that he quickly inspected. It was fully loaded. He inserted it into his waistband and switched off the light.

Elias cracked the door open carefully. He initially didn't see anyone in the warehouse. He opened the door wider and spotted the guy guarding the door at the entrance to the garage.

Ducking back into the room, Elias pulled the unconscious henchman to his feet and leaned him out the door. "Hey," Elias yelled. "I need a hand here." He pulled the man back into the room and dropped him to the floor.

The man guarding the door saw the man apparently walking back into the room and walked over to join him. When he reached the door and began to enter, he was suddenly jerked into the room.

As he spun around to face his threat, he stopped raising his weapon as he found himself staring into the business end of a .22's barrel.

"Don't say anything unless I ask you," Elias warned as he took the man's gun.

"I thought you were dead," the man stammered.

Elias shoved the gun barrel into the man's mouth. "I said, don't talk unless I ask you. Understand?"

The man nodded and Elias pulled the barrel out of his mouth.

"How many of you are there?" Elias asked. "Tell me or you'll end up dead like your friend here." Elias tilted his head in the direction of the man on the floor.

Not wanting to join him, the man replied quickly, "There are four of us left."

"Where are the other three?"

"In the conference room."

"Take me there and I won't kill you," Elias said seriously as he shoved the man through the door and into the warehouse.

They walked the short distance to the conference room's doorway. Elias held the man in front of him as a shield as they walked into the room.

"Surprise! Surprise!" Elias said calmly as the room's occupants looked up. Their eyes widened and mouths gaped at seeing Elias' return from the dead. Without hesitation, they withdrew their weapons and fired at Elias, killing their unfortunate crony in the process.

With seemingly cool ease, Elias fired two shots. Fire and the other henchman were killed instantly with deadly headshots. Smoke fired as he dove behind a desk. The bullet narrowly missed Elias' head and embedded itself in the door frame.

Dropping the dead man he was holding, Elias withdrew the .45. He slowly approached, firing both weapons through the cheap wooden desk. When he looked over the desk, he saw Smoke's body riddled by bullets and sprawled on the floor.

Elias quickly reached into his pocket and withdrew an ace of diamonds. He threw the card on Smoke's body. Then he turned and ran to the front entrance. When he burst through the door, he found Fat Freddy parked next to it. He had an anxious look on his face.

"Get in!" he yelled as he threw his Uzi submachine gun on the floor under his seat and looked nervously around for any witnesses. Sirens from approaching police cars signaled that the gunshots had alerted someone in the industrial complex.

As Elias turned his back to the building and began to enter the car, the warehouse door opened. It was the first henchman who had regained consciousness. In his hand was his hideout gun that he was bringing up to point at the fleeing assassin, Elias.

A rifle crack filled the air as a bullet connected with the henchman's skull, knocking him off his feet. He was dead when he hit the ground.

Without hesitation, Fat Freddy punched the gas pedal and the car took off like a racehorse at the crack of the starter's gun.

"That was a mistake, Manny. You never leave anyone alive!" Fat Freddy yelled sternly as the car careened around a corner. "Dead men don't talk – or shoot."

Elias had a perplexed look on his face. "Yeah, I forgot about the first guy. I knocked him out."

"You don't do that! You take them out!" Fat Freddy seethed. "That was too close."

"I'm confused."

"You should be!"

"I don't get it. Who killed the guy?"

Fat Freddy was sure that he knew and he also knew that he'd be hearing about it. "Must have been your guardian angel."

Elias didn't respond. He was thinking about his near miss with death.

Fat Freddy glanced at Elias. He decided to lighten the mood. "I used to have a guardian angel, but I think I drove mine to drink." He chuckled softly.

"No, seriously. Who killed the guy?" Elias asked.

"I'm sure we'll know about it shortly," he said as he pulled onto I-71 and headed south toward Wooster.

Two hundred feet away from the warehouse, a van driven by Parella slowly pulled out of the parking lot from a commercial business. It had provided good concealment from the view of the warehouse where Elias had been taken. But the spot had also provided cover for the sniper. It was an insurance policy that Diamonds used in case Elias got himself in a jam. And this time it paid off.

"Nice shot," Parella said as he watched the shooter disassemble the sniper rifle and place it in its case.

"That's what I get paid to do," the sniper said.

"Jimmy will be pleased."

"I'm sure," the sniper said a moment before calling Diamonds.

"It's Santoro. The goods are safe." Santoro hung up.

Pleased, Diamonds sat back in his chair. He had the look of a satisfied snake which had just swallowed a large rodent.

The Next Morning
The Farm

"Listen, you dumb schmuck! You don't leave anyone alive!" Diamonds had been ranting from the moment he stepped out of the vehicle and walked into the farmhouse. That had been fifteen minutes ago. He had been pleased with the hits on Smoke and Fire until Fat Freddy had called him the previous evening on his way back from the hit. That sense of well-being had gone up in smoke when he heard that Elias had left one alive and almost ended up dead because of it.

Parella was standing with his back against the wall. He was smirking as he enjoyed seeing Fat Freddy and Elias take a verbal barrage from Diamonds.

"What if that guy had killed you or you two got involved in a shootout? And the police showed up before you left? All of my good planning would have gone down the toilet!"

"It was a mistake," Elias said as he owned up to it.

"Yeah, I know a lot of mistakes. And they live in the bottom of the Detroit River now." Abruptly, Diamonds pulled out a .45 from under his sport coat. He pointed it at Elias. "Just give me one reason why I shouldn't off you right now for not following my orders. Just give me one."

"Now, wait a second, Jimmy!" Fat Freddy interrupted. "He took on a risky job and pulled it off. It was just one mistake – he did the rest on point."

Diamonds whirled around and pointed the .45 at Fat Freddy. "And now you shut up! It only takes one mistake to blow it all.

Besides, I'm talking to liquid stupid here."

Fat Freddy shrunk back. He knew better than to open his mouth when Diamonds was having one of his legendary rages.

"Now, Elias, what do you have to say for yourself?" Diamonds stormed, red-faced.

"Like I said, it was a mistake. It won't happen again." Elias didn't want to tell Diamonds, that for some reason, he didn't want to kill someone who was unarmed. He didn't know where that feeling was coming from.

Jamming the gun's muzzle under Elias' chin, Diamonds screamed, "It better not. Otherwise, you're history, Moore, like you shoulda been a long time ago!"

As Diamonds withdrew the weapon, Elias asked, "Why did you call me, Moore?"

Realizing that in his anger he had addressed Elias by his real name, Diamonds moved quickly to recover. "I said moron, you stupid putz! Now, you can't even hear straight!" he fumed as he recovered from the slip.

Diamonds peered at Elias to see if the comment caused any triggers for restoring Elias' memory. Softening his rage, Diamonds asked, "Hey, I haven't asked you in a while. How's that memory thing working for you? Any news? Remember anything?"

"No, I still don't, Jimmy," Elias answered. "I wish I did."

"Aw, that's too bad," Diamonds said with a sense of relief. "Listen, I got another job for you two if you think you'll leave nothing but dead bodies behind." Diamonds paused and looked at the two men who were nodding their heads in unison that they understood the message loud and clear.

"Good. I want you to whack the Caniglia Brothers." Diamonds looked intently from Fat Freddy to Elias. "No one lives. Understand?"

"Got it," Fat Freddy answered.

"Understood," Elias replied.

Taking a draw on his ever-present cigarette and exhaling a plume of blue smoke, Diamonds said to Parella. "Show us the map."

Parella stepped over to the table and spread out a map on it. "Here's where the Caniglias operate in Mayfield Heights," He pointed to an intersection. "They have a warehouse here."

"But, that's not where you're going to hit them," Diamonds said as he pointed to another location on the map. It had a red circle drawn around it. "This is where the brothers live - 2032 Dorchester in Chagrin Falls. It's heavily protected. High fence all around the property. Surveillance cameras everywhere. Might be at least six bodyguards on the grounds."

From a folder he was holding in his hand, Parella produced several pictures, including aerial photos of the grounds taken recently through the use of a drone. He placed them on the table and Fat Freddy and Elias eyeballed them.

"Looks pretty tight to me," Fat Freddy said after looking at them for a few minutes.

"It could be very messy," Elias added. "If we make too much noise and stay too long, the police will be all over us. We won't get away."

"Exactly. That's why you'll use a stealth bomber," Diamonds

smirked. His ego was pleased that his two killers had seen no easy way to handle the challenging hit.

"Of course, a drone. What a great idea!" Fat Freddy smiled.

"No! I said a stealth bomber. You're going to fly that stealth bomber into the house!"

"No, we'll hit them in their car in the driveway," Fat Freddy suggested proudly.

"You're missing the point. You're going to use the stealth bomber and walk right into the place," Diamonds said assuredly with an evil grin.

"Okay, Jimmy. Tell us about this stealth bomber," Elias said as he realized that Diamonds was toying with them.

"Very easy. A garbage truck."

"Garbage truck?" Fat Freddy asked.

"That's what is so beautiful about this hit. You're going to use it to dispose of the trash that lives there. Here's how it's going to work. You're going to steal one of Ace Garbage's trucks in Woodmere. That's the same company that picks up the Caniglia's trash now. We'll get you uniforms. Then, you drive up to the house and park by the gate. You take off the two-wheeled trash carts and walk over to the call box.

"Call the house on the gate intercom, they open the gate and you walk up to the house with your weapons in the trash carts. You might get searched. I don't know. One of their bodyguards will greet you by the garage and watch you empty the trash from the containers there. You take him out and go out to the patio behind the house. The Caniglias like to have breakfast there and that's where you take them out. That makes it easy. You will virtually be hidden in plain sight."

"And we make our getaway in a slow garbage truck?" Fat Freddy said with a look of concern on his face.

"I smell stupid," Diamonds stormed. "Think about it. You're using silencers. No one is going to suspect anything. You just drive away calmly, like nothing happened."

"What about surveillance cameras, Jimmy?" Elias asked.

"That's what I like. Somebody is thinking here and asks a good question," Diamonds smiled. "Not too much we can do about the cameras. You can wear oversized sunglasses and ball caps. We can get you some fake tattoos and scars for your faces to throw off whoever looks at the film."

Sitting back in his chair, Diamonds looked at the two men. "Satisfied?"

Elias spoke first. "Sounds like a good plan. I don't see why we couldn't pull it off."

Fat Freddy's head was jerking back and forth from Elias to Diamonds. "We can ace this one," Fat Freddy said confidently.

"You better."

Two Days Later
Woodmere

It was early morning as Fat Freddy drove up the exit ramp from I-271 and turned right onto Chagrin Boulevard in the southeast Cleveland suburb of Woodmere. The area was congested with traffic and lined with a number of commercial buildings.

"Keep your eyes open," Fat Freddy cautioned.

The two were searching for The Original Pancake House. The Ace Garbage truck would be parked behind it, with the keys in the ignition. The two employees would be inside enjoying a large breakfast and blind to anyone stealing their truck. Diamonds had made sure of it. He had Parella slip the two men five hundred dollars each to look the other way that morning.

"There it is," Elias pointed to the restaurant. "The truck's out back as Jimmy promised."

Fat Freddy drove the car into the parking lot next door where Elias exited and walked to the garbage truck. Like Fat Freddy, he was wearing an Ace Garbage coverall, dark sunglasses and a dark ball cap. They had pulled work gloves on their hands and applied fake scars to their faces with the kits that Diamonds had given them.

When he reached the truck, Elias opened the door and peered in to see if the keys were in the ignition. Seeing them, he waved at Fat Freddy, then entered the cab. He started the engine and followed Fat Freddy down Chagrin Boulevard to a vacant building where Fat Freddy parked the car behind the building.

Both men exited their vehicles and walked to the rear of the car, which Fat Freddy opened. They reached in and pulled out four

.22's and one sawed-off, double-barrel shotgun. The .22's were each fitted with silencers. The shotgun would be used in case of an emergency. It was stolen and couldn't be traced to them. They took extra rounds of ammunition from the trunk and two cloth pouches with hooks.

Next, they lowered the two-wheeled trash containers from the rear of the garbage truck and opened the lids. They hung the cloth pouches inside the containers and placed their weapons and extra rounds inside. Fat Freddy tied a wire to the shotgun and lowered it inside the container, securing the loop end of the wire to one of the hooks. Then, they opened two container-sized trash bags which they hung into the containers so that the weapons would be hidden. The edges of the trash bags were pulled over the rim of the containers.

"I think we're ready," Fat Freddy said.

"How far away are we?"

"About ten minutes or so. You drive and I'll navigate. We'll make a couple of turns as we head into the valley."

The two men entered the cab and Fat Freddy opened a map while Elias started the truck's engine and drove it onto Chagrin Boulevard. Within fifteen minutes the truck pulled over in front of the Caniglias' estate in Chagrin Falls and parked. The two men exited the truck and lowered the two trash containers.

Fat Freddy walked to the intercom and pressed the call button.

"Yes?" a voice answered.

"Trash pick up," Fat Freddy answered.

There was a brief pause before the voice said. "You're early."

Fat Freddy thought quickly. "We had a route change. If you don't want us to come in, we'll see you next week."

"No, no. It's fine. I was just asking," the voice spoke as the camera mounted above the gate moved and pointed first at Fat Freddy and then at Elias.

"You don't look like the guys who usually pick up," the voice said.

"Hey, I just told you that there was a route change. We're the new guys on this route. If you don't want us to come in, we'll be back next week."

"Come on in," the voice spoke. "I'll meet you at the garage."

"Yeah, whatever," Fat Freddy said as the gate opened and the two men pushed their wheeled containers up the long driveway to the garage. As they walked, they knew that they were under close surveillance by the cameras. When they neared the garage, they saw three armed guards waiting for them.

One of them spoke as the two walked up to the garage. "Mind if we frisk you?"

"What for?" Fat Freddy said with indignation.

"We don't know you two and our employer wants us to be careful."

"Nobody touches my body but beautiful women," Fat Freddy said as the two garbage men edged their way closer to the open garage door.

"Freeze!" the man said as he walked over to Fat Freddy. "You're going to have to make an exception today, Sissy Boy!" he said in a taunting tone as the three guards aimed their weapons at the two.

"Go ahead. No sweat off my back. I probably smell so I'd suggest you wash your hands after you're done," Fat Freddy retorted.

The man approached Fat Freddy first and patted him down. Next, he moved on to Elias. Finished, he spoke. "They're clean." He lifted the lids of the two containers and quickly peeked inside. "Empty," he said as he closed the lid on the second one.

"Too bad Oscar the Grouch didn't pop out at you!" Fat Freddy huffed as he thought about the Sesame Street character who lived in garbage cans.

The man ignored the comment and pointed to a corner of the garage. "Trashcans are over there."

"I told you there was nothing to worry about," Fat Freddy said irritably as he and Elias casually wheeled their carts to the corner of the garage while the three men stood in the doorway, carefully watching them.

Fat Freddy and Elias flipped off the lids of the five trashcans along the wall and each picked up a can. When they walked over to their wheeled containers, they flipped open the lid and emptied the cans in their containers, letting both cans drop inside. When their hands emerged from the containers, they were holding their .22's in their right hands. Fat Freddy also gripped the shotgun in his left hand, although he didn't want to use the noisy weapon yet.

It happened so quickly that the three guards couldn't react fast enough. As they began to raise their weapons, the .22's popped and the three guards dropped dead to the ground.

Fat Freddy walked over and gave each an extra shot to the head to ensure they were dead. "That's three down. There's three more, plus the two Caniglia brothers."

Meanwhile, Elias had walked over to the door leading into the main house. He slowly pushed it open and saw that no one was in the hallway. He nodded at Fat Freddy, who had joined him, and the two hitmen walked through the doorway with their weapons pointed in front of them.

As they neared the main hallway, which ran through the center of the house, Elias saw movement out of the corner of his eye. He spun to face the front door and saw a guard pointing a .45 at him. Elias charged the guard, snapping off two quick shots at him before he could fire. The bullets caught the guard in the head, killing him instantly as he fell to the floor.

Elias bent over the body and retrieved the .45. Suddenly, he heard the plop-plop of Fat Freddy's .22 and turned to see another guard drop his .45 and tumble down the staircase to the floor.

"Thanks, Freddy," Elias said as he ran over to check the body to confirm it was lifeless.

"I'm just your guardian angel." Fat Freddy's cherubic face was filled briefly with a smile before turning deadly serious. "Three to go."

Without warning, the intercom system buzzed.

"Somebody's at the gate!" Elias said with concern.

"And that can't be good news for us!" Fat Freddy replied as he stared at the box near the front door as it buzzed again.

A voice from the rear of the house yelled, "Answer that!"

The intercom buzzed again.

The voice at the rear of the house swore several times. "What are you guys doing up there?" Then Elias and Fat Freddy heard the owner of the voice answer the intercom. "Yeah. Who is it?"

"Ace Garbage, but we see one of our trucks is already here. It's not part of their route, it's ours."

Before the two trash men at the gate could comment further, the man in the back swore again. He turned and yelled out to the patio to the Caniglia brothers who were enjoying their breakfast. "We got two sets of garbage men. I'm betting the first set are frauds."

"Cover the front!" Tommy Caniglia shouted toward the house as the guard ran through the dining room and then to the front of the house where he saw the bodies of his two cohorts. Both of the Caniglia brothers stood and reached into a storage box on the patio, retrieving semi-automatic weapons.

At the same time, Elias and Fat Freddy had raced down the main hall and entered the kitchen that opened onto the patio. Tommy Caniglia's weapon sprayed bullets at the two figures he saw standing near the open patio doors.

Fat Freddy dove to the right and Elias dropped behind the kitchen island.

"We can't stay here long. Those shots will attract the police," Fat Freddy called as another round broke the glass in the window over his head and shards fell over him and to the floor. Several jagged glass shards were imbedded in his coveralls. Three penetrated the material far enough to prick his skin, causing it to bleed.

"I'll draw his fire and you take him out!" Elias said after he inserted a new clip in his .22. He stood and fired once before ducking back below the island. It was enough to draw Tommy Caniglia's attention and he sprayed the island.

That's exactly what they wanted. Fat Freddy stood and fired two blasts from his shotgun, catching Tommy in the stomach and propelling him backwards into the pool. He was now dead, too.

"Two to go," Fat Freddy called as he reloaded while looking out to the patio for Tommy's brother, Joey.

"This one isn't going to be easy," Elias said as he looked back over his shoulder and down the main hallway. "Crap!"

Elias saw the guard advancing down the hallway. He was aiming at Fat Freddy, whose attention was focused on the patio.

Elias fired twice, killing the guard.

Fat Freddy turned to look behind him and saw the man on the floor. "Thanks for covering my butt!" Fat Freddy said as he looked again for Joey Caniglia.

Sirens in the distance announced approaching police cars.

"We can't wait!" Fat Freddy said as he rushed onto the patio, swinging the shotgun. Elias followed him. As they looked back at the house, they saw a rear door to the garage ajar.

"He must have gone in there," Elias yelled and moved swiftly to the door. When he arrived, he yanked it wide open and peered inside the garage. "Nobody," he said as he walked into the garage.

The garage door was still wide open from when they had first arrived with their trash containers.

"I think we're done here," Fat Freddy nervously stated. "There's no way we'll get away in that garbage truck," he said as he looked down the tree-lined drive to the front gate.

"Open the gate!" Elias yelled as he pointed to the intercom and the gate release control.

"What?"

"We're getting out of here," he yelled as he rushed over to the corner of the garage to a cross-country motorcycle. He started it as Fat Freddy pushed the gate control button and then jumped on the back of the motorcycle.

"This isn't good for my hemorrhoids," Fat Freddy whined as he clutched the shotgun and settled in.

"Not my problem," Elias said as he gunned the engine and they roared out of the garage toward the opening gate where two garbage men were staring with their mouths wide open in disbelief.

It happened about halfway down the driveway. Joey Caniglia stepped out from behind one of the large trees and began to spray bullets at the oncoming motorcycle and its occupants.

Having no choice, Elias began to lay down the bike on the drive. As he did, two blasts from the shotgun echoed near his ear as Fat Freddy fired. The first blast missed Joey, but the second one hit him, knocking him off his feet.

Shaking his head as he stood up the motorcycle and helped Fat Freddy to his feet, Elias spoke. "Nice shot, But I can't hear anything," Elias said as Fat Freddy rushed over to the downed Caniglia as fast as his short legs could move.

Fat Freddy tossed the shotgun into the shrubs and pulled out his .22, putting two bullets into Joey's head. He reached into his pocket and pulled out an ace of diamonds. He then threw it on the ground next to the body.

When he turned, Elias had pulled the motorcycle up next to him. "Let's go."

"Yeah, ride it like we stole it!" Fat Freddy yelled as his plump frame mounted the motorcycle again.

"We did," Elias grinned as he raced the bike down to the end of the drive.

"We left trash for you," Fat Freddy yelled at the two real garbage men as they slowed to ride through the gate and then quickly down the road.

Three minutes later, Elias pulled the motorcycle off the road and into a wooded lot with a stream running through it. "Better get these coveralls off of us," he said as they took them off and buried them in a shallow depression with their caps and handguns.

"You sure went slowly enough when we rode by those garbage men," Fat Freddy said as he followed Elias to the stream where Elias knelt and washed the fake scarring from his face.

"I wanted them to get a look at our scars. That should help throw off anyone looking for us," he said as he finished scrubbing his face with the cold water. "Did I get it all?"

"Yep. How about me?"

"You're good. Let's go."

The two men raced back to the motorcycle and rode the short distance back to where their car was parked. While Fat Freddy unlocked the doors and sat behind the wheel, Elias grabbed two incendiary devices from the rear of the vehicle. After he set the timers and placed them on the motorcycle, he joined Fat Freddy in the car.

As they drove away, Elias commented, "It's probably overkill on that bike. I brought those along to destroy the garbage truck."

"I love blowing things up!" Fat Freddy smiled as he slipped off his gloves and drove onto the ramp for I-271 South. He was relieved that they had pulled off the hit despite the last minute snafu with the real garbage men arriving. He knew Jimmy Diamonds would be pleased that their mission had been accomplished.

"Hey, Manny," Fat Freddy called.

"Yeah?"

"Do you remember what going on garbage detail means?"

"No."

"Man, your memory sure is gone. That's mob talk for a hit. Kind of funny we pulled off a hit as garbage men," Fat Freddy laughed as he amused himself.

Elias didn't comment. He sank back in his seat and watched the passing traffic, wondering why all of this didn't give him any satisfaction like it should. After all, he was a professional hitman. So why did it all feel so wrong?

The Next Morning
The Farm

From the edge of the woods, Elias could see Desiree. She was standing on the shoreline, skipping flat stones across the water. She wore a cotton T-shirt in a bright salmon color with tan shorts. They seemed to heighten the allure of her long legs. Her blonde hair was pulled back and she wore a white terry band around her forehead.

Smiling, Elias walked quietly up to her.

"Having fun?" he asked.

She jumped, but didn't turn around as she recognized Elias' voice. She dropped the stones in her hand and stood, staring at the calm lake water.

He wondered why she didn't answer. "What? No 'Hello, Manny'?"

"It's more like 'Goodbye, Manny'," she said as she turned to face Elias. Her eyes were red from crying.

Reacting and not thinking, Elias closed the distance between them and swept her up in his muscular arms. He held her close as he comforted her. "What's wrong? What's this goodbye stuff?"

"I'm leaving," she said as she buried her face into his broad chest.

Pulling back, Elias reached under her chin with one hand and lifted her face to look into her eyes. "What do you mean?"

"I'm being transferred to another camp. It's a promotion for me, but I have some reservations."

"Would one be me?"

She was quiet and turned her head away before she spoke. She didn't want to look into his eyes. "Yes."

Despite himself, Elias smiled. "I'm glad to hear that," he said as he pulled her tight against him and she leaned her head against his chest. "I didn't even get a chance to take you on a first date yet."

"You seem like such a nice guy, Manny. It's been a long time since I've met someone nice like you. It's a shame it has to end this way."

"Your promotion – is it nearby?" he asked hopefully.

She silently shook her head no.

If she only knew what I really do, she wouldn't think I'm such a nice guy he thought to himself. He really liked her. She was daylight compared to the darkness where he resided. He decided to encourage her even though it was difficult. He'd miss seeing her at the lake, but knew nothing could come of this, anyway.

"They'll be other nice guys," he said as he gritted his teeth. "And to get promoted, how great is that!"

She didn't respond.

"I know you'll do well, Desiree. You've got to go for it!" he said with feigned optimism. He preferred that she stay in her current position.

"I guess I'd better go. This is hard enough on me," she said as she began to pull away.

"Not yet. We just started talking," he protested as he reached to pull her back.

Suddenly she stood on her tiptoes and kissed Elias on the lips. Before he could react, she turned and began running away.

"Hey," he yelled. "At least you could have let me enjoy the kiss."

"Sorry," she called over her shoulder as she continued running down the lane toward the camp.

"What was that all about?" Elias spoke aloud to no one. He turned and began jogging.

On the hill overlooking the lake, a man had been watching Elias and the woman. He didn't like seeing them together. It could complicate things. The man stepped back into the woods.

Emerald Necklace Marina
Lakewood, Ohio

The car descended into the valley that cut through the steep cliff lining Rocky River before it emptied into Lake Erie. Following the route on his GPS to the western Cleveland suburb of Lakewood, Fat Freddy reveled in the fresh, natural scenery of the valley.

"This is really something. You've got this beautiful park sitting below a crowded suburb," Fat Freddy observed as he drove into the parking lot along the riverbank and parked as dusk approached.

"Not what I expected," Elias said as he stepped out of the car and took in the adjacent wooded area and steep cliffs.

Scouring the parking lot for trouble as he exited the car, Fat Freddy said, "Okay, now. Keep your wits about you. Santoro could be watching us."

Elias exited the car and thought about the week that had elapsed since the Caniglia murders. Diamonds had met with them at the farmhouse. He had been in a rage like none before that Elias had witnessed. He was glad when he was told to step outside while Diamonds, Parella and Fat Freddy talked. After an hour, Diamonds and Parella had left. Fat Freddy was unusually quiet and wouldn't discuss what had transpired during the meeting.

A day later, Diamonds and Parella returned to meet with Fat Freddy. That time, Elias was included in the meeting. He learned that their next target was Santoro. No one would answer Elias' questions as to why they were going to hit Santoro. Nor could anyone provide him with Santoro's photo. It was a strange mystery to Elias.

Ever vigilant, Elias looked around. He saw several fishermen along the riverbank and several couples, walking hand in hand in the park. He didn't sense any immediate danger. "Strange that no one has a picture of Santoro," he said to Fat Freddy.

"Yeah, that's one thing that makes Santoro so dangerous. The master of disguise. Santoro can walk up to you and off you before you know who's pulling the trigger," Fat Freddy warned. "Of course, that's the way you are, too. Nobody knows what you look like or where you came from. That's what makes you both so dangerous."

The two cautiously walked toward the Nelly Belly Restaurant and marina office. As they rounded the backside, Fat Freddy stopped. "I forgot something in the car. You wait here and I'll be back."

Surprised, Elias looked at Fat Freddy. "And what if Santoro walks up to me? What do I do?"

"Kill Santoro," Fat Freddy said as he quickly walked away. Fat Freddy felt several twinges of guilt as he walked away. He was using Elias as bait. He knew that Santoro would want to take out the competition.

Elias calmly looked around. He observed two families on the

outside patio and no one else. He walked to the steps leading to a gazebo and the marina. That's when he became stunned by what he saw next.

There was something familiar about the woman walking from the marina to the gazebo, but he couldn't place it immediately. As they neared one another, Elias then recognized her. A familiar smile crossed his face and his eyes widened.

She was wearing a short toga-style dress. It was oatmeal-colored and had a rough weave to it. It was sleeveless and tied at the waist with a thick gold cord. The cord matched her sandals. Her gleaming blonde hair was the color of wheat and brushed long to her shoulders. Rather than walking, she seemed to glide effortlessly across the sidewalk. He enjoyed watching her move.

As she approached, a smile crossed her face as she recognized Elias, too. He could see that her skin was flawless and a dusky tan. Its color and texture begged him to touch it and slowly caress it. He had missed his previous visits with Desiree, and now here she was.

"Desiree," he called out as he moved swiftly toward her and forgot about his mission. He was so excited to see her that he completely forgot about Santoro. "What a happy coincidence! What are you doing here?" he asked as he embraced her.

"Did you miss me?" she asked as she warmly returned the embrace.

"No!" yelled Fat Freddy urgently as he stepped around the corner of the restaurant and ran toward the couple.

"What?" Elias asked, confused as he turned his head away from Desiree and toward Fat Freddy.

Suddenly, Desiree released her embrace and spun the unsuspecting Elias around to face the oncoming Fat Freddy. Using Elias as a shield, she pulled a .22 from her dress pocket and fired off two shots at Fat Freddy. They connected.

Fat Freddy's body continued moving forward under its own momentum and fell to the ground, bleeding heavily from his wounds.

Pulling away from Desiree, Elias turned around to face her. His jaw dropped when he saw that she had a weapon in her hand. It was pointed at him.

"Desiree, what are you doing?" he asked, bewildered.

Before she could respond or act, a gunshot roared from Fat Freddy's weapon as he pulled himself up on his elbows and fired.

She fell backwards from the impact of the round to her lower right side.

"What in the hell are you doing?" Elias asked angrily as he rushed toward her. Desiree struggled to a sitting position. She began to raise her weapon that was gripped tightly in her now trembling right hand.

Confused, Elias screamed, "Don't, Desiree! There's some sort of mix-up here!"

"There's no mix-up, Manny. None at all," she said as she calmly took aim at Elias' chest.

Before she could fire, Fat Freddy unloaded another round. This one was to her head. The bullet entered her head from the upper portion of the right side of her neck, under the jaw line, passed upward through the body of the tongue, pierced her brain and struck the skull approximately three inches below the top of the head, fracturing it. The bullet remained in her head. Blood began draining from the entrance wound in her neck onto her shoulder and her right arm. Blood accumulated in her mouth and then flowed through her lips as she fell backwards to the ground. She was dead.

"Why did you do that?" Elias asked as he ran to Fat Freddy and knelt down next to him. Fat Freddy was gasping.

"You stupid schmuck! Don't you know who that was?"

"Yeah. That's Desiree. She worked at the girls' camp."

"How do you know that she worked at the camp?"

"She told me."

"You believe everything people tell you, Manny?" Fat Freddy struggled for breath.

"No! But –"

"Did you ever think about following her back to the camp to see if that's where she went?"

"No."

"That was a mistake. Remember what Jimmy said about mistakes?"

"Yeah, they're buried in the Detroit River." Elias was shocked and now edging into a deep emotional trauma. "So, what gives?"

"She's as deadly as a black widow spider!"

"What?"

"Yeah, and so are her kisses, lover boy."

Elias glared at Fat Freddy. "How did you know that we kissed?"

"I was on the hill. Jimmy told me to watch over you and that's what I did."

"And you never told me?"

"Orders from Jimmy."

Elias shook his head. "So, who is she?"

"Santoro."

"The hitman?"

"One and the same, my boy," Fat Freddy winced in pain.

Elias' mind was racing with an avalanche of mixed feelings, and he remembered Newt's advice to not trust anybody. He learned that lesson the hard way now. "But why would she try to shoot me? I thought Santoro was Jimmy's back-up? On our side?"

"She pulled a Benedict Arnold on us. She switched sides."

"Why?"

"They offered her more money. It's always about the money."

"How do you know she switched?"

"She disappeared on us. She had an RV parked on the hill not too far from the farm. The farmhouse was wired for sound, which you didn't know about."

Elias shook his head negatively.

Fat Freddy continued. "That's how she knew what we were talking about. She also kept you under observation. She decided to get cute with you at the lake. Reeled you right in like a sucker. Just like a cat playing with a mouse before killing it."

"I had no idea," Elias said as he stared at the dead and bloodied body of the attractive, blonde woman for whom he had grown so fond.

"She stopped giving Jimmy updates, so Jimmy told me to check out the RV. I hiked up to where he told me to find her RV and all of her personal stuff was gone."

Sirens signaled the approach of the police and an ambulance.

"What do we do now?"

"Here, take my cell phone and car keys and get outta here. You call Jimmy and let him know what happened here."

"What about you? You need an ambulance."

Fat Freddy knew that his wounds were fatal, but decided not to tell Elias because he knew Elias wouldn't leave if he knew the truth. He knew Elias was good at heart, not cold like the others in the organization.

"I already called 911 and I'll be fine," he lied. "Let me give you a piece of advice, Manny."

"Yes?"

"You can't trust anyone."

"Can I trust you?" Elias asked.

Fat Freddy didn't answer right away. He took two deep breaths and winced in pain as he did. "You can't trust anyone. In this business, we're like Jimmy's piranhas. They turn on each other when one is weak. You got to stay tough or you'll be eaten alive!"

Elias nodded his head as he heard Fat Freddy's breathing become more rattled.

"Hey, do you see a Bible around?" Fat Freddy asked between gasps.

"Why?" Elias asked dumfounded by the question.

"I think I should look through one and see if there are any loopholes. I've been a bad boy," Fat Freddy cracked as he allowed a groan to emit.

"For what it's worth, I'll put in a good word for you. After all, you saved my life. That was a good thing, Freddy."

"You know you were the only one who never called me Fat Freddy. I liked that about you, my boy. Showed me your inner being. You did become like a brother to me. For real. I want to do something for you," he moaned through clenched teeth.

"You don't have to do anything. You need to rest. It sounds like you'll be on your way to the hospital shortly," Elias said.

"Listen, kid. I feel sorry for you, Manny. You don't deserve any of this. I do. I want you to go on my computer back at the farmhouse and look up this name. It's Emerson Moore. That's all I can tell you. Emerson Moore. Look it up, and soon. Now go!"

Before Elias could respond, a voice boomed, "Hands up!"

Elias looked up and saw two police officers with guns drawn approaching him. He quickly raised his hands.

"Are you armed?" one asked.

"Yes." Elias slowly lowered one hand and raised his shirt to show the handle of a .22 protruding from the waistband of his slacks. "I have a concealed/carry permit," he offered as an explanation even though it was a counterfeit.

As the other officer held his service weapon on Elias, the first one reached and retrieved Elias' gun.

"Step over here with me," the officer said as more officers arrived and checked on Fat Freddy and Santoro.

"They're both dead," one of the arriving officers called out.

"You part of this?" the first officer asked Elias.

"No, I was just walking by," Elias lied, stunned by the revelation that Fat Freddy had died.

"Just walking by and you have a .22 on you?" He didn't buy Elias' answer.

"In case of muggers," Elias responded.

"You see any of this go down?"

"No. I was fishing along the river and ran over after I heard the shots," Elias lied again.

"Sure you did." The officer eyed Elias and quietly assessed that he looked dangerous. "So, where's you're fishing rod?" he asked as he looked around Elias toward the river.

"The gunfire startled me and I dropped it in the river."

Seeing the ambulance crews arrive, the officer decided to vacate the area and allow the remaining officers to secure the scene. "Let's the two of us walk up to the building. The detectives will be here any minute. They'll want to talk to you."

As they headed up the steps to the patio in front of the Nelly Belly Restaurant, the officer asked, "What's your name?"

"Smith. John Smith."

The officer eyed Elias skeptically. "Okay, Mr. John Smith. Take a seat here." He pointed to one of the chairs at a nearby table.

"Sure, but can I use the bathroom first? Or, I can go behind one of the bushes?" Elias asked as he grimaced like a man who was on the verge of peeing his pants.

The officer frowned. "I guess so." He turned back to his fellow officers in the distance and said, "I'm escorting Mr. John Smith to the men's room."

The officer and Elias walked into the restaurant and to the rear where the entrance to the men's room was located. The officer held the door open and both walked into the men's room.

The officer saw that no one was in the bathroom and that the window was set too high for his reluctant witness to escape.

"I'll let you have some privacy and be right outside," the officer said.

"Thanks," Elias offered, as he walked quickly to the urinal.

As soon as the door closed, Elias turned and raced to the sink where he grabbed the tall waste can and overturned it, dumping the contents on the floor. He stood the can on the sink and below the window. Then he jumped onto the sink and stepped onto the overturned waste can.

His heart stopped when he heard a knock on the door and the officer calling, "You done yet?"

"Almost," Elias yelled back with a grin.

He quickly and quietly slid the window up and hoisted himself through, dropping to the ground on the other side. Then he raced to the nearby parking lot and to the car, thinking how glad he was that he and Fat Freddy earlier had parked close to the building. He pulled the keys out of his pocket and started the car, then drove out of the parking lot at normal speed and through the maze of police cars and ambulances.

Inside the Nelly Belly Restaurant, the officer banged on the restroom door a second time. "Let's go, Smith."

When he didn't get a response, he opened the door and walked in. The first thing he saw was the open window with the overturned waste-basket on the sink. Knowing exactly what happened, he reached for his radio and sounded the alarm. It was too late. Elias had escaped from the valley and was driving through Lakewood.

When he neared Cleveland Hopkins Airport, he pulled the car into a vacant parking lot and withdrew the cell phone that Fat Freddy had given him. Remembering that Diamonds had pre-programmed the cellphone with his name as "Dad," he called Diamonds.

"Yeah?"

"I've got some bad news," Elias started.

Diamonds was stunned to hear Elias on the phone. He guessed the news before Elias told him. "What?"

"My friend has passed."

"That's what I figured when it was you instead of him on the phone." Diamonds' eyes were like slits as he heard the news of Fat Freddy's death. He'd miss his longtime associate, but just briefly. Diamonds didn't dwell too much on death. It was a part of normal life as far as he was concerned.

"What about our other friend?" Diamonds asked.

"Passed also."

Diamonds smiled when he heard that Santoro, the double-crosser, was dead. He was anxious to hear the details, but wouldn't chance it on an open line. "Get back to the place. I'll see you there."

"Will do." Elias disconnected and threw the cell phone down. As he drove south on I-71, he thought about the day's events. He felt an emptiness in his stomach. He was saddened by the loss of his confidant and mentor. He was going to miss the chubby wiseguy and his stupid jokes. He had sensed a growing closeness between the two of them – a camaraderie that he would miss terribly.

Then his mind turned to Santoro. He was still reeling in shock from the revelation that Desiree was actually Santoro and had been toying with him the entire time. I've been so naive, he thought to himself. Too trusting. Fat Freddy's words and Newton's advice echoed in the back of his mind. Don't trust anyone. He'd let down his guard and become too vulnerable, he realized.

Now that he didn't have Freddy, who did he have left? Diamonds? He already knew Diamonds didn't care about him or Freddy at all.

He knew he couldn't trust him, but without his memory, he didn't know where to go or what else to do. So he headed back to the only home he knew – the farm.

Two Hours Later
The Farm

Elias had finished explaining in detail to a red-faced Diamonds what had transpired at the marina in Lakewood. Diamonds was filled with rage at the death of Fat Freddy. Diamonds, who was puffing on a cigarette like a steam locomotive, interrupted him several times through the explanation to berate Elias and unleash a flurry of expletives.

"That stupid schmuck," Diamonds stormed. "He should never have left you by yourself. He broke the rules!" Diamonds jabbed a finger at Elias. "See what happens when you break the rules, when you don't do as I say? Someone gets killed!"

"Like I said, Jimmy, I'm sorry."

"Sorry don't mean a hill of beans to me, Manny!" Diamonds screamed at the top of his lungs. His anger was boiling over.

"Jimmy," Parella started. He had been standing to the side of Diamonds during the tirade.

"Shut your mouth. If I want you to speak, I'll ask you!" Diamonds threw his spent cigarette on the worn kitchen floor and ground it out with his right foot. He walked over to the front window and looked out at the moonlit night.

"And that freaking Santoro. She turned on me. She deserves to be dead." Diamonds' head whipped around and he pointed his finger at Elias again. "You teased death tonight and walked away alive. You should never have been by yourself."

"Freddy had to get something," Elias started to explain.

"Shut up! He broke the rules. You were never to be by yourself. See what happens when you break my rules. I just told you a minute ago. Aren't you listening to me?"

"I am, Jimmy," Elias replied.

"You better be!" Diamonds started walking toward the door. "Okay. I've got to sort through things. I'll be back." He pointed a finger at Parella. "You stay with Elias."

"What?" Parella asked with a surprised look on his face.

"Now don't YOU start on me. You do as I say!" Diamonds snapped at Parella.

"But, Jimmy!"

"Outside!" Diamonds grunted as he walked through the doorway, followed by Parella. They didn't stop to talk until they reached Diamonds' vehicle.

"Why do I have to stay?" Parella asked.

Diamonds tilted his head and looked at Parella. "Don't you remember anything?"

"Sure, why?"

"Why did I have Fat Freddy glued to Elias' side?"

"So if Elias' memory started to come back, he'd call you."

"And now, do you think I'm going to leave Elias by himself? Who's going to call me and let me know? Elias? I don't think so," Diamonds grumbled.

"Can't you get someone else?" Parella pleaded.

"And who am I going to trust? It was you and Fat Freddy who've been the closest to me. You're up to bat." Diamonds leaned so close to Parella that Parella could smell his garlic-enhanced breath. "Don't strike out on me!" he warned. "Got it?"

"I got it, Jimmy."

"Good. And don't worry – he's getting to be more trouble than he's worth. One or two more hits and I'm putting him out to pasture. For good."

Diamonds entered the vehicle and drove away while Parella walked back into the farmhouse with a new sense of authority. He found Elias at the stove, making coffee.

"Coffee?"

Parella was in a foul mood at having to play babysitter. "Where's the liquor?"

Elias pointed at a cabinet and Parella walked over. He found a half-empty bottle of Jameson Irish Whiskey and set it on the table. He grabbed an empty glass off the kitchen counter and walked back to the table where he sat and poured himself a large drink.

At the kitchen counter, Elias finished making his coffee and poured himself a cup. Carrying it, he walked over to the table and began to pull out a chair.

"Sit somewhere else," Parella stormed.

Letting go of the chair, Elias headed for the front door.

"Where do you think you're going?"

"Porch."

"You don't go anywhere without telling me," Parella warned Elias, who had walked through the doorway onto the porch. "Or you'll end up like your little fat buddy," Parella yelled after Elias. "Some call Jimmy the Teflon King because nobody can stick anything on him. Your fat little buddy was the Teflon brain. Nothing stuck to it!" Parella laughed at his joke.

Plopping onto one of the rockers, Elias spent the next two hours sipping his coffee and sifting through his daunting emotions that resulted from the evening's events. When he walked into the house, he found Parella head down on the table. Next to him was the now totally empty liquor bottle. He had passed out.

Shaking his head, Elias walked to the stairs and went up to the second floor.

The Next Afternoon
Put-in-Bay

His ringing cell phone interrupted Mike "Mad Dog" Adams' enjoyment of the BBQ chicken sandwich he was eating at the Goat Soup and Whiskey Tavern on Catawba Avenue.

"Hello," Adams answered.

"Mike, it's Yogi Sandes."

"Hi, Yogi." Adams and Sandes had known each other as kids on Cleveland's west side. Sandes was a detective on the Lakewood police force and would often get together with Adams to catch up on the good old days or to watch Adams' show at the Round House Bar.

"Hey, I just had something interesting come across my desk."

"What's that?"

"That newspaper friend of yours who went missing a while back?"

"Emerson Moore?"

"Yeah."

"What about him, Yogi?"

"Last night, we had a shootout down at the Emerald Necklace Marina. Two of the shooters didn't make it."

"Okay, and what's this got to do with Moore?" Adams asked before taking a gulp of his cold beer.

"There was a witness to the shooting, but he disappeared."

"Snatched by aliens?" Adams couldn't help himself.

Sandes chuckled. "No, Mike. The guy took off on us. I won't bore you with the details. There was one very interesting thing."

"What's that, Yogi?"

"He was armed, but we got his .22. I just got back the fingerprint report and the fingerprints on the .22 belong to Emerson Moore."

Adams almost spit out the beer he was swallowing as he sat straight up in his chair. "Are you sure?" he asked anxiously.

"Oh yeah. We dug up some photos of Moore and showed them to the officers who had disarmed him. They said it's the same guy, but he's now got a beard and long hair."

A large smile crossed Adams' face as he realized that his friend was alive. At the same time he was confused. What had Moore gotten himself into this time? Was he undercover on a story? Why would he let his friends and his aunt believe that he was dead?

"Any leads on where he went?" Adams asked.

"No. We're checking the surveillance cameras to see what kind of car he drove. If we're lucky, we could get the plate number."

"You said there were two people killed. Innocent bystanders?"

"No. One was a woman who went by the name of Santoro, one of the top contract killers for the mob. Kind of a freelancer. Worked for the highest bidder. The other victim, however, was even more interesting."

"Oh?"

"Yeah. It was Fat Freddy Fabrizio. He worked for Jimmy Diamonds in Detroit. He disappeared into thin air just like Diamonds after he escaped while being transferred from Detroit to state prison, as did your buddy, Moore."

"Emerson must still be linked to Diamonds," Adams guessed.

"Yeah. But we can't figure out what kind of hold Diamonds has on him. Why would he run away from us and disappear? Why not ask us for help?"

"That's a hard one to figure out," Adams said. "Can you keep me in the loop on this without getting yourself in trouble, Yogi?"

"To a point, I can."

"Thanks, and let me know about that license plate number if you guys come up with it."

"Sure. One more thing you'll find interesting."

"What's that?"

"Fabrizio had some playing cards in his pocket."

"Two pairs? Black aces and black eights?" Adams guessed, remembering the 'Deadman's Hand' that Wild Bill Hickok reportedly held when he was murdered during a poker game in the late 19th century.

"No. Fabrizio had several aces of diamonds in his possession. Could tie Fabrizio to the Caniglia brothers' murders in Chagrin Falls. Maybe Moore, too. They said there were two killers involved and they found an ace of diamonds there near one of the bodies. I bet it's a message from Jimmy Diamonds."

"Yeah, I heard about those cards showing up. There was one out near the airport."

"Right," Sandes agreed.

Adams thanked Sandes again before ending the call and calling Sam Duncan.

"Hello?" Duncan answered on the second ring.

"Sam, where are you?" Adams asked.

"In Detroit running down leads on Emerson."

"I've got some exciting news, Sam."

"I could use some."

"Looks like Emerson's alive."

"I knew it! He's got more lives than an alley cat!" Duncan was smiling. "Where is he? Have you seen him?" Duncan began to pepper Adams with questions, almost relentlessly.

"Whoa! Whoa!" Adams said as he tried to rein in Duncan's enthusiasm. He then relayed what he had heard from the Lakewood police detective.

After listening closely, Duncan wondered aloud. "Maybe Emerson's in Ohio and not Michigan. Why wouldn't he contact us?"

"Yeah, that's the big unknown. We've got a problem here."

"How's that?"

"Do we continue to search for Emerson and possibly upset his undercover project or forget his undercover project and find him anyway?" Adams asked. "Maybe there's a reason he doesn't want to be found or reveal himself just yet."

"I say find him. If there's any chance he's in trouble, we need to help."

"I was thinking the same thing, Sam. Something's screwy with this whole thing. You'd think he'd get a message to one of us if he were undercover. He wouldn't want his aunt upset and in mourning."

"Okay, I'll wrap up here and drive over to Cleveland. I've got some friends in the FBI there and I'll see what I can stir up."

"Good."

"Time to soar with the eagles, Mad Dog!" Duncan was excited about the renewed prospect of finding their friend.

"Don't soar too high, eagle man," Adams cautioned. "Remember foxes don't get sucked into jet engines. Be smart as a fox."

"Funny!"

"But true. Stay in touch," Adams said as he disconnected from the call. He turned back to his sandwich as his mind spun with ideas about what Moore might be up to.

Four Days Later
The Farm

The Ford pickup turned left and eased its way up the drive. After a short distance, Adams pulled over. He was pleased that Duncan's diligence paid off. His work with the FBI and some of his more nefarious contacts led them to the farmhouse near Wooster. Duncan had reconnoitered the farm the previous afternoon with a small drone. Its recorded images showed two individuals. One was of a bulked up and bearded Emerson Moore.

"We better leave it here," he said as he turned off the ignition and opened his door. He and Duncan exited the vehicle and walked around to the tailgate that Adams had lowered.

"Ready to rock and roll?" Duncan asked as he grabbed a Kevlar vest and threw it on.

As Adams fastened his own vest, he replied with a large smile, "It's bad-ass time. We don't need to get any police involved on this rescue mission."

"Hooyah! Vigalantes!" Duncan grinned. "Unleash hell!"

"We'll do a little sneak-and-peek, then plan an op," Adams said as he strapped on an ammo belt.

"Nothing like a body snatch mission to raise the adrenaline level."

Inside the farmhouse, Parella heard the alarm sound. It signaled that a vehicle had turned into the drive and was approaching. Parella ran upstairs and unlocked his bedroom door. When he returned, he was holding an AK-47.

"This should take care of any intruders," he smiled wickedly at Elias.

"Where's mine?" Elias asked.

"You still have that new .22 I gave you?" Parella was referring to the replacement .22 he had given Elias. There were several weapons in a locked trunk in Fat Freddy's old room.

"Yes."

"That's all you need. Papa will handle this one. Watch and learn a few things. That's where Doublewide made his mistake. He should have been taking advice from me. Now, that fat freak is dead."

Elias bristled at the use of the term "Doublewide." "Tony?"

"Yeah, what?" Parella whipped his head around to glance back at Elias and then turned back to face the driveway.

"Freddy didn't like you calling him by that name."

"So, who cares? He's gone."

"I care," Elias said with a stony look on his face.

"Shut up and focus on what we got going on here." Parella grabbed his cell phone and opened one of the apps. "Look here."

Elias bent over and saw a live shot of two men walking warily along the side of the drive.

"I didn't know we had live surveillance cameras here," Elias said as he watched the live feed.

"There's a lot you don't know nothing about, altar boy!" Parella had an all-knowing smirk on his face. "That's the two guys that one of our snitches told us about. They've been poking around, trying to track us down."

Elias looked at the two men. "Who are they?"

"A couple of former Navy SEALs. Think they know it all. The one on the left is a guy named Mike Adams. The other one is Sam Duncan."

Parella peered closely at the two as they made their way up the drive. "We're going to have a little surprise for them," he said. "Follow me."

The two ran out of the house and toward the drive where it came out of the woods.

"Over there," Parella said softly as he pointed toward an area near the drive that had a mound of dirt and shrubbery. "Good place to set up an ambush," he said as he ran over, followed by Elias.

When they reached their concealed area, Parella pulled out his cell phone and looked at the app again. "Shhh," he said. "They should be coming around the corner in a few seconds."

They crouched low. Soon they heard the soft crunching of approaching footsteps.

"I hear that you're pretty good with that .22," Parella said as he glanced at the weapon in Elias' hand.

"Deadly."

He pointed to the spot where he expected Adams and Duncan to emerge. "How about at that range?"

"Deadly," Elias said again with a serious look on his face.

"Good. It's your kill then. When they sneak around, you take them out."

"Can do," Elias said as he raised his weapon and aimed at the spot.

As Adams and Duncan, walking in a crouch, emerged around the corner, Elias and Parella stood to confront the intruders.

Caught by surprise and recognizing Moore immediately, Adams yelled, "Emerson!" as he and Duncan lowered their weapons.

Elias fired twice with fatal accuracy. Adams and Duncan fell to the ground.

"Yippee ki-yay," Elias said as he blew across the open end of the gun barrel and stood. "Easy kill. Like shooting fish in a barrel."

Four Hours Later
The Farm

Diamond's vehicle descended into the valley as it neared the farm. He had received the text message that all was clear and he wanted to see the bodies of the two intruders before they were burned.

The vehicle turned into the drive and slowed as it drove past the parked pickup truck, belonging to Adams and Duncan. Diamonds allowed a smile to cross his face as he looked at it.

He drove up the drive and parked in front of the farmhouse.

"Jimmy!" Elias greeted Diamonds as he exited the vehicle.

"Nice job, Manny," Diamonds couldn't hide his satisfaction in having Elias kill his two friends. His investment in training Elias was now paying improved dividends. He couldn't have planned this better himself. "Where are the bodies?"

"We dragged them behind the barn," said Elias.

Walking around the vehicle, he followed Elias up the stairs. "Where's Parella?"

"Inside. Making coffee."

"Who wants coffee? It's time to celebrate! We'll have a few

shots!" Diamonds said as he followed Elias into the house. He stopped when he saw Parella sitting at the kitchen table. His eyes were lifeless and there were two bullet holes in his head.

"Think you're smart, don't you?" Diamonds snarled as he held a .45 in his hand. He had pulled it out of his shoulder holster as he followed Elias into the farmhouse. He had a knack for being a survivor, thanks to his sixth sense.

Elias started to turn around as he reached for his .22 at the same time.

"Uh, uh. I wouldn't do that," Diamonds said as Elias turned and saw Diamonds' .45 pointed at him. "You're not as smart as you think."

Diamonds looked around the room. "Where are your two friends?"

"They never showed up," Elias lied.

"Then, you want to tell me whose vehicle I passed down the driveway?"

"Fishermen?"

"I should put a bullet through you right now," Diamonds growled. "Where are they?"

"Right here," Adams said as he and Duncan stepped out of the hallway. They had semi-automatic weapons pointed at Diamonds.

"I'd suggest you put that .45 on the table," Duncan added. "Now!"

A sweat broke out on Diamonds' face. He had been in tough situations before, but these three were going to make it interesting for him to turn the tables on. He slowly placed the .45 on the table and asked, "Mind if I sit, Manny?"

"No, go ahead," Elias said. "And by the way, I'm not Manny Elias. I'm Emerson Moore, in case you forgot."

"So, your memory came back?"

"Yes, and you can thank Fat Freddy for that!"

"How's that?" Diamonds asked as he arched his eyebrows.

"Before he died, he told me to get on his computer here and search the name Emerson Moore."

Diamonds burst out with a series of expletives.

Once Diamonds calmed down, Moore continued. "You can imagine my surprise when I saw several images of myself and that I've been missing a good while. And that I have friends and family mourning for me, missing me."

"It came back right away? Your memory?"

"I'd say most of it. The trauma of learning that Desiree was Santoro and seeing her killed, along with Fat Freddy, probably helped jolt my memory. Couple that with getting on the computer and being able to see myself, accelerated its return. I'm Emerson Moore and I'm back, you sick dirtbag!"

"How did you get on the computer? That was locked in Fat Freddy's room!"

"Fat Freddy gave me the keys. I'd get on the computer when Parella was down at the barn or taking a shower."

Diamonds swore again. "And you just played along with us?"

"Yeah. I needed to position myself to capture you so I could return you to the police. You're going to do some serious prison time – like maybe a lifetime. And we'll make sure you don't get away this time."

Ignoring his comment, Diamonds asked, "What happened with Parella? You killed him in cold blood?"

"Isn't that what you trained me to do?" Moore asked. He didn't wait for a response. "We both stood to fire. I whispered to Parella to drop his weapon. When he swung it around to take me out, I gave him a double tap just like I was trained."

"Stupid schmuck," Diamonds said as he looked at Parella's body.

A noise on the porch caused Moore, Adams and Duncan to look toward the screen door. Standing in the doorway was one of Diamonds' henchmen. He was holding an Uzi assault pistol. He was ready to open with spray firing.

Glass panes in the front window and kitchen window broke as two more henchmen stuck the muzzles of their assault weapons through the broken glass.

Diamonds nonchalantly reached across the table and picked up his .45. He had a devilish smile on his face. "You don't think that I've survived this long by just being handsome, do you?" He rose from his seat. "No, it's from always being one step ahead of my adversaries," he smirked. "Drop your weapons."

"Better do as he says, Emerson," the wily Adams said as he bent down to put his weapon on the floor.

Adams' action was replicated by Duncan, who added, "No other choice, E."

Reluctantly, Moore followed suit and placed his .22 on the floor.

"That's being smart, boys," Diamonds sneered as the gunman in the doorway entered the room and covered the three. The other two gunmen rushed in and one patted down the three men. He found a hideaway gun strapped to Adams' ankle and a knife hidden on Duncan.

"They're clean, now," the gunman said as he set the two items on the kitchen table.

"Good. I think I have a few scores to settle here," Diamonds said as he withdrew a cigarette from the pack in his shirt pocket and lit it. He took a deep pull on the cigarette and exhaled a large cloud of white smoke. Then he spoke. "Take them to the barn. I'm going to have a little fun."

The group walked slowly from the house and across the open lawn to the barn. When Diamonds saw a closed door, he opened it, revealing a large empty room with no windows. He walked around the room and was satisfied by what he saw. "Bring them in here."

The three captives were marched into the room and made to sit on the dirt floor.

"See if there are any plastic zip ties, rope or chain around here," Diamonds told one of the henchmen.

Within a couple of minutes, he returned with a handful of plastic ties. "I saw some chains. I'll bring them in," he said as he handed the ties to Diamonds and walked out of the room.

Before approaching the captive trio, Diamonds looked at his remaining gunmen. "Pay attention now. If one of them so much as looks cross-eyed at me, shoot him dead."

The two nodded their heads in understanding.

"Hold your hands out in front of you," Diamonds said as he approached Moore.

Moore complied and Diamonds wrapped the zip tie around his wrist, pulling it tightly. He repeated the process without incident on Adams and Duncan.

The clanking noise from the chains being carried into the room grabbed Diamonds' attention.

"I found three sets," the henchman said as he walked into the room.

"Wrap them around their ankles and secure it with the zip ties. Then, take the free end and wrap it to the post." Diamonds was referring to a six-by-six post set in the ground and supporting the floor overhead. "These boys aren't going anywhere," he said with a determined look.

"I wouldn't be too sure of that," Duncan cracked.

Without hesitation, Diamonds whirled around and fired his .45, hitting Duncan in the shoulder. "Want to try again, pretty boy?" Diamonds' eyes had a wild look to them.

Duncan didn't respond as he winced from the bleeding wound.

Each of the three chains was wrapped around the post and secured by a zip tie.

Then Diamonds walked over to Moore and pushed him over from his sitting position. "Thought you had me, didn't you?" He didn't wait for a response as his right shoe connected with Moore's ribs. "Hold him for me!" Diamonds ordered two of the men, who rushed over to hold Moore prone on the ground as Diamonds launched a series of kicks at his ribs.

"You little piece of crap! You've cost me a lot of grief!" He kicked at Moore several more times, screaming obscenities. When he tired, he stepped back and looked at the beaten reporter. "You have no idea how I've looked forward to your memory returning. My revenge wouldn't be as sweet without it."

A faint moan escaped from Moore's lips as he curled into a fetal position.

"This is just the start. You haven't seen anything yet." Diamonds turned and looked at Adams. "I'm going to give you one break because I've liked your singing."

"Don't do me any favors," the burly Adams quipped.

"I'm not!" Diamonds countered.

"Just so you know. When I'm done with you, you'll be squealing like a pierced pig," Adams pushed.

Adams didn't see one of the henchmen with a shovel moving near him. Adams did see Diamonds look behind and nod. Before he could react, the henchman swung the shovel and caught a glancing blow to the side of Adams' head, knocking him immediately into a prone position.

"I take it back. No breaks for you!" Diamonds laughed sinisterly. He looked at the three henchmen. "See if you can find a car tire around here somewhere."

"Got a flat?" Duncan called as he ignored the pain from his wound.

"Nope. Going to stuff your head, arms and legs through it while we beat you," Diamonds said. "Then, I'm going to douse the tire in gasoline and light you up. You're the first to go."

Duncan didn't flinch. He just shot Diamonds a confident look.

"Adams, I think we'll try a little oxygen deprivation with you. Put your head in a plastic bag and watch you struggle for your last breath before we pull the bag off and let you breathe. The funny thing is that you won't know which time we won't pull the bag off of your head," Diamonds spoke with evil glee.

"And your buddy, Moore, is in for a special treat if I can find a staple gun in here. I'm going to put staples in his feet, fingers, chest and ears. The ears are real sensitive to staples. Then, maybe a little battery acid in the eyes. I wish I had my piranhas here, but I'll make due. We'll see what we end up doing before we burn you all and bury your bodies in the woods. No one will ever find you."

Diamonds laughed in anticipation. He couldn't believe how easy this was. "And Moore, you'll watch your two friends die first and be burned. See what you can find," he ordered two of the henchmen who walked out of the room.

"Close the door after us and stand guard, although I don't think these clowns are going anywhere," Diamonds said to the third henchman as he took one final glance at his captives before walking out of the room. "We're getting the tools we need, but we won't be long. Think about what you have to look forward to."

The third henchman stepped out of the room, closed the door and took up position outside of it.

"Okay, battle buddy. You're going to have to get out of the zip ties," Duncan said softly to Adams, as he saw Moore painfully struggle to a sitting position. Neither E nor I are in condition to do it."

"No problem. That's why we had all of that training." Using the technique he learned during SEAL training, Adams bent over and used his teeth to position the zip tie so that the center was positioned between his wrists, Then he raised his hands over his head while chicken-winging his arms behind his back and contracting his shoulder blades to try to touch them together. Suddenly and abruptly he pulled his hands down, breaking the zip tie and freeing himself.

"Piece of cake when you know what you're doing," Adams smiled.

"Nice trick. What about the chain?" Moore gasped quietly.

"No problem. I've got a friction saw," Adams said as he reached for his shoe and unlaced one of the laces.

"What?"

"If you were trained as a SEAL, you'd know this stuff, E," Duncan said.

Placing an end of the lace in each hand, Adams began sawing at the zip tie binding the chain to his ankles. "I always use 550 cord bootlaces. They get the job done in emergencies like this." Within a minute, the friction from the sawing motion caused the zip tie to fall apart.

Carefully, so that the chain didn't clank, Adams unwrapped the chain from around his legs. Once free, he knelt next to Duncan and prepared to saw off the zip tie from his wrists.

"Hold it, Mike. I can't get to it, but pull on my belt buckle."

Adams smiled. "Knife?"

"Yeah."

Adams reached down and pulled the hidden knife out of its hiding place. Gripping the buckle end, he used the two-and-a-half-inch blade to cut through the zip tie on Duncan's hands and then the tie on the chain around his feet. "Nice, I need to get me one of these."

While Duncan unwrapped the chain, Adams moved over to Moore.

"How are you feeling, Emerson?"

"Very sore. I think I have a couple of cracked ribs," Moore replied as Adams cut through the zip tie on Moore's wrists and freed him.

"You'll be fine," Adams said as he moved to Moore's feet and repeated the action. Then, he helped unwrap the chains from Moore's feet while Duncan retrieved his knife from Adams and took up a position next to the closed door. He held the belt buckle knife in his hands.

Helping Moore to his feet, Adams and Moore walked over to the other side of the door. Adams was now holding the shoelace in his hands, ready to use it as a garrote.

"Ready to unleash hell?" Duncan quietly asked. He had torn off the sleeve of his shirt and wrapped it around his upper arm, securing it with his belt to slow the bleeding. He was ripe for a fight.

"Ready when you are," Adams replied.

"Me, too," Moore replied. "It's payback time, but I want to take Diamonds alive."

"That might not be possible, E. He'll go down shooting," Duncan offered.

"Sam's right, Emerson. Diamonds' life expectancy is about as long as a house fly's," Adams added.

Outside the barn, Diamonds was overseeing the efforts of his two henchmen in loading lumber from a pile next to the barn into an old front-loader. Its engine was running and making noise. One of the henchmen then followed Diamonds to a spot halfway between the woods and the barn where they dumped it. They were preparing to burn their victims once they had been tortured to his satisfaction.

Inside the barn, the henchman guarding the door heard a shriek from inside the room. He quickly turned and pulled open the door. Stunned by seeing that the captives were missing and the chains strewn on the floor, he stepped into the room – a big mistake. When he entered, Duncan used his good shoulder and pushed him toward Adams, who quickly placed the garrote around the man's neck and pulled it tight.

As the man began to swing his weapon toward Duncan, Moore jumped in and wrestled it away while Duncan drove his knife's blade directly into the man's chest, quickly killing him. They dropped the body to the ground and Moore searched it, finding a .45 and a couple of extra clips.

"That was easy," Moore said as he stood with the .45 in his hand.

"A little overkill, if you ask me," Duncan said as he picked up the Uzi assault pistol from the floor. "I've been meaning to ask you. When did you become so skilled?"

"It was that Special Forces training I had in Florida," Moore responded as he moved to the door and reconnoitered the area. "All clear."

"Doesn't compare to what we SEALs went through," Adams said proudly.

"Whatever!" Moore snapped playfully. "Let's go."

The three men walked out of the room, closing the door behind them. They saw that Diamonds and his henchmen had placed a number of items for their torture in the middle of the barn. There were a couple of chain saws, a blow torch, rope, chains, ice picks, two cans of gasoline and a couple of car batteries.

Moore surveyed the area. "We'll set up our kill zone here," he pointed to an area inside the barn door. "We'll catch them in a crossfire, but I still want to take Diamonds alive."

"We know you do, but it really depends on what he does, Emerson," Adams cautioned. "He might have other ideas."

"Let's keep that in mind. I want to see him pay for what he's done."

"There's a number of ways to do that. And his death is one way, too," Adams said.

Duncan nodded in agreement.

Hearing the front-loader approaching, Moore yelled softly, "Time to dance, guys!" and he took a position behind a tractor that gave him a clear shot.

Duncan and Adams took up positions behind an empty hay wagon.

The front-loader stopped outside the open barn door and its engine shut off.

Leading his two henchmen into the barn, Diamonds noticed that his henchman wasn't standing in front of the closed door to the captives' room. "Now, where did he go?" Diamonds roared as his anger began to soar.

"Maybe, he's taking a leak," one of the other henchmen suggested.

"The only leak he's going to get is when I fill him with holes," Diamonds said as he raised his .45 and walked into the killing zone.

"We already did!" Moore yelled from behind the tractor. "Drop your weapons!"

"Like hell!" Diamonds bellowed as he and his men opened fire on the tractor. As they swung to face the tractor, Duncan fired the Uzi assault pistol, killing one of Diamonds' men. Hearing the gunshot from behind him, Diamonds' other man whirled and sprayed the area by the hay wagon with bullets, sending Duncan and Adams ducking.

Moore realized the predicament his friends were in and stood. He fired off several rounds, killing the henchman. At the same time, Diamonds saw Moore exposed from concealment. He fired twice. The first shot missed. The second connected with Moore's abdomen, knocking him to the floor as he dropped his weapon.

Diamonds rushed over to Moore and stood over him. "This isn't exactly the way I planned to kill you, but I'll still enjoy it," he said evenly. His eyes were glazed over in anger. He had an evil smile on his face as he pointed his weapon at Moore's face and prepared to fire. "Either way, the ace of diamonds wins every time."

While in pain from the wound to his abdomen, Moore didn't flinch. He stared belligerently at Diamonds. "But I really screwed up your game, didn't I?" Moore laughed as he faced certain death.

The look on Diamonds' face suddenly went from evil glee to shock and his eyes rolled back into his head. He grunted and dropped the gun in disbelief as he reactively looked down at his chest where the five prongs of a pitch fork where protruding.

Behind Diamonds stood a triumphant Adams. His hands were wrapped around the pitchfork's handle. He shoved it in further and blood poured from Diamonds' chest as the mobster fell mortally wounded upon the floor.

"Looks to me like you're a flawed five-point diamond," Adams joked morbidly as he stood over the rapidly dying Jimmy Diamonds.

"I'll see your diamonds with a club and a spade," Duncan quipped as he walked over to Adams, who was kneeling next to Moore.

"How you doing, Emerson?" Adams asked as he gingerly pulled up Moore's shirt, revealing a gaping, profusely bleeding wound.

"Fading fast," Moore replied weakly.

"Stay with me, Emerson. It's not serious," Adams said as he downplayed the critical nature of the wound.

"Watch out!" Despite the pain he felt, Moore pushed Adams to the side and pointed his weapon at Diamonds, who with his final breaths was aiming his .45 at Adams. Moore gave Diamonds a double tap to the head, killing him instantly. Moore fell back to the ground, groaning as he did.

"Thanks, Emerson. I should have been more careful." Adams took a deep breath as he realized how close he had come to meeting his maker.

Moore moaned in response.

"There's a first aid kit in the pickup. I'll take that front-loader and drive back to get it," Duncan said before racing off.

Meanwhile, Adams turned over Diamonds' body and searched it. He found a cell phone and dialed 911, quickly giving the address of the farm. After hanging up, he took off his T-shirt and applied it to the wound as he attempted to stop the blood flow.

Adams leaned over Moore. "Take it easy, Emerson."

Moore half-nodded before sinking, unconscious, into a dark oblivion.

When Duncan returned with their vehicle, he parked it and ran into the barn with the first aid kit. He opened it quickly and began binding up the wound.

Soon ambulances and the Wayne County Sheriff's department arrived on the scene.

Magruder Hospital
Port Clinton, Ohio

Three days had passed since Moore had been wounded. He spent the first day in Wooster's Community Hospital after surgery on his abdomen before being driven to Magruder Hospital, the closest hospital to Put-in-Bay. He would convalesce there for several more days before his release. His first visitor had been his Aunt Anne, who was thrilled by his return from the dead.

She had also nagged him about shaving the beard and cutting his long hair. After several visits from her, he relented and allowed the hospital staff to comply with his aunt's wishes. When he was cleaned up, he realized that it was just another step back into normalcy as Emerson Moore – and a break from his tumultuous recent past as Manny Elias.

Moore opened his eyes and looked around the room. The nurses had trouble keeping the steady stream of visitors, flowers, and balloons at bay, and the room was bursting with colorful blooms and reminders of the people who cared about him.

He saw the fruit basket from his boss, John Sedler, who had flown in from Washington the previous day and left without a story after two hours with his ace reporter. Moore had refused to talk about what had happened during the time he was missing. He didn't want to share the dark deeds he committed, so he locked them up in the deep abyss of his mind and chalked it all up to his still shaky memory. He would be answering no questions from the press, either, which was ironic given his profession. Moore also feigned memory loss when law enforcement officials showed up to question him.

Spotting his aunt's knitting basket by the visitor's chair, Moore knew she would be back. The nurses had to practically force her to go home to rest after she elatedly fussed over her recovering nephew. He would never take her motherly nature for granted again. He was so grateful to have his life back – and his friends and family.

As soon as he contentedly closed his eyes to get some sleep, he heard someone storm into his hospital room. When he opened his eyes, he saw Boozer hulking over him.

"I found you," Boozer roared. "I've been looking for you, S.O.B., ever since I caught my Connie and you kissing in front of our trailer!"

Moore winced as he tried to raise himself. "Listen," he began to explain.

"I ain't listening to anything you have to say," he said as his eyes widened in fury.

Boozer's demeanor suddenly changed and he started laughing. He turned toward the doorway and shouted softly, "Sorry, guys. I can't keep a straight face!"

Laughter filled the hallway as Adams, Duncan and Connie walked together into Moore's room.

"Had you going, didn't I?" Boozer chuckled as he turned back to look at Moore.

"Yes, you did," Moore replied as he sighed in relief. "I am a bit disadvantaged here."

"I bet you soiled your shorts," Boozer chuckled again. Leaning toward Moore, Boozer explained. "Connie told me about those guys getting her drunk awhile back and trying to take advantage of her. She said that you saved her butt and she was just thanking you with the kiss. I didn't know any of that. I just jumped to conclusions. Sorry about that."

"No problem," Moore smiled as Connie walked over to the bedside, leaned forward and gently kissed Moore on the cheek.

"How's my hero?" she asked with a wide smile.

"Much better!" Moore replied. Then he said softly, "I like your kind of medicine. With Boozer's permission, of course."

Connie smiled again, and Boozer nodded good-naturedly. "Although I don't need any man's permission to do anything I want to do!" Connie said in a tone that meant business.

Moore beamed. He knew that Connie was a very independent woman.

"When your buddies told me you were here, I wanted to stop in and thank you, though it's been a good while. It was their idea to trick you," Boozer continued.

"That doesn't surprise me," Moore said as he looked at his two grinning friends, standing at the end of his bed.

"Can't let you get too comfortable, E," Duncan said.

"Yeah, you'll lose your edge," Adams chuckled.

"Oh, I don't think that's ever going to happen to me," Moore countered.

"After all of that special forces training you went through, you should be prepared for any tough investigating assignments *The Post* throws your way," Duncan suggested.

Nodding his head, Moore agreed, "Yep. You can just call me Iron Man from now on."

"Ironing Man? You get a job at the dry cleaners?" Adams joked.

Moore threw his friend a smile.

After a few minutes of chatting, Boozer and Connie excused themselves and left. Adams and Duncan continued to converse with their bed-ridden friend for ten minutes. Suddenly, another person entered the room. It was Jimmy Diamonds' girlfriend, Veronica.

Duncan commented first, "I think I'm going to get a bed here so beautiful blondes come and visit me."

"You'd have to pay them first," Adams quipped.

Smiling demurely, Veronica approached Moore while Adams

and Duncan stepped back. "Hello, Manny, uh... Emerson. I better call you by your real name now, Emerson."

Moore smiled. "You can call me any name you want." He introduced her to his two friends, who sensed she wanted to talk privately with Moore and took their leave.

"How do you feel?" she asked.

"A little tender, but much better. Especially since my memory returned."

"I knew what they were doing to you and I couldn't say anything. Jimmy would have killed me," she explained. "And I couldn't leave or he'd kill me. Either way, I was stuck."

"Don't worry about it. I understand," Moore responded.

"I'm glad your memory is back, Emerson" she smiled. "Sometimes I'd rather forget my past, but you – you sound like you had a real good one to remember."

"Thanks. What are your plans now, Veronica?"

"I have an aunt in Portland, Oregon. She has a small business and I'm going to move there and help her run it. It'll be a different lifestyle for me, but I think I'm going to like it. The mob life isn't as glamorous as I thought it would be."

"I'll say, and the Portland gig should be a lot safer."

She looked nervously around the room and back to Moore. "I guess I better be going," she said. She leaned in and kissed Moore on the cheek.

"What was that for?"

"I always thought you were cute from the moment I saw you at Jimmy's place in Grosse Ile. And, well, you set me free when you got rid of Jimmy. I wanted to thank you for giving me my life back, and showing me there's still good in the world."

"I'll say one thing about Jimmy. He knew a beautiful woman when he saw one."

Veronica smiled again. "Thank you." She turned and walked to the door.

"Good luck," Moore called as she walked out, disappearing from Moore's life.

The Keys
Put-in-Bay

A mist was rising off the warm waters of Put-in-Bay. Behind Perry's Monument, the early morning sun was also rising, signaling the dawn of another day in this island paradise. Two men were seated at The Keys, overlooking the bay and the marina.

An island vacationer stopped by the table and spoke to the bearded man. "You're Mad Dog, aren't you?" the man asked excitedly.

"That would be me," Adams replied.

"Man, I just love your show. You performing today?"

"Thank you. Yes. Stop by the Round House around two o'clock."

"I'll be there," the man said, starting to walk away from the table and happy that he had a chance to talk to the entertainer.

Adams called after him, "They've got beer there colder than you ex-wife's heart!" Adams chuckled as he saw the man nod and walk toward DeRivera Park.

"You never stop, do you?" Moore asked after he sipped his coffee.

"Ah, you know. The folks like it when the Mad Dog has a little fun with them." Adams peered at his friend and took a more serious tone. "I've been meaning to ask you. How are you feeling about the murders you committed?"

"That's something I've been wrestling with," Moore said with a concerned look on his face. "I rationalized it as self defense, but of course they wouldn't have pulled their guns if I hadn't pulled mine."

"Losing sleep over it, are you?" Adams probed.

"Yes, I have been, and I find myself frequently waking up in the middle of the night. I'll walk outside the house and sit on the dock. Just sit there and think about Freddy and Desiree and most of all about what undoubtedly I've done."

Moore stared with a blank look on his face out to the bay as the Jet Express rounded Gibraltar Island, making its familiar way to the dock. "I could rationalize and say that I was helping the justice system by taking out bad guys!"

"Yeah, that's what I was thinking. You saved the courts and police money and time, Emerson," Adams noted with a nod of approval.

"But everyone deserves their day in court. Innocent until proven guilty, not gunned down with an assumption of guilt. I do feel remorse for what I did," Moore volunteered. "Except for Jimmy Diamonds. It's funny, ironic I guess, but I don't feel bad at all about killing him."

"He deserved it. Especially after what you told me about him when you were in the hospital. You're not going to go public with what happened? All of those people you killed?"

"No. If I did, I'd end up doing prison time even though I had my memory issues and just killed the bad guys."

"Don't go stupid on me," Adams cautioned Moore.

"All of the witnesses to the murders I committed are dead. Only you and Sam know and I'm sure you're not going to tell anyone."

"You know you can count on us to keep quiet. One for all and all for one."

"I'll take all of this to my grave," Moore said before taking another sip of coffee. He was enjoying this respite by the bay. "We'll stick to my story that I had amnesia and was being held hostage by Diamonds at the farm until the shootout. It's all true, after all."

"What about that gorgeous blonde who visited you in the hospital?"

"Veronica? She doesn't really know anything. She never saw me do a hit."

"What about that Newton guy, and the doctor?"

Moore shook his head. "Even if they saw my picture and made the connection, they wouldn't talk. Their silence earns them a good living with the mob. Besides, implicating me means implicating themselves. No, I'm not worried about them."

After a pause, Moore continued. "You know this would be an interesting story for my newspaper."

"It would. So would the story about you getting the electric chair. Don't you go a half a quart low on intelligence now," Adams warned.

"My mouth's zipped," Moore said.

"And so is mine, unless one day I need to use it to leverage something out of you," Adams grinned. "Blackmail amongst friends is always handy," he joked.

The burly singer rose suddenly and walked over to a woman who had just sat down at a nearby table. She was struggling to take off her sweater.

"Here. Let me help you with that," Adams said as he assisted her.

When Adams returned to the table, Moore teased him. "Aren't we being the gentleman today?"

"Nothing gentlemanly about it! I excel in helping women out of their clothes," he smirked.

"You're incorrigible!" Moore retorted.

"You want to spell that for me?" Adams grinned back.

"I heard that there was a cash award for finding me. I assume you and Sam were paid."

Nodding his head, Adams said, "Yes, we were, but we donated it to charity in your name."

"I'm impressed. You do have a soft heart," Moore said.

Adams leaned toward Moore as he placed a finger to his lips. "Shh. Don't tell anybody," Adams whispered.

Moore's cell phone rang. When he reached to get it, he winced.

"Still painful?" Adams asked.

"When I move the wrong way," Moore responded.

"You know, Emerson, it's going to be interesting to see how you handle your future exploits."

"How's that, Mike?"

"Now, you're a trained killer. You've acquired some deadly skills."

"That's correct, but I'm not sure that I'm any smarter. I'm sure I'll still manage to get myself in some jams. But maybe it will be easier to get out of them."

"True dat!" Adams smiled.

"I'm enjoying my time off." Moore's cell phone rang again. He picked it up and looked at the caller ID. "It's my boss, John Sedler."

"Looks to me like your time off lasted about as long as a carnival ride," Adams chuckled as he watched Moore answer the phone.

"This is Emerson," Moore answered, wondering if the call would signal the start of another adventure.

Coming Soon
The Next *Emerson Moore* Adventure

Golden Torpedo